NICK DRAKE | THE PINK MOON FILES

For Naoko, Alex and Nick

NICK DRAKE | THE PINK MOON FILES

JASON CREED

OMNIBUS PRESS
London • New York • Paris • Sydney • Copenhagen • Berlin • Madrid • Tokyo

Exclusive Distributors
Music Sales Limited,
14/15 Berners Street,
London, W1T 3LJ.

Music Sales Corporation,
257 Park Avenue South,
New York, NY 10010, USA.

Macmillan Distribution Services,
56 Parkwest Drive
Derrimut, Vic 3030,
Australia.

Every effort has been made to trace the copyright holders of the photographs in this book but one or
two were unreachable. We would be grateful if the photographers concerned would contact us.

Typeset by: Phoenix Photosetting, Chatham, Kent
Printed in the EU

A catalogue record for this book is available from the British Library.

Visit Omnibus Press on the web at www.omnibuspress.com

Contents

Introduction

I first visited Tanworth-in-Arden – the small, peaceful village in which Nick Drake grew up, died and was buried – in 1993, when I was 21. It was the first time I'd been on a 'pilgrimage' to a stranger's grave and, not wanting to rush the experience, I headed first to the village's only public house and ordered a pint.

The landlord immediately identified me as a non-local and enquired about my visit, and I soon found myself chatting to him about Nick Drake, of whom he had no vivid memories, and Nick's mother, Molly, whom he recalled with fondness. He also recalled a great number of people who had visited over the years, from as far afield as America and Europe, to pay their respects to Nick Drake. They too, like me, would first head for the pub and ask where they might find his grave. So I finished my drink and asked, and he happily pointed me in the right direction.

It took me a while to find, probably because I was expecting to see some large monument befitting a legend. But, no: just a small, weather-worn headstone beneath an old, bending tree, remembering Nick and his parents, who share the ground with him. And then I noticed the inscription on the back of the headstone:

*NOW WE RISE
AND WE ARE EVERYWHERE*

1

I stayed for a while, perhaps wondering why I had come, or what exactly one is supposed to say to a gravestone, or maybe just waiting for someone else to turn up; but nobody did.

Next I made my way to Far Leys, once the Drakes' family home. I wanted to take a photo of the house for a fanzine I was planning on putting together. I made my way through the village (the landlord had also given me directions to the house), which was neat and picturesque; the sort of place where everyone knows everyone by name, and a stranger's face gets noticed.

I found Far Leys to be a grand old house at the end of a quiet lane, the rear of which looks out onto lovely views of the Warwickshire countryside; rolling hills and green fields. I parked at the rear, where the garden stops and the fields begin, found a gate, climbed over it and, after a short walk, had a clear view of the rear of the magnificent house that stood on the hill opposite me. I snapped away.

As I returned to my car, glad now that I had come, I was greeted by two members of the village constabulary (possibly the entire force) who'd had a tip-off that a man was snooping around. They searched me and the car and found nothing incriminating, which seemed to disappoint them.

What exactly did I think I was up to, they wanted to know. And so I explained: I'd come to see Nick. As a fan, I'd come to see the grave, get a pic of the house, pay my respects. What could be more normal? It must happen every day...

But, of course, they'd never heard of Nick Drake.

It was shortly after my visit to Tanworth that I began producing *Pink Moon*, a fanzine dedicated to the life and music of Nick Drake. My introduction to Nick Drake was via Paul Weller, name-checking him in an *NME* interview around the time of his *Wild Wood* LP, in 1993. It took me a while to get into Nick's music, as it was so different to anything else I'd been into up to that time. I started with *Five Leaves Left*, and still vividly remember lying on my bed, listening to it repeatedly, staring at the cover, trying to get my head round this strange new sound. I felt a connection to Nick and his music immediately, but didn't know what it was. I had a vague idea I might write about him, meet him and interview him. I didn't know he was dead at the time.

My next purchase was the *Way To Blue* compilation. The variety of the music on this CD pulled me in and hypnotised me, and I was hooked. I began to feel I had to find out as much as I could about this enigmatic artist. The songs sounded like they'd been written by, for, or about, someone like me, and yet their beauty and sophistication was of a level I had not heard before.

Next stop was Chas Keep's *Record Collector* article, and the *Fruit Tree* box set which contained all the tracks available, at the time, and a lengthy biography. And so something of the mysterious life behind the songs was revealed. I had already learned from the *Way To Blue* sleeve notes that Nick had died, but I don't remember being shocked or surprised, just sad, and perhaps disappointed I would never get to meet him. My mission now was clear; I had to find out all I could.

I started placing adverts in the music press, requesting info from collectors and fans. I bought old copies of music papers from Nick's day and tracked down some articles written before and after his death.

I soon had a good collection of material and, by way of a tribute, decided to put it together in a fanzine. I decided to call it *Pink Moon*, because I liked the mystery of that title. The name was later changed to *Pynk Moon*, after the style of *Bryter Layter*, to give it its own identity, but shall be referred to as *Pink Moon* or *PM* throughout this book. I had enough material for three issues, and had no intention of continuing the fanzine after that. I assumed that I had already collected all the Drake-related written material that existed in the world. I was wrong.

The first issue appeared in 1994. It was an A5 booklet of 24 black and white pages, with a pink, paper cover. The contents, as for the following two issues also, consisted of a biography I had written myself, 'borrowing' information from all the other biographies I had recently read, and photocopies of all the articles and pictures I had gathered together. I put more adverts in the music press, offering the first issue for £2, and waited.

Letters began to trickle in, then flooded in; sometimes up to 20 a day. I was amazed by the excitement and interest generated by my humble tribute, and glad to hear from so many other people like myself, from all around the world, who were huge fans of Nick Drake and desperate for a source of information on him. What also surprised me was the volume of new material that was submitted to me for future editions. It began to look like *Pink Moon* would take on a life all of its own.

New material was created by fans who wanted to share their thoughts and feelings, whether via articles, essays or poetry. Press articles from all around the world were reproduced, and I began to have contact with people who had known and worked with Nick, such as Robert Kirby and David Sandison, both of whom contributed interviews. And so it continued for 19 issues that sold approximately 10,000 copies all around the world. The format never changed, nor did the price.

Many of the articles that featured in the pages of *Pink Moon* appeared in other publications first. At this point I would genuinely like to thank all the people who didn't sue me (or even complain!) when I used their material without asking. Although, in later days, *Pink Moon* became quite independent with its own unique and original content, it would never have got started without the 'contributions' of others. My excuse is that it was only intended as a small tribute, and I honestly never expected to sell more than 50 copies; it never really occurred to me, in my youthful enthusiasm, to get permission to reproduce articles, and a lot of them came from defunct magazines anyway. Hopefully, reproducing some of those articles in this book will go some way to making amends. If it's any consolation, I never made any profit from *Pink Moon*; perhaps just a couple of pounds for a few cigarettes, and a couple of beers, at the end of the week (ah, happy days). The fanzine was always produced and sold as cheaply as possible, with all profits going back into advertising or producing future issues. It was never a job, just a hobby I did in my spare time.

In the year 2000, the last issue, number 19, was published. At the time it was not intended to be the last. To this day people ask me why I stopped producing the fanzine, and my reply is that I don't really have an answer. In some ways I guess I grew out of my desire to learn as much as I could about the mysterious Drake; my life changed and I had other interests; I became a little tired of the mechanics of physically producing the fanzine three or four times a year. Whatever the reason, it just came to a stop.

So, what is this book? It's a compilation of articles, interviews and other writings, as they appeared in the fanzine, some with a little additional commentary, or editing from me, some revised and updated by the authors for this book, where they wanted to improve on the originals; and some new material as well.

The articles are either presented in chronological order, or grouped together in sections, such as 'Live Performances' or 'Film and Television'.

My criteria when selecting material was to choose work that I felt best captured the spirit of, or expressed a truth about, Nick Drake. For example, there's an article by Charles O'Meara, from 1988, which includes an interview with Joe Boyd, who shares a memory he has of a smiling Nick enjoying a late-night poker game with a 'cockney criminal type' who was a mutual friend of theirs; or there's the haunting review of Nick playing live, by Brian Cullman; or the only recorded interview with Nick, by Jerry Gilbert. These are invaluable snapshots of the past, and memories like this are as close to Nick as people can get, without listening to his songs, and should be recorded for posterity.

There's a myth cultivated over the years that Nick was lauded by critics, but shunned by the record-buying public, which contributed to his depression and downfall. I've lost count how many times I have read statements to this effect. However, when we go back and look at the archive material, the actual critical reviews of the day, we find that few writers actually knew what to make of Nick at all. Worse than critical, we find them in some cases indifferent; and you can hardly blame the public for not rushing down to Woolworths. The book starts with these fascinating reviews – the first material to be published about Nick, from 1969.

Nick did have some supporters, of course – Connor McKnight, Jerry Gilbert and David Sandison – who wrote about him while he was alive, urging the public to check him out. Their works also feature in these pages.

This is simply a book about Nick Drake, by people who appreciate Nick Drake, for fans of Nick Drake. I hope you enjoy it.

Jason Creed, August 2010.

The Albums

Five Leaves Left

In his article, 'Requiem For A Solitary Man', in *NME* on February 8, 1975, Nick Kent wrote of the release of Nick Drake's debut album, *Five Leaves Left*: "... Island Records loved it, critics drooled, everybody who made it their business to know exactly what was happening in music nodded in their arch pseudo-sage-like pose and predicted great things and Drake immediately became the object of the 'But, my dear, have you heard?' conversations. The public largely ignored the album of course ..."

But was it true? Let's take a look at the moment when a critic first drooled over Nick Drake's stunning debut. This is taken from the *Melody Maker* (author unknown), July 26, 1969, and is the review in full, not just a snippet:

> *NICK DRAKE: Five Leaves Left (Island)*
> *All smokers will recognise the meaning of the title – it refers to the five leaves left near the end of a packet of cigarette papers. It sounds poetic and so does composer, singer and guitarist Nick Drake. His debut album for Island is interesting.*

This one is from *NME*, October 3, 1969, by "G.C.":

> *NICK DRAKE: Five Leaves Left (Island ILP/ILPS 9105; 37s 5d)*
> *Nick Drake is a new name to me and probably to you. From an accompanying biography, I read that he is at Cambridge reading English, was*

'discovered' by Fairport Convention when they played on the same bill, and spent some time travelling in Europe, a trip which has greatly benefited his songwriting. I'm sorry I can't be more enthusiastic, because he obviously has a not inconsiderable amount of talent, but there is not nearly enough variety on this debut LP to make it entertaining.

His voice reminds me very much of Peter Sarstedt, but his songs lack Sarstedt's penetration and arresting quality. Exceptions are Mary Jane, a fragile little love song, and Saturday Sun, a reflective number on which the singer also plays a very attractive piano.

Five Leaves Left was released in September 1969. The original vinyl album featured the second pink label design with sleeves printed by E.J. Day. There was a misprint on the album cover, putting 'Way To Blue' and 'Day Is Done' the wrong way round, but the track listing on the label was correct. On later "palm tree" issues, the mistake appeared on both the label and the cover. The track listing for the album was chosen by its producer, Joe Boyd, after the record was mixed, and was based on what sounded good to his ear, rather than any predetermined concept of Nick's. It was discussed with, and approved by, Nick. The lyrics to 'Three Hours' appeared on the inside of the gatefold sleeve (titled 'Sundown'), alongside the lyrics to 'River Man', and both sets contained verses which were not actually sung on the finished record. The unsung verse from 'River Man' was:

> *Betty fell behind a while,*
> *Said she hadn't time to smile, or die in style,*
> *But still she tries,*
> *Said her time was growing short,*
> *Hadn't done the things she ought*
> *Where teacher taught*
> *And father flies.*

The unsung lyric from 'Three Hours', titled 'Sundown', went:

> *We had all the time, but failed to make sense,*
> *From one side to the other we fell to the fence,*

The one hope of failure had turned for the best
While three hours had taken the hope of success.

There has been some debate over whether *Five Leaves Left* was ever released on cassette. Alvin Smith remembers that it was, although he has long since lost his copy, and has been trying to verify its existence ever since. In a letter to *Pink Moon*, Alvin wrote: "…Just yesterday I had a phone call from my pal Phil Smee (album-cover designer extraordinaire) with some light to shine on the *Five Leaves Left* cassette story. Seems Phil is about to design a forthcoming Free CD on Island and had spent the afternoon in conversation with a representative from the label. This bloke claims, with some degree of insider knowledge, that because the printed (*Five Leaves Left* LP) label was pink (which I definitely recall to be the case), it must, at the very least, have been issued at the time of the vinyl and, furthermore, it could have been in a batch of four (with Fairport Convention, Free and Spooky Tooth) which were Island's initial cassette releases – not far off the first by any label…"

The first artist to cover Nick's songs, before any were even released, was Elton John, in 1968, as part of a Warlock promotional album. He recorded 'Time Has Told Me', 'Saturday Sun', 'Day Is Done' and 'Way To Blue'. Only 100 white label acetates were pressed, one of which apparently changed hands for over £700 in the Nineties.

A more recent tribute was the brilliantly titled *Five Leaves Theft*, released in 1998. The CD covers all ten tracks from *Five Leaves Left*, in the correct order, and features 'some of Italy's popular stars'. The cover versions, all sung in English (apart from a bit of 'Way To Blue', which is in French), bear little resemblance to the originals, being the artists' own interpretations, in a modern, lo-fi style. The album was released by Baracca & Burattini (cat. no. 4918962).

Bryter Layter

Bryter Layter was released in November 1970. It should have had a pink label, according to the catalogue number and the fact that Cat Stevens' *Tea For The Tillerman*, released the same month, had one. However, by the time of an article in *Record Collector* magazine in 1996, no one could find one, and it had become the 'Holy Grail' for collectors of Nick Drake.

Critical reviews of the album were again sparse, but a vast improvement over those for *Five Leaves Left*. It seems a few individuals, outside of his close circle of friends and colleagues, were picking up on Nick's talent.

This review, by Jerry Gilbert, is from *Sounds*, March 13, 1971:

NICK DRAKE: Bryter Layter (Island ILPS 9134)
I get the feeling that only a Joe Boyd-Paul Harris alliance could have produced such a superb album as this. And once again a great slice of the credit must go to Robert Kirby, whose splendid arrangements are as noticeable on this album as they were on Nick Drake's last album. On their own merits, the songs of Nick Drake are not particularly strong, but Nick has always been a consistent if introverted performer, and placed in the cauldron Joe Boyd has prepared for him, then things start to effervesce. Also joining guitarist Nick Drake on various tracks are Dave Pegg, Richard Thompson, Ray Warleigh, Mike Kowalski, Paul Harris, Ed Carter, Lyn Dobson, John Cale, Chris McGregor, Pat Arnold and Doris Troy; it seems nothing has been spared to make this album a success, and Joe Boyd and Nick Drake have certainly succeeded in their intentions. There has been a long gap between Nick's first and second albums, and anyone who has seen Nick performing at Witchseason concerts in the interim will recognise tracks like Hazey Jane. And this, like all his songs, does take time to work through to the listener, with help from the beautiful backing which every track receives.

Bryter Layter review, from *Melody Maker*, March 13, 1971, by Andrew Means:

NICK DRAKE: Bryter Layter (Island ILPS9134).
This is a particularly difficult album to come to any firm conclusion on. For one thing the reaction it produced depends very much on the mood of the listener. It's late night coffee 'n' chat music. The ten tracks are all very similar – quiet, gentle and relaxing. Nick Drake sends his voice skimming smoothly over the backing. The range of musicians used is apt to catch one unawares. Among the talents employed are Dave Pegg

(bass) and Dave Mattacks (drums) both of Fairport Convention, Richard Thompson (ld gtr) ex-Fairport, John Cale (celeste, piano and organ) ex-Velvet Underground, Ray Warleigh (alto sax), Chris McGregor (piano) and Pat Arnold and Doris Troy (backing vocals).

Bryter Layter review, *Record Mirror*, March 20, 1971, by Lon Goddard:

NICK DRAKE: Bryter Layter (Island ILPS 9134)
A beautiful guitarist – clean and with perfect timing – accompanied by soft, beautiful arrangements by Robert Kirby. Nick isn't the world's top singer, but he's written fantastic numbers that suit strings marvellously. Definitely one of the prettiest (and that counts!) and most impressive albums I've heard. Remember what Mason Williams did with Classical Gas? A similar concept here, but Nick does it better – it's refined. Happy, sad, very moving.

Long after the release of *Bryter Layter* an early pressing of the album, with alternative artwork and a catalogue number, was discovered in a second-hand shop. The front cover features a Keith Morris face-shot of Nick, relaxed and smiling, on a background of red and blue dots over a pattern of tiny hexagons.

Jonathan Nelson, who reproduced the artwork for *Pink Moon*, wrote: "The cover houses two, one-sided white label demo copies of *Bryter Layter* and belongs to a dealer in London. A friend of the dealer bought it some years ago from a Record & Tape exchange for only a couple of pounds!

"On the non-music side of one of the discs is an almost illegible hand-scratched message, but most interestingly, suggesting a working title, on one of the labels is, handwritten, 'Nick Drake Poor Boy.'

"The cover is fully printed, roughly cut and stapled with the opening along the top edge. The rear of the cover uses the same photo as the standard, but smaller, with the same cream base-colour, blue dots and red hexagons and a different block layout for the text, which is black on the plain cream. It has the Robert Kirby misprint – 'All bass arrangements,' (rather than 'brass') – like the standard copy, and also states cover design by Nigel Waymouth."

11

'Nick Drake'

'Nick Drake' (Island SMAS 9307), released in America in 1971, was a compilation album featuring tracks from *Five Leaves Left* and *Bryter Layter*, distributed and marketed by Capitol Records. The vinyl LP came in a gatefold sleeve; the front cover shows the now-familiar picture of Nick, by Keith Morris, leaning against a wall as a running man blurs past. Around the photo is a cream background, and above in large letters *'Nick Drake'*. On the rear cover is a photo from the same session, with Nick leaning against the wall, but with a woman, in a headscarf, walking by. The centre of the gatefold features a large, colour, head and shoulder shot of Nick, laughing and reclining in a field of long grass.

The track listing for this rare compilation is: (side one) – 'Cello Song', 'Poor Boy', 'At The Chime Of A City Clock', 'Northern Sky'; (side two) – 'River Man', 'Three Hours', 'One Of These Things First', 'Fly'.

Apparently a cardboard cut-out of Nick was placed onstage at the launch party. A favourable review of the album, by Steve Holland, was published by *Rolling Stone* magazine in 1971.

Pink Moon

Pink Moon was released in February 1972. If you're not familiar with his story you could be forgiven for thinking that, by the time of the release of his third LP, Nick Drake was a household name. Far from it, he was barely any more famous than on the release of his debut. He may have inspired a small, cult following, but nothing more. Again this is reflected in the lack of Drake-related material in the press. There was a full-page advert for the album in *Melody Maker*, and two reviews, that I've been able to find, published in this country. A third review, published in a French magazine, seems to appreciate Nick's work the most.

The first review by Jerry Gilbert is from *Sounds*, March 15, 1972:

NICK DRAKE: Pink Moon (Island ILPS 9184)
Island appeared to have forgotten about Nick Drake until he ambled into the offices one day and presented them with this record. No one knew he'd recorded it except the engineer and it's a long way removed from the mighty sessions that Joe Boyd used to arrange for him. Nick Drake

remains the great silent enigma of our time – the press handout says that no one at Island even knows where he is living, and certainly he appears to have little interest in working in public again. The album consists entirely of Nick's guitar, voice and piano and features all the usual characteristics without ever matching up to Bryter Layter. One has to accept that Nick's songs necessarily require further augmentation, for whilst his own accompaniments are good the songs are not sufficiently strong to stand up without any embroidery at all. Things Behind The Sun makes it, so does Parasite – but maybe it's time Mr Drake stopped acting so mysteriously and started getting something properly organised for himself.

Melody Maker, May 1, 1972, by Mark Plummer:

NICK DRAKE: Pink Moon (Island)
John Martyn told me about Nick Drake in ecstatic terms and so it seemed the natural thing to do, bag the album when it came in for review that is. It's hard to say whether John was right or not. His music is so personal and shyly presented both lyrically and in his confined guitar and piano playing that it neither does or doesn't come over. Drake is a fairly mysterious person, no one appears to know where he lives, what he does – apart from writing songs – and there is not even a chance to see him on stage to get closer to his insides. In places he is a cult figure, and among the new younger sixth form and college audience there are pockets that go overboard to catch the latest glimmer of news that moves along the verbal news meanderings. The more you listen to Drake though, the more compelling his music becomes – but all the time it hides from you. On Things Behind The Sun he sings to me, embarrassed and shy. Perhaps one should play his albums with the sound off and just look at the cover and make the music in your head reciting his words from inside the cover to your own rhythmic heart rhymes. Nick Drake does not exist at all. Four lines of Know – 'Know that I love you, Know that I don't care, Know that I see you, Know I'm not there.' It could be that Nick Drake does not exist at all.

From the French magazine *Best*, by Herve Muller, May 1972 (translated by Jerome Dumont):

In today's wave of singer-songwriters of a more or less 'folk' inspiration, Nick Drake is far from being a well-known name. However, while stable-

mate Cat Stevens would acquire a growing reputation, Drake recorded two albums, Five Leaves Left and Bryter Layer, which made a strong impression on a lot of people ... but failed to sell. It has to be said that Nick Drake himself didn't do much to help: he is barely known at Island, and at the moment nobody knows where he lives. He is to reappear occasionally every six months or so, a laconic, vaguely mysterious character, and his live appearances are almost nonexistent.

It's most probable that, were he willing, Drake could be as famous as some of the greatest names of the genre. The first two albums, with their subtle compositions and deep sensibility, the delicate beauty of the melodies, the voice full of rich inner warmth, and Nick's beautiful guitar playing, revealed a genius, supported by a cast of some famous musicians – like Lyn Dobson – and often very elaborate arrangements. It is quite revelatory that on his new album – far from the general mood – Drake has chosen to be alone, accompanying himself on guitar and piano. This is just as well, and fits perfectly with the intimacy of his style: the songs of Nick Drake are like whispered poems, and their profound charm, all in nuances where humour and emotions are confusingly entwined, has something ethereal. The spell is completed just by the magic of his voice and music, but another asset of Nick's is being a wonderful poet who, by comparison, makes so many 'wordy' singers seem ridiculous.

I won't pick any favourite track here, as they're all extraordinary, the instrumental Horn included. 'Saw it written and I saw it say, Pink Moon is on its way ...' May it be true.

At The BBC

On August 6, 1969, the Nick Drake *Peel Session* was broadcast. This was the first of two sessions that Nick would record for BBC radio; and there would have been a third, had he turned up to play it. The tracks he played, unaccompanied, were 'Cello Song', 'River Man', 'Time Of No Reply' and 'Three Hours'. It was recorded at Maida Vale, Studio 5, the day before the broadcast; the producer was Pete Ritzema and the engineer Mike Harding.

A *Pink Moon* reader, who worked for the BBC, discovered and sent in photocopies of the records that the BBC kept on Nick; among them an audition report featuring comments from a production panel, who, on October 10, 1969, judged whether his material was suitable for future recording and broadcasting. They gave him a unanimous pass. These are the producers' comments:

Sings his own songs and accompanies himself on guitar. Attractive vocal quality somewhat reminiscent of Donovan. Quite professional behaviour on the session. (Pete Ritzema)

Nice artiste – excellent guitar work – pleasant voice. YES.

Self-accompanied vocalist singing current folk music. Good of its kind, but of limited appeal. Probably his own compositions. YES.

Vocal/guitar. Guitar excellent. Voice, moody and rather down and a little bit uninspiring. Suitable to broadcast, but would probably only be in specialist late night programmes. Not a general appeal contribution. Type of artist who would appear on 'John Peel' record label – underground, folky. YES.

At last something that holds one's interest from the start. Some good playing with a quiet voice which none the less rivets one's attention. The second number has a husky vocal quality with a competent guitar backing. YES.

A very good voice well used in the interpretation of his songs. Good intonation and diction. Very competent and pleasing guitar accompaniment. YES.

Very competent guitarist. Interesting material. Presumably he composes his own music, and consequently sings it with intimate feeling. Ideal for 'Top Gear' type programmes. PASS.

Contemporary balladeer who accompanies his own songs on guitar which he plays very well. YES.

Contemporary singer/guitarist. Material good and he plays well. Unanimous pass. Jimmy Grant, 20/10/69.

The following, dated October 22, 1969, was from Marjory Lipscomb (of 'Light Entertainment' at the BBC) to the late Anthea Joseph, who worked for Joe Boyd at Witchseason, informing her that Nick had received 'favourable reports' for his 'trial broadcast' on the John Peel programme. The letter in full reads:

Dear Miss Joseph,

(Nick Drake)

We refer to the above artist's recent trial broadcast in John Peel Programme.
    The recording of his part in this programme has now been played to our Production Panel, and we are pleased to inform you that his performance received favourable reports. As a result, his name has been added to the list of artists available for broadcasting generally.
    You will, no doubt, appreciate that the selection of artists from the

large number suitable for broadcasting is governed by our programme requirements; however, if we are able to offer any engagement we shall, of course, get in touch with you immediately.

Yours sincerely,
Marjory Lipscomb,
Assistant to Light Entertainment Booking Manager.

The *Peel Session* has never been officially released and it's believed that the original tapes were lost or destroyed. At least one, almost complete, copy does exist though. *Pink Moon* reader Steve Greenhalgh wrote to me in March 1997: "My then future wife and I saw Nick perform live in Manchester. It must have been the end of 69, or 1970. I think it was a university gig – UMIST or Owens. Fairport Convention were headlining as I recall. Nick was the 'warm up' act. He perched on a high stool, never said a word, and started playing. Unfortunately the booze was flowing freely amongst his potential audience who, for the most part, continued talking amongst themselves. After a couple of numbers (one of which I think was 'River Man') Nick stopped playing, vacated the stool and sloped off the stage carrying his guitar gingerly by the neck…

"In those days, I had a reel-to-reel tape recorder and used to tape lots of sessions from the Peel shows (*Top Gear* on Saturday and his Wednesday evening shows).

"Initially, these were recorded with a microphone placed at optimum distance in front of the radio speaker – crude but, sometimes, reasonably affective. It was in this way I caught most of Nick's session broadcast on 6th August 1969 on the Peel Wednesday early evening show.

"I have to confess that I only began listening to the programme during Nick's first number, 'Time Of No Reply', so I only have the latter half of this track. I then recorded in full, 'Cello Song' and 'River Man'. Tragically, after a few minutes of his last number, 'Three Hours', which featured some amazing guitar, the tape ran out."

Trying to make these recordings public in 1997, Steve Greenhalgh founded the 'Northern Sky Nick Drake Appreciation Society' of which anyone could become a member for a £9.50 registration fee. For their money, members would receive a certificate and a 'free' cassette copy of the Peel session. However, Steve ran into 'difficulties' over the distribution; he returned all monies and the tapes never saw the light of day.

Regarding the original recording by the BBC, David Barber later said that the tape had probably been destroyed after the broadcast, because the BBC in those days didn't bother to keep a library of their recordings, but recycled their tapes instead.

John Peel himself was quoted as saying he believed the tapes still existed somewhere in the BBC vaults.

Another file that the BBC kept on Nick lists his appearance, on April 13, 1970, on the *Night Ride* programme, but there is no mention of the songs recorded. Nick was accompanied on this session by flute player Iain Cameron, who remembers this session in his article 'Meeting & Listening to Nick', which appears later in this book. There is no known recording of this show in existence.

Nick received £15,15 shillings for each of his BBC appearances. It also mentions a recording date (March 28, 1972, to be broadcast on April 14, 1972, which ties in with the release of the *Pink Moon* album) for an appearance on Bob Harris' *Sound Of The Seventies*, for which Nick would have received another £15,15 shillings, had he turned up. But, as it says on the lower half of the page, upside-down, in barely readable handwriting: *Unreliable – Did not appear for recording on 28/03/72 – has a habit of disappearing without trace.*

The final page is a form which Nick was supposed to complete and sign before recording. The form was never completed, but lists Nick's address at the time as: 3 Aldridge Road Villas, W11.

Live Performances

It's often reported that Nick played only a few gigs before giving up performing altogether, but how many did he actually play? It's impossible to get a precise figure nowadays, but we can at least get a 'ballpark' one.

Nick's earliest performances, aside from his folk song busking days in the South of France, were at Cambridge, where he teamed up with Robert Kirby to play functions and balls. These early concerts, at which Nick was, by all accounts, a happy performer, are remembered elsewhere in this book by Iain Cameron and Robert Kirby.

Nick also played the odd pub whilst he was at Cambridge, and one occasion was remembered by Alan Frasier in a letter to *Mojo* magazine: "Back in the Sixties, probably in late 1968, I was in Cambridge for some reason, and happened to take in a concert from some artist I'd never heard of before. It must have been in a pub. I only caught his surname, Drake, but came away thinking he was one of the finest performers I'd ever heard. I kept an eye out for this guy, and when Dylan's Nashville Skyline came out in mid 69 I saw that one musician was credited as Pete Drake. (I think this English Drake performed at least one Dylan cover.) This put me on the wrong track for a while, but I eventually found out that Pete was an American, and not the guy I'd seen.

"Anyway, this guy Drake's recording career completely passed me by for some reason, and it wasn't until February 1997 when I saw the cover of *Mojo* 39 in a newsagent that I finally realised just who I'd seen that night nearly 30 years before!

"I can't recall any details of the set list (apart from that Dylan cover) but now after getting the *Fruit Tree* set, buying Patrick Humphries' book, and corresponding on the internet with Drake fans, I have a pretty good idea of what I must have heard that night. After a life of Dylan fandom, I was surprised to find out that Drake's sets aren't documented with the same rigour, so I still can't find out the exact venue and date of the performance. My vague memories have infuriated a Drake fan or two, as none of those I've corresponded with actually saw him live as I did. Even so, I can strongly confirm Gabrielle Drake's assertion that Nick was a brilliant performer, or at least he was that night. It's just a pity I never caught his first name."

Another 1968 performance was at the Roundhouse, London, as part of a festival for peace. Nick was given a 10-minute slot at about two in the morning, and, of course, Ashley Hutchings was in the audience. Speaking on Alan Taylor's *Joe Boyd – A World Of Music*, broadcast on BBC Radio 2, Ashley said: "Well, I was at the Roundhouse with Fairport – it was one of those many charity concerts – and I was wandering around, and I felt this voice, and I looked at the stage and I moved closer, and I saw this, what I thought was, very commanding figure, very handsome young chap, erm... very upright. The closer I went to the stage, the more I was drawn into his music, his personality. I mean, he was very... a very quiet, unassuming performer, but everything came together: his guitar playing, his singing, the way he looked and the atmosphere. The aura, if you like, that he created, made me, drove me, to go and talk to him afterwards when he came off stage and say, 'I really liked that,' you know, 'Have you got a deal?' or whatever. I mean, I had no vested interest, I was a young musician, but I got details from him and passed them immediately on to Joe Boyd, because I felt that he just had something very special."

Next stop was the Royal Festival Hall (September 24, 1969) where Nick supported Fairport Convention, thus going from low-key gigs to a prestigious 2,500-seater venue. It was Fairport Convention's return to the stage after the band had been involved in a road accident which claimed the life of their drummer Martin Lamble. Gabrielle Drake said Nick's performance was mesmerising, and Joe Boyd agreed.

Also in 1969, Nick played at a folk club in Hull, in a pub called the Haworth. The gig was witnessed by folk singer Michael Chapman, who later said that Nick struggled because the crowd were not a 'Drake' crowd, and wanted rousing songs. He describes Nick as playing beautifully and remaining silent between the songs.

Nick's last known gig of 1969 was at a social club in Smethwick, near Birmingham. *Pink Moon* reader Robert Jones was in the audience: "The venue was the Guest, Keen & Nettlefolds works social club, Thimblemill Road, Smethwick. The occasion was the end of season dinner for their rugby club. Both of these facts may seem strange to people today, they even seem strange to me when I look back, but I've seen some very good bands in stranger places. Nick Drake was due on between the end of the meal and the start of the disco.

"My friends and I arrived at about 8.30 p.m. knowing that the meal would be over, and that we would probably be able to get in for very little. Nick came on at about 9.00 p.m.; at this time they were still clearing away tables and arranging chairs around the room. Not a good start for an artist who needs to be listened to. He placed his chair in the left-hand corner of the stage and without a word proceeded to play. I'm not sure what he started with – almost 30 years is a long time – but something in me says that it was 'The Thoughts Of Mary Jane'. By this time he had an audience of about 10 to 15 people in front of the stage; the rest of the people in the hall continued to arrange chairs, clean up after the meal, or just chat amongst themselves. For Nick, who was obviously very nervous, this must have seemed like total rejection; although he did have a small, but very attentive audience. Nick put on a brave face whilst being ignored by the majority of the people in the room, but you could tell he was feeling the strain. He managed to get through about five or six numbers against the constant chatter in the background, and his audience of 10 to 15 remained loyal, enthralled by the obviously huge talent in front of them.

"I'm afraid that we were of little consolation to Nick as he looked out at the majority of the crowd who were totally oblivious to his undoubted talents. After his five or six numbers he just packed away his guitar in its case and walked off the stage without a word."

John Martyn was interviewed by Rob O'Dempsey for Issue 5 of *Musin' Music* magazine, and was asked about Nick's performances: '... He never felt comfortable in front of an audience; it was embarrassing to go and see him, because he was obviously in such utter discomfort; he just didn't like going on and playing. He primarily played for his own amusement. Heaven knows how Joe Boyd discovered him, because I know for a fact that he didn't play in public, and one of the things that contributed to his utter detestation of the whole thing was that he was once booked to play a Coventry Apprentices Christmas Ball ... In those days, let me see, 'Purple Haze' was 'in', and here he was singing 'Fruit Tree' and all these gentle, breezy little ballads, and I can just imagine them swigging back the Carlsberg Special and totally giving him an awful hard time. I know that that gig lived forever in his mind; he'd talk about it quite regularly ... I'd hate to be affected that badly by one social experience ... Dreadfully sensitive fellow; dreadfully sensitive.'

Nick's first booking of 1970 was at Ewell Technical College on Saturday, January 24, supporting Genesis and Atomic Rooster. This gig was advertised in *Melody Maker*, but there are no eyewitness reports to prove that he played this one.

On February 6, he played the Free Trade Hall in Manchester, and *Pink Moon* reader Dave Burrows was in the audience: "I saw Nick Drake in concert; the sixth of February 1970, the Free Trade Hall, Manchester. A one night stand on one of the ubiquitous Fairport tours. A triple bill – 'Fairport Convention and Friends' – the friends being Nick Drake and John and Beverley Martyn. The Martyns didn't make it to Manchester (car breakdown, I think) so Nick had a solo support slot.

"Fairport were hot in Manchester in 1970 and the Free Trade Hall was packed at the kick-off. I remember the hushed atmosphere and intensity rather than the specifics of Nick's performance. I can't name any songs that he played but I recall his gangly, loose-limbed gait as he walked on and off the stage. There was some great guitar playing and a husky, resonant voice – in a 'live' setting similar to Bridget St. John. I wish I could remember more, but it's a long time ago."

On February 21, he supported John and Beverley Martyn at the Queen Elizabeth Hall, for what was billed as 'a concert of contemporary music'. The audience numbered about 1,500. Nick's set included two, as yet, unreleased songs: 'Hazey Jane I' and 'Things Behind The Sun'. David Sandison, Nick's press officer at the time, later said: "He was embarrassing, if you wanted a big sort of 'Hi! Here's my new single,' or, 'Here's a track off my new album.' He was embarrassing because he was very gauche, and there were long pauses between the numbers, because he was either retuning or thinking about it. But it was intense. I would love to have seen that set in a smaller room, rather than in a room with 1,500 people. It's too impersonal. But it was engrossing because the songs were engrossing and the mood was engrossing. But the contrast between him and John and Beverley Martyn who came on with a full band … couldn't have been greater."

In March, 1970, Nick was supposed to go on the road with Sandy Denny's band Fotheringay. He was booked to play five gigs (listed below), but again there is no evidence to prove that he played any of them. A copy of the programme for this tour, featuring a rare photo of Nick, sold on eBay recently for around £60.

Birmingham Town Hall, March 16
Leicester De Montfort Hall, March 18
Manchester Free Trade Hall, March 20
Bristol Colston Hall, March 22
London Royal Festival Hall, March 30

Next, Nick was booked for an all-nighter at Bedford College on Friday, May 8, where he was on the same bill as various groups and artists, including Spencer Davis, John Martyn and Graham Bond. Another advert appeared in *Melody Maker* for this one, but again no evidence of an appearance exists.

Also, probably in the earlier part of 1970, Nick played a regular Saturday night spot at Cousins, on Greek Street, London. There are three known bookings at which he supported the Third Ear Band, John Martyn and John James. We know that Nick played at least one of these gigs because he mentions it in his interview with Jerry Gilbert. He was also supported there by a young musician called Brian Cullman, who recalls the experience later in this book.

Another (rumoured) performance in 1970 was a short, unbilled set at an open-air concert in Yorkshire which was headlined by Free.

Nick's last known booking was a return to Ewell Technical College on Thursday, June 25, where he supported Ralph McTell. Nick did play this time and Ralph has gone on record saying how extremely nervous Nick appeared to be and that, halfway through playing 'Fruit Tree', he suddenly got up and walked offstage.

So, as per usual, contradictions abound. Embarrassing or mesmerising? Of course, we have to conclude that Nick was never cut out for live performance. Out of the 20 gigs listed above, he played at least 10.

Magazine Articles & Memories

Something Else for Nick?
Jerry Gilbert, *Sounds*, March 13, 1971

Nick Drake is a shy, introverted folk singer, who is not usually known to speak unless it is absolutely necessary. But Nick is not the kind of folk singer who will drift into your friendly neighbourhood folk club; in fact, if you've seen him perform, the chances are that it was on the bill of a sell-out Festival Hall concert.

Last week I spoke to Nick, and eventually discovered that it has been precisely these kind of gigs that had hung him up – the reason why he has shied away from public performances almost without exception.

"I think the problem was with the material, which I wrote for records rather than performing. There were only two or three concerts that felt right, and there was something wrong with all the others. I did play Cousins and one or two folk clubs in the north, but the gigs just sort of petered out," Nick explained.

Nick pointed out that he was not happy with the way the gigs were working out and he couldn't get into them properly. Why, then, was he performing at such esteemed venues as the Festival Hall?

"I was under some obligation to do them, but it wasn't the end of the world when I stopped. If I was enjoying the gigs it would have made much more sense."

Don't, however, gain the impression that Nick is not a superb artist. Placed in the right context, his songs produce quite a stunning effect over a period of time. He has worked on two albums with Witchseason producer Joe Boyd, the latter having been released only last week. Entitled *Bryter Layter*, it features some of the musicians who have contributed to the success of the John and Beverley Martyn albums, notably Paul Harris; and Robert Kirby's arrangements are just as important as Nick Drake's songs.

Says Nick: "I had something in mind when I wrote those songs, knowing that they weren't just for me. The album took a long time to do, in fact, we started doing it almost a year ago. But I'm not altogether clear about this album – I haven't got to terms with the whole presentation."

What's the next step for Nick? "I think there'll be another album and I have some material for it, but I'll be looking around now to see if this album leads anywhere naturally. For the next one I had the idea of just doing something with John Wood, the engineer at Sound Techniques."

Would there be any gigs to promote the album? "I don't think that would help – unless they were done in the right way. I'm just not very sure at the moment, it's hard to tell what will turn up. If I could find making music a fairly natural connection with something else, then I might move on to something else."

In Search of Nick Drake
Connor McKnight, *Zig Zag 42*, June 1974

Six months ago I walked wearily into the office of *Zig Zag*'s production consultant. Weary because it was 1.30 in the morning, and because the then current issue of the magazine was virtually complete; after days of last minute toing and froing, it was all over for another four weeks. He was playing a record that began, imperceptibly, or so it seemed to me, to fill the entire room with music of ravishing beauty. I asked who it was and he replied Nick Drake. Two hours later I left his place with my head reeling, after keeping him up so I could listen to Nick's other albums. I also, fortunately, persuaded him to lend me Nick's latest album *Pink Moon* and when I got home I played it again to try and dispel my incredulity that there was music this good that I hadn't been aware of till now. It worked and I went to bed anxiously waiting for the next day, which offered another chance to listen to some more. My feelings about Nick Drake and his music haven't altered since then.

Island in the person of their press officer informed me that they didn't know where Nick Drake was, what he was doing, or what he intended to do, but did send me some photos and their old press releases about him. One in particular was an extraordinary testament, at least in terms of the normal guff that record companies issue, so I phoned the man who had written it, because by now I had to know as much as possible about how this beautiful music came to be made. This is what I uncovered.

Nick was discovered, as the saying goes, at the Roundhouse, where he was playing during a twelve-day festival for peace arranged by one of the more hip members of the aristocracy. Tyger Hutchings, then playing bass with Fairport Convention, had gone to see Country Joe, and heard Nick playing. He was sufficiently impressed at what he saw that he went backstage, talked to Nick and got a telephone number from him. He also, more importantly, mentioned Nick and his reactions to Joe Boyd, who was then head of Witchseason Productions. Joe Boyd rang Nick and asked him to send Witchseason some tapes of his songs. The tape he sent in had been put together on a home recorder. Joe remembers that it contained among others, three songs that were to appear on Nick's first album *Five Leaves Left*. Joe called Nick back and told him how impressed he had been with the tape, and asked him to visit Witchseason as soon as he could. Now that is pretty much the story that has been told of every musician in his first encounters with a record company since Elvis did his famous one minute mile to get to the Sun studios in 1954. Two bits of the story are different. The first was that Nick was visiting Witchseason and not a normal record company.

Joe Boyd had been the first head of Elektra in this country, but had left in 1966 to become a producer, working on, among other things, the Floyd's first single 'Arnold Layne', which was released in 1967. With the growth of the underground, there was a need for individuals who were a part of that culture to take on the business aspects, and this Joe did, so Nick was going to an enterprise that was part of the movement itself, rather than exploiting it. Witchseason's impact on British music of that era was profound. It was one of the first units to offer the artist a complete service – management, agency, publishing and recording, and in terms of the taste that it exhibited in the artists it signed, it was equally innovative – Fairport Convention and The Incredible String Band. But that is another long, long story.

The second difference was that whereas Sam Phillips had first started the great Presley history with the remark, when he was considering who to record 'Without You', 'What about the kid with the sideburns?' Joe Boyd had a very special response to what he sensed of Nick Drake from the tape. "I've always had a very strong taste for melody and it has obviously been reflected in the people I have worked with. And it was Nick's melodies that really impressed me. There was also a considerable feeling of sophistication and maturity about his songs and the way they were delivered. While the tapes were in the office, I was playing them to someone who came in and he made a remark to the effect that they sounded like Donovan, and although a lot of people went on to echo that sentiment it was one that had never occurred to me, because I really did feel that I was listening to a remarkably original singer. And from the point of view of a producer, I felt that they lent themselves perfectly to good arrangements. So when he came into the office we decided to do an album."

The album was *Five Leaves Left*, and I think, together with Family's *Doll's House*, although it received nothing like as much acclaim, it is one of the best first albums ever made. The songs are stunningly evocative; Nick latches onto a theme and develops the inspiration it furnishes him, with a fierce, but always coherent intensity. His voice provides all the melody, with the arrangements underpinning its subtlety. It's a curious thing about Nick Drake's songs that they are almost impossible to sing, for he teases notes and phrases in such a way that they only seem to exist for the moment; and as soon as that moment has passed all that remains is a disembodied memory. His voice lacks stridency, but never falters, and this comes from his very gentle attack, so it seems that all the notes are slurred. The arrangements on the album demonstrate Robert Kirby's literally fantastic empathy with Nick. They are sombre and melancholy, devoid of gaiety, but exhibit a total apposition to the voice.

Joe Boyd had already sensed that arranging would be the key to a successful production, and the first attempt was made in the summer of 1968, using material from a new demo tape that Nick had got together in the spring. The arranger they used was the same guy who had arranged James Taylor's first album (anybody know his name?) and had been recommended to Joe by Terry Cox then with Pentangle.

They recorded three songs which Joe recalls as having 'nice' arrangements, with the quotation marks he would wrap around the word evident in his voice. In spite of enthusiasm from Polydor, it was generally agreed that another soul would be needed. Robert Kirby was a friend of Nick's from Cambridge; Nick had told Joe that he wanted to use him on 'Way To Blue', one of the tracks that they were attempting to record. Joe remembers being fairly sceptical, but agreed to meet Kirby in Cambridge, where Kirby explained that he wanted to use just six strings and Danny Thompson on bass. Joe's scepticism turned to delight when he heard the results of the one track and so Robert Kirby went on to do the arrangements for all but one song on that album and all the material on Nick's next, *Bryter Layter*, with results little short of magic. Joe describes Nick as being very shy and tentative, with Robert Kirby throwing out ideas until one stuck, but detected in Nick's quietness a determination to wait and keep working until the music was exactly how he wanted it to be. The album took nearly a year to finish. "That was partly because Sound Techniques had just had 8-track equipment installed, partly because Nick was very unhappy at Cambridge where he was still an undergraduate, but most of the delay came from his reticent, yet strangely determined approach to recording." Another relationship that was forged during the making of the album which has had a profound effect on the subsequent work of Nick was with John Wood, who was the engineer at Sound Techniques, where Joe Boyd did the major part of his work. Joe describes the relationship thus: "John was tremendously interested in Nick's work, and very, very protective towards him. Their relationship is still a mystery to me. Every time I come back to England I try to arrange it so that John and I could do some work with Nick if he wanted to, but ..."

The tape was played to Island at Sound Techniques, who agreed to release it, although the general feeling was that in spite of the relationship with Island, Witchseason could easily have obtained another record company's interest. Island's efforts can possibly be gauged by this peerless piece of prose that was sent out with the record. It reads in part: "Nick Drake is tall and lean. He lives somewhere in Cambridge, somewhere close to the University (where he is reading English) because he hates wasting time travelling, does not have a telephone – more for reasons of finance than any anti-social feelings and tends to disappear for three or four days at a time, when he is writing, but above all ... he makes music!" The record sold almost nothing. One feeling at the time still current in quarters that ought to know better is shown in a reply to my question as to why it didn't sell. "It only sold six copies because there are only that many people miserable enough to buy it."

Joe Boyd explains the problems encountered in trying to bring Nick's music to the public: "The conventional approach is to get the artist performing, but Nick had very little experience of playing live, and the one occasion when he tried was disastrous. It was the first gig the Fairports did after the car crash, and Nick opened the show. He did three numbers, and then 'Things Behind The Sun', which I remember, because I was really upset that it wasn't on *Bryter Layter*. Nobody really seemed interested, and of course Nick's enthusiasm for performing was minimal. It became very hard to get bookings for him. We also tried to establish some interest in him as a songwriter, for that way he would at least make some money, but again it was to no avail." Curiously enough, one person who did express interest in doing an entire album of Nick's songs was Francoise Hardy, to the extent that she brought her musicians over ready to record, but the only published material had been recorded by Nick already and he couldn't or wouldn't write fresh material for her, so she abandoned the project. So Nick was left in hiatus, surviving on the £15 a week provided by Island. Thank God he didn't perish, because he went on to make an altogether brilliant album, *Bryter Layter*.

If Nick's career was helped initially by the sympathetic handling he received from Witchseason, it is also true that Witchseason bloody nearly ruined it, and it was only Joe Boyd's personal commitment that saved it. John Martyn, in last month's issue, reflected the general state of the malaise afflicting Witchseason, but Joe's comments maybe enlighten it a bit more. "1970 was Witchseason's last year and was insane. I realised my limitations as a manager, and was generally pretty unenthusiastic; the Fairports were in the shit with all the splits, and the String Band also required a lot of my time. I just generally took against working that year – I OD'ed on record producing, I did twelve albums! The only ones that were the real thing were *Bryter Layter* and Mike Heron's solo album, *Smiling Men With Bad Reputations*, and of the two Nick's took by far the greater amount of my time."

I think the album is near perfect. It exhibits the abundant quality that was evident on *Five Leaves Left* – beautiful tunes beautifully sung, with arrangements that are audacious in what they attempt, and brilliant in what they accomplish.

Most of the musicians came from loose affiliations with Witchseason's other bands, for example the Fairports, and musicians like Chris McGregor who had worked on Dudu Pukwana's album with Joe. Paul Harris was over to do John and Beverley Martyn's *Road To Ruin* and John Cale was linked via Joe Boyd's work with Nico. The record was again engineered by John Wood and arranged by Robert Kirby. The album had taken a year to get finished, but this was probably as much to do with the availability of players as with Nick's search for, and insistence on, perfection. I asked Richard Thompson who overdubbed some guitar on one of the tracks what Nick was like to work with. "He is a very elusive character. It was at Trident I think, and I asked him what he wanted, but he didn't say much, so I just did it and he seemed fairly happy. People say that I'm quiet, but Nick's ridiculous. I really like his music, he's extremely talented, and if he wanted to be, he could be very successful."

It is at this stage that it is necessary to say, in a spirit of regret rather than one of vicarious and morbid interest in such things, that Nick as a person has difficulty communicating with other people, and is, sadly, a very insecure person. Which explains both his remoteness, and may also explain the stark beauty of his work. The title of the album with its overtones of enervating gloom says it all.

The year proved too much for Joe Boyd and Witchseason was folded, the whole shop going to Island, but since Island were supporting Nick, and he didn't need management or agency anyway, it didn't have too much bearing on matters. What is interesting is a story told me that one of the clauses in the heads of the agreement for the sale was that Island

31

undertook to release *any* album by Nick Drake. Joe Boyd neither confirmed nor denied the story, saying gnomically, "Chris Blackwell has always been right behind Nick." Whatever the truth is, it says much for Joe's commitment to Nick that Island did continue to support him, and maybe goes some way to dispel the doubts left by John Martyn's remarks last issue. Anyway, Joe Boyd left for the States, and the general feeling was that without his help, the musical career of Nick Drake would fritter out.

It was not to be. During 1971, Nick rang up John Wood and said that he wanted to make an album. He had been in touch with John off and on, and John agreed. "He arrived at midnight and we started. It was done very quickly. After we had finished, I asked him what I should keep, and he said all of it, which was a complete contrast to his former stance. He came in for another evening and that was it. It took hardly any time to mix it, since it was only his voice and guitar, with one overdub only. Nick was adamant about what he wanted. He wanted it to be spare and stark, and he wanted it to be spontaneously recorded."

Nick was very depressed during the recording of the record, and, one can assume, during its gestation; and because Nick Drake is an artist who never fakes, the mood is reflected in the album. Without the arrangements it is impossible to avoid the searing sensibility behind the record. The album makes no concession to the theory that music should be escapist. It's simply one musician's view of life at the time, and you can't ask for anything more than that.

Dave Sandison, who was Island's press officer at the time of the album's release, had this to say. It is worth quoting, because it is so rare to find sincerity in these releases, and also what he says is true.

"The first time I ever heard Nick Drake was when I joined Island and picked out his first album *Five Leaves Left* from the shelf and decided to listen to it because the cover looked good.

"From the opening notes of 'Time Has Told Me' to the last chord of 'Saturday Sun', I was held by the totally personal feel of the music, the words, and the vague feeling of intruding on someone's phone conversation.

"The first time I ever saw Nick Drake was at the Queen Elizabeth Hall, when he came on with his guitar, sat on a stool, looked at the floor and sang a series of muffled songs punctuated by mumbled thanks for the scattering of bewildered applause from the audience who didn't really know who the hell he was, nor cared too much. At the end of his last song, his guitar was still holding the final notes as he got up, glanced up, then walked off, his shoulders hunched as if to protect him from the embarrassment of actually having to meet people.

"The first time I ever met Nick Drake was the week his second album *Bryter Layter* was released. I went to the old offices of Joe Boyd's Witchseason company in the beautiful Charlotte Street, W1, with the intention of telling Nick how much I liked the album, and that I wanted him to do a couple of interviews.

"He arrived an hour late, shuffled in, and shrugged disinterestedly when I suggested a coffee around the corner. When we got there (it was about lunchtime), I asked him if he wanted a cup of tea, something to eat, anything? He looked down at the dried ring of saucer-stain on the table, and smiled to himself, meaning 'no'.

"For the next half-hour he looked at me twice, said maybe two words (one was to agree to an interview, which was done and was a total disaster), while I rattled on at him about every kind of nonsense, trying to get some kind of reaction, until I ran out of voice, paid the bill for my coffee and sandwich, and walked him back to Witchseason.

"That was more than a year ago. Since then, I have seen Nick twice. Once, when for some reason still never explained he came to Island's offices, stayed for maybe half an hour, addressed perhaps three monosyllabic words to people he knew from Witchseason, before leaving as mysteriously and silently as he'd come.

"The second time was a week or so ago, when he came in, smiling that weird little smile, half-mocking, half-bewildered, and handed over this, his new album. He'd just gone into the studios and recorded it without telling a soul except the engineer. And we haven't seen him since.

"The point of this, is this: nobody at Island is really sure where

Nick lives these days. We're pretty sure he left his flat in Hampstead quite a while ago. We have a bank agreement for him so that he's always got his rent money and some spending bread, so there's no need for him to make more appearances than he does.

"The chances of Nick actually playing in public are more than remote.

"So why, when there are people prepared to do anything for a recording contract or a Queen Elizabeth Hall date, are we releasing this new Nick Drake album, and the next one (if he wants to do one)?

"Because we believe Nick Drake is a great talent. Quite simply that. His first two albums haven't sold a shit, but if we carry on releasing them, maybe one day, someone in authority will stop to listen to them properly and agree with us, and maybe a lot more people will get to hear Nick Drake's incredible songs and guitar playing. And maybe then they'll buy a lot of records and fulfil our faith in Nick's promise.

"Then. Then we'll have done our job."

(David Sandison, November 1972)

Al Clark ended his review of *Pink Moon* in *Time Out* with this observation: "Sadly, and despite Island's efforts to rectify the situation, Nick Drake is likely to remain in the shadows, the private troubadour of those who have been fortunate enough to catch an earful of his exquisite 3 a.m. introversions."

Little has been heard of Nick since then. He seems to have retired into a world in which music doesn't exist as a form of expression any more. He spent some time in 1973 working with John Wood, but little came of it that satisfied him, and he occasionally spends time with John and his wife at their home in Suffolk. Joe saw him late last year. "He rang me to ask if he could stay with me since his car had broken down in Pimlico. John Wood had previously told me that Nick had said that he had some tunes but no words, and when he arrived I talked to him and mentioned this to him. He just looked at me and said sadly, 'I haven't got any tunes any more.'"

John wouldn't talk much about Nick, because he feels protective towards him, except to say, "Nick has terrible trouble leading any sort of a life at all these days."

If Nick Drake never recorded another song, he has left me at any rate, a gem of a legacy, music that is honest and true to himself, and because it is so, the complete affirmation of what music is about.

Nick Drake: Death of a 'genius'
Jerry Gilbert, *Sounds*, December 14, 1974

Nick Drake died in his sleep two Sundays ago, leaving a legacy of three superb, stylised albums on the Island label. He had been ill – perhaps weary is a better expression – for some time, but at the time of his death his enthusiasm had never been as high for he was totally immersed in the prospect of completing his fourth album.

"He was a genius," proclaimed arranger Robert Kirby when I spoke to him last week. "There was absolutely no one to touch him in England." Kirby worked on Nick's first two albums.

Nick Drake was a complete enigma. He seldom spoke and few knew what was going on inside his head. John Martyn tells of trips Drake would make down to his home in Hastings, stay the weekend and then leave as mysteriously as he had arrived, having uttered scarcely a word.

He hated performing, and although in the heyday of Joe Boyd's Witchseason management he would be found opening shows for bands like Fairport Convention at the Festival and Queen Elizabeth Halls, personal appearances had petered out almost entirely by the end of 1970.

There was an ominous portent in a lot of his work and for Nick Drake the outside world was something he found difficult to look squarely in the face. He seldom raised his eyes from the ground and would walk around with a curious enigmatic half-smile most of the time.

My one attempt to interview Nick back in 1970 was a total disaster – no words, just the smile.

Nick's first album, *Five Leaves Left*, was widely acclaimed, as was the quite remarkable *Bryter Layter*. The final album was *Pink Moon*: Drake arrived at Island's Basing Street offices one day, introduced himself, handed over the finished master and disappeared. No one even knew he'd made the album except engineer-producer John Wood, who probably knew Nick better than anyone.

That album was, for the most part, a grim acceptance of death, intensely personal – as with all his music. Robert Kirby is right when he says that Nick Drake should not be built into a legend or some kind of posthumous superhero in the way that Jim Croce was. He would never have wished for that.

Yet whilst respecting Nick Drake's life in obscurity it is important to at least hint at the influence he had upon musicians like John Martyn and mention the extrovert brilliance as recalled by Robert Kirby when Nick was out of the public eye, sitting back relaxing and playing blues and ragtime pieces like you wouldn't believe.

"People don't realise but he had remarkably broad tastes," says Kirby. "One of the biggest shames is that no one will ever hear him play blues.

"He was the happiest I'd ever seen him just before his death, but he was usually despondent simply because he had nothing to do and couldn't see a direction for himself. I think London upset him, he didn't like it here at all, in fact he was upset by a lot of things that he saw and heard, he was just too sensitive.

"He was ready for death alright, I just think he'd had enough, there was no fight left in him. All his songs were epigrams – little extracts of philosophy and you could either take them optimistically or pessimistically.

"Yet I get the feeling that if he was going to commit suicide he would have done so a long time ago."

The Final Retreat
David Sandison, *Zig Zag 49*, January 1975

The amount of coverage Nick Drake's death had in the weekly musical comics just about sums it all up, really. Jerry Gilbert did a beautiful piece for *Sounds* – and they cut it down to half a dozen paragraphs. No one else mentioned his departure with much more than a cursory nod of acknowledgement.

OK, so the guy did no more than a dozen gigs before more than 150 people, and they raised no ripple you'd notice. He released three albums in four years, and together they probably didn't sell enough to cover the cost of one. What the hell do you want? Front page in *The Times*?

So you look at the facts and have to agree that when The Bay City Rollers have a new number one and Gary Glitter's made his comeback after what we've been told is a crucial throat operation, there's precious little space left for the accidental death of some recluse folkie.

But.

The biggest three-letter word in the dictionary, that. But, Nick Drake was a lovely cat. But he wrote songs that'd tear your soul out if you relaxed for a second. But in a world full of bullshit, hype, glittery horrors with the talents of dead oxen and the integrity of starving rats, Nick Drake was a man of sincerity, an artist of tremendous calibre and one of the few entitled to be called unique. But what the hell do they care?

Connor McKnight cared enough to research a superb piece on Nick Drake in *Zig Zag 42*. Jerry Gilbert cared enough to pressure *Sounds* into printing a shortened obituary. A lady who worked with me at Island Records when Nick's second album *Bryter Layter* was released cared enough to cry when I told her he was dead. Joe Boyd and John Wood, his former producer and recording engineer, care like hell. And I do too.

I have no intention of making this short appreciation much more than that. This history, if you haven't read it and care to, is contained in Connor's story and is as complete as time allows. There is some to add.

Since *Zig Zag 42*, when Connor's story ended, Joe Boyd, John Wood and Nick Drake did get together in the Sound Techniques studios and put down some tracks.

Nick and Joe had got together in February 1974, while Joe was on a fleeting visit to London. At the time Nick told Joe that not only didn't he have any words left, he also didn't have any tunes any more. What Joe didn't tell Connor is that he was shocked enough by this response to give Nick a good talking to. Joe describes it as a pep talk, but what he did was to tell Nick that he was wasting and abusing a real and valuable talent and that he ought to stop pissing about and knuckle down to work.

In July, Boyd was in London again and heard from Nick. He wanted to go into the studio and try out four new songs he'd pretty well got together. Nothing elaborate was done in that session – just guitar and voice tracks.

"Nick couldn't sing and play at the same time," Joe recalls. So they recorded the guitar and then the voice. It was shaky, but the melodies – the factor which elevates Drake's work above any of his rivals – were as beautiful as ever. Apart from a general dissatisfaction with the vocals, Nick, Joe and John were happy.

Boyd had to return to the States for more work and left Nick with every intention of returning in the autumn to continue what they decided was the beginning of a fourth album. Success with a number of projects, not the least being the Maria Muldaur albums, forced Joe to spend all his time in American studios, so the planned grand reunion never came off. By the end of November, Nick Drake – described by everyone around him as being more happy than they'd known him for a long time – was dead from an accidental overdose of sleeping pills.

Joe Boyd is still clearly upset about Nick's death and honest enough to express sorrow that he didn't make it back. His relationship with Nick was pretty special to him. "In a lot of ways it was a frustrating one, because although I felt I was able to get through to him and deal with him as a musician, I was never really able to handle him as a person. I don't think I ever gave him the feedback he needed."

It was a problem most people encountered, mainly because of Nick's own personality, which changed discernibly through his last few years. John Martyn was someone originally close to Nick, someone with whom Nick communicated eagerly, both as a musician and as a person. But even John, and his wife Beverley, were eventually unable to handle Nick's moods. He'd turn up at their home in Hastings, unannounced but welcome, sit around for a couple of days without saying more than a few monosyllabic words, and leave as unexpectedly and as abruptly as he'd arrived. It upset both of them; they tried to help and draw him out, but they got nowhere fast.

My few dealings with Nick at Island were at the time when he was withdrawing more and more away from all but a few people. He was non-communicative to the point of pain and spent a lot of time in a secret world of his own making. He'd vanish for long periods. Traced to a house full of flats in Hampstead, you'd discover that no one even knew his name, or that he'd taken the flat in an assumed one.

But to contradict any generalisations made about his mental state, he would keep in touch with Joe Boyd and John Wood, still call Robert Kirby, the old friend from his days at Fitzwilliam College, Cambridge, who was brought in to arrange *Bryter Layter*. And he still managed to come up with the songs which made his last album *Pink Moon*.

The album was stark – just Nick's voice, his guitar and occasional piano. It reflected his mood at the time, and the dissatisfaction he felt about the way *Five Leaves Left* and *Bryter Layter* had sounded. At the time of *Bryter Layter* I got the impression from Nick that he didn't like the strings, or the way the album was presented. Fine, if his studio relationship with Joe Boyd and Robert Kirby had been as bad as Tim Hardin's was with the people at Verve.

In Hardin's case, the rhythm and vocal tracks had been laid down, Hardin had split and strings shoved on when he was far away.

Nick Drake personally supervised every aspect of Kirby's arrangements, working with him and – as Joe Boyd tells it – mainly getting Kirby to chart out what Nick had, in the main, already planned. *Bryter Layter* took a year to make because Nick Drake spent that long making damn sure it was precisely the way he wanted it.

So if Nick Drake failed to realise the sounds he heard in his head, *Pink Moon* trusted to the Drake audience to hear them for themselves. Maybe he did it that way so he could play it at home and hear the different arrangements himself.

But what Joe Boyd calls 'the steady progress of retreat' was going on, and Nick spent more and more time at his parents' home in Stratford-upon-Avon [*he means Tanworth-in-Arden – ed.*], and latterly in Paris. His deal with Island had ended, and with it the regular 15 quid a week salary/pocket money Joe had arranged with Chris Blackwell before handing over the Witchseason stable to Island. Joe isn't sure how Nick made ends meet. There certainly weren't any royalties coming in.

Nick had enough friends to ensure that he had somewhere to stay and watch out for him. Joe and he had talked about getting a new deal together so that he could get some kind of advance, but a hoped for meeting between Nick, Joe and a still-interested Chris Blackwell never came off because Nick just didn't want to commit himself to any kind of contract.

And that's pretty well the way it ended. Unfinished, inconclusive and typically up in the air.

If you haven't heard Nick Drake's work, dare I suggest you go out of your way and do so? It won't change the ending of the story, but it could change you. Don't take my word for it – Joe Boyd says it far heavier than I ever could: "Of all the albums I ever made, the two albums I produced by Nick are the ones I'm most proud of. I listen to them often because Nick Drake was extraordinarily good. Nothing he ever did was less than striking, and he had the gift of writing melodies of incredible beauty."

Joe Boyd, it may be worth reminding you, has been responsible during his career for some of the definitive British folk and rock albums, including Fairport's *Unhalfbricking* and *Liege & Lief*, for John and Beverley Martyn's *Stormbringer* and the best Incredible String Band albums.

Two pictures of Nick Drake pretty well sum up what I think his relationship with us norms was. The first was on the cover of *Five Leaves Left*. Nick stands, supporting and being supported by a wall, static and observing while a figure blurs past. Nick tended to let a lot of the world blur past – and was probably smart to do so.

The second was the back view of Nick – shoulders hunched, hand in scruffy jacket pocket, trouser turn-up torn – used to illustrate the ads for *Pink Moon*.

We spent a day with Nick, taking innumerable excellent arty shots of him with a romping Gus the Labrador, or sat on park benches with a wistful, far-away (and bored?) look in his eyes. But that retreating back said it all.

And it still does.

Nick Drake
Frank Kornelussen, *Trouser Press*, January 1978

The English folk scene has always seemed obscure and mysterious from this side of the Atlantic Ocean. The traditional music of the British

Isles began a renaissance in the Fifties and Sixties with Ewan MacColl, A. L. Lloyd, Ian Campbell and Martin Carthy. They paved the way for the singer/songwriter/guitarist, who, with a nod towards Bob Dylan, updated the traditional folk style and synthesised it with blues and jazz. The early sixties wave was led by Bert Jansch, John Renbourn, Davy Graham, Ralph McTell and Donovan, to be followed by Fairport Convention, John Martyn, Pentangle and the Incredible String Band.

Some of these people reached nationwide, even worldwide success. Many remained in relative obscurity, rarely if ever playing in the States. They remained in the folk club and small concert scene in England. Their music was often intricate, introspective and unlike the 'folk music' we are accustomed to. One of them was Nick Drake, who remains to this day an almost anonymous figure, even in his own country.

Nick Drake was born June 18, 1948 in Burma, where his father was working. The family moved to their British home at Tanworth-in-Arden when Nick was about six years old. Though always a quiet boy, Nick did well at his boarding school, especially in athletics (where he still holds records for his school). His mother, Molly, played piano and wrote songs. The urge for music rubbed off on Nick and he played clarinet and saxophone in his teens. By the age of 16 he had begun to play guitar, working at it with a friend. He listened and learned from Bob Dylan, John Renbourn and Bert Jansch. By the time he was 18 Nick had a fairly large repertoire of standard folk songs as well as some of his own, which steadily grew in number.

While living at home he made a lengthy tape for his parents of some 25-odd songs. Among them were 'Saturday Sun', 'Day Is Done', 'Way To Blue' (later used for his first LP), 'Princess Of The Sand', 'Joey' and 'Mayfair'. Also included were 'Don't Think Twice', 'Tomorrow Is A Long Time', 'Let's Get Together', '500 Miles', a duet with his sister Gabrielle, Bert Jansch's 'Courting Blues', and a Renbourn-style country blues, 'Black Mountain'.

Nick began college around 1968, and it was there things began to happen for him. He became good friends with other musicians, learning from them and playing with them. Paul Wheeler, a songwriter and guitarist (his 'Give Us A Ring' is on John Martyn's *Road To Ruin*), remembers Nick as 'one of the lads' but with eclectic tastes. He met Nick through Robert Kirby, a talented musician who helped Nick with arrangements for his songs (Kirby was a recent member of Strawbs). Wheeler cites Jackson C Frank, an American singer who lived in Britain, as an influence, and recalls Traffic and Randy Newman as two of Nick's favourites.

Though Nick was considered shy and quiet, Paul Wheeler didn't find him withdrawn. He enjoyed Nick's dry humour and was impressed when he first heard 'Time Has Told Me'. Another very close friend, Brian Wells, also claims Nick was happy at Cambridge, but Wheeler describes it as a 'precious environment'. Paul brought his friend John Martyn by once or twice, and he also was impressed with Nick, especially with 'River Man' which he calls 'my fave' of Nick's.

In 1968 Ashley Hutchings, then bassist for Fairport Convention, heard Nick performing at a benefit in London's Roundhouse, asked Nick for his number and promptly told producer Joe Boyd how impressed he was with him. Boyd had already established himself through Witchseason Productions, recording LPs by Fairport, John Martyn and the Incredible String Band (as well as being the latter's mentor/manager). He called Nick and asked for a tape, which Nick obliged. Joe described his initial impression of Drake's music as 'melodically unusual and sophisticated'. There was no doubt that Nick had to be nurtured and recorded.

Five Leaves Left was begun in mid–1968. Almost a full year's work went into it, and the LP was released in July, 1969. John Wood says Nick was 'fairly shy' though he 'had a very definite feeling how he wanted things to be'. Three or four tracks were cut, and it was collectively decided to augment some songs with string arrangements. An arranger was brought in with disastrous results. Nick's mention of Kirby's abilities brought raised eyebrows from Boyd and Wood, but they gave in. Kirby worked on four songs, and declined working on 'River Man' which was done by Harry Robinson.

Five Leaves Left was received with admiration by critics but didn't sell very well. In late 1969 Nick made his first important public appearance at the Festival Hall concert which welcomed Fairport Convention back to the public eye. Joe Boyd remembers it as 'a fateful occurrence – he played fantastic – he was brilliant, he was nervous. It was a magical kind of thing, the audience was mesmerised'. Nick himself was surprised and bewildered.

For a first LP, *Five Leaves Left* is an astounding album. Nick's strange, jazzy sound was superbly juxtaposed against his rhythmic and melodic music. His lyrics were distant yet strangely to the point, described by one reviewer as 'exquisite 3 a.m. introversions'. 'River Man' is the epitome of Nick's style, bossa-nova full of beauty and uncertainty:

Going to see the river man
Going to tell him all I can
About the ban on feeling free
If he tells me all he knows
About the way his river flows
I don't suppose
It's meant for me

Sometime after the LP's release Nick quit college and moved down to a bedsitter room in Hampstead, nearby close friends John and Beverley Martyn. He had decided to forsake his English studies and become a professional musician. It was there he wrote most of the songs for his second LP, *Bryter Layter*.

Paul Wheeler called *Bryter Layter* a 'city LP'; that city is London. Nick remained there, seeing John and Beverley most often and dropping in on friends like Keith Morris (who took most of the photos on Drake's albums). But Nick was alone. John Martyn says 'he was the most withdrawn person I've ever met'. London seemed to deepen Nick's feelings of loneliness, yet it sharpened his music.

Bryter Layter was released in January, 1971; again, almost a year's work went into it. Joe Boyd got Nick to respond in the studio, using 'house' musicians Richard Thompson, Dave Pegg, Dave Mattacks, Ray Warleigh, Paul Harris and even John Cale. Cale loved Nick, according to Boyd, although Nick was 'a bit bewildered by him'. Both Boyd and Wood consider *Bryter Layter* the finest LP they or Witchseason ever produced. Boyd comments, 'The music was so good.' Wood says it's the only LP he did which he wouldn't alter at all.

43

The songs were intensely personal images and amazingly elusive. At times, as in 'Poor Boy', Nick pokes fun at his own faults. In 'Hazey Jane I' he sings to an unknown girl:

> *Do you curse where you come from?*
> *Do you swear in the night?*
> *Would it mean much to you if I treat you right?*

Perhaps it's 'Northern Sky' which most epitomises Nick, lyrically and musically. John Cale's arrangement complements Nick's desires and feelings:

> *I never felt magic as crazy as this*
> *I never saw moons knew the meaning of the sea*
> *I never held emotion in the palm of my hand*
> *Or felt sweet breezes in the top of a tree*
> *But now you're here*
> *Brighten my northern sky*

London became too much for Nick, and he moved back to his parents' home soon after the LP's release. He was deeply depressed and troubled, physically ill as well, and spent some time in hospital. Still, he felt he had more music in him and he had songs ready for another LP. Though still weak and depressed, he carried out his plans. Joe Boyd had sold Witchseason and was no longer around to guide and help things along. John Wood says, "Nick rang me out of the blue and said he wanted to make a record." Nick took a flat in Muswell Hill, and stayed there while he worked on *Pink Moon*. He refused to tell anyone where he was, and it was only by accident they eventually did find out.

Pink Moon was exactly what Nick wanted; Wood describes it as 'stark and honest. The other two LPs were a little too pretty or sweetened up for Nick.' These songs said more about him. The LP was indeed stark. It was, however, well done and contained some of Nick's finest songs, only his voice, guitar and piano being used. It was recorded in three days with a minimum of overdubs.

The album seems to bear out Nick's mother's idea of his being a true

Gemini, two people living in two worlds (his music and his home life). One song expresses extreme joy, another sad and bitter longings. Some songs, like 'Know', do both. 'Place To Be' and 'From The Morning' are hopeful love songs to life; 'Parasite' is a caustic self-putdown. The title track expresses a strange doomsday:

> *Saw it written and I saw it say*
> *Pink moon is on its way*
> *And none of you stand so tall*
> *Pink moon gonna get ye all*

Keith Morris, Nick's friend, says the LP was a 'cry to be heard'.

The months after *Pink Moon*'s release (in February, 1972) brought Nick into a period of deepening depression. His mother said he appeared to be desperately unhappy. Around April Nick suffered a breakdown and was voluntarily hospitalised for about five weeks. He claimed he had no music left in him, though his parents heard him working over songs in the music room. Still, he stated he had given up performing and recording, thinking only of perhaps writing songs for others. Nick was never really able to cope with the life of a professional musician; he wanted recognition but not the trappings and put-ons of being in the public eye. He was never comfortable with recording companies, going so far as keeping his studio sessions secret and only sending Island the completed tapes of *Pink Moon*.

With the help of his parents, friends and prescribed medication, Nick got along after his release from hospital. In early 1973 he contacted John Wood, saying he wanted to record again. Joe Boyd was back in England and came by to produce the sessions. Wood described them as 'rough going'; Nick said he felt like a zombie, that he couldn't feel anything. He also refused to record his voice at the same time as his guitar, over-dubbing some rough vocals almost a year later. Nick produced four songs from these last sessions. Though the vocals are a little shaky the guitar work is superb. The songs are nearly complete and very good, definite proof that he did have music left in him. Once again the songs show the two sides of Nick Drake, sunlight and shadow. In 'Voice From The Mountain' he sings:

45

Tell me, my friend, my friend, tell me of love
A tune from the hillside, a tune full of light
A flute in the morning, a chime in the night
I know the game, I know the score
I know my name, but this tune is more

'Rider On The Wheel' is also an optimistic view of life. 'Black Eyed Dog', though, shows the darkness Nick dwelled in; the title is a medieval symbol of death. The guitar figure is modal and sparse, and he sings:

Black eyed dog he called at my door
Black eyed dog he called for more
Black eyed dog he knew my name

One should hesitate to read too much into this; desperation is a feeling common to many people. The final number, 'Hanging On A Star', is a simple song of rejection, a sort of cry for help.

Writing in *Zig Zag* magazine in June, 1974, Connor McKnight called on Nick to try again, stating that he and his music were still loved and respected. Drake's parents remember that in his own quiet way Nick was moved by it. He silently showed it to them, and in the weeks after began to work on songs again. They had thought, "Nick's back on the note." Perhaps it was this article and a pep talk from Joe Boyd which prompted Nick to work on those final tracks. Nevertheless he was starting to come out of his shell just a bit.

John Martyn wrote a song for Nick, the title song of his LP *Solid Air*:

You've been getting in too deep
You've been living on solid air
You've been missing your sleep
And you've been moving through solid air

John seems to have known Nick as well as one could. Nick is sometimes considered to be very down and low-keyed in his songs, but John says it's not true: "He was quite conscious of the image portrayed in his songs. He was not a manic depressive who picked up a guitar; he was a singer-guitarist in every sense. He was unique in his own way. I loved him very much: it was a privilege and honour to know the man." John Wood seconded those feelings saying: "I was proud to have worked with him."

Still, Nick's gradual process of withdrawal had taken its toll. Though his spirits were better, he was moody and uncertain. His mother said he struggled very hard against his 'illness'. In October, 1974, Nick went off to Paris with an acquaintance. There he met some people who took to him and put him up for several weeks. Nick loved Paris, loved the Seine, and returned home with plans to move there. He talked about writing again, played guitar – even studied French using a record course.

Nick Drake died in the morning hours of November 25, 1974. He had been prescribed a drug, Tryptizol, for his depressions. Tragically, neither he nor his parents were warned that even a slight overdose could affect the heart. He had been happy, though his mother thinks he suffered through a bad night, and that it was purely accidental and out of desperation that he took the pills. The coroner called it suicide; his parents and friends are certain it was anything but.

Nick once said, "In moments of stress, one forgets so easily the lies, the truth and the pain." His death was a tragic waste. There will probably be no monuments for Nick Drake, but he doesn't really need them. He left them for us. His music, embodied in his three albums, stands as a testament to his soul, talent and beauty.

Nick Drake
Brian Cullman

In the summer of 1970, I played a professional club for the first time, opening for Nick Drake at Cousins, a dark underground club on Greek Street in London. I got the job through the good graces of Nick and Andy the Greek, who ran the place. I'd met both of them through John Martyn, an extraordinary guitarist and songwriter. When I arrived in London that spring, fresh from high school, I somehow had the good fortune to stumble through his doorway in Hampstead, and for much of that summer he and his wife Beverley took care of me: fed me, nursed me through an unhappy romance, and listened with dignity if not patience as I began trying to write songs on an oversized Gibson Hummingbird that seemed, in the London of 1970, an overt display of opulence. (When I opened the case at Cousins, my guitar got an ovation.)

For all of my enthusiasm and earnestness, I was terrible, and in retrospect the kindness of that audience seems formidable, almost an act of international good will. Nick Drake was also very bad, but for different reasons. His shyness and awkwardness were almost transcendent. A tall man (he stood over 6ft 3ins), his clothes – black corduroy jacket and pants, frayed white shirt – hung around him like bedclothes after a particularly bad night's sleep. He sat on a small stool, hunched tight over a tiny Guild guitar, beginning songs and, halfway through, forgetting where he was and stumbling back to the start of that song, or beginning an entirely different song, which he would then abandon midway through if he remembered the remainder of the first. He sang away from the microphone, mumbled, and whispered, all with a sense of precariousness and doom. It was like being at the bedside of a dying man who wants to tell you a secret, but who keeps changing his mind at the last minute: come closer; no, on second thought, go away.

There was a new song he sang that night that he kept starting and stopping, never completing; he finally just sang the opening lines over and over again: "Do you curse where you come from? Do you swear in the night?" (from 'Hazey Jane I'). It was chilling and morbidly fascinating. No one took their eyes off him for a second – there was a real sense of keeping him there with our gaze and our attention, that if we looked away, however briefly, he might disappear or forget that we were there and go to sleep.

Nick had a talent for disappearing. Once, late at night, I was out driving with John and Beverley and a guitarist friend of theirs, Paul Wheeler, on our way to an all-night Indian restaurant; we passed Nick driving along in an old white Chevy and signalled for him to join us. I remember the smell of curries and hot breads very clearly, remember the white linen tablecloths and the white linen turbans on the waiters, the ubiquitous cats sliding back and forth from the kitchen, and the strong smell of hashish being smoked upstairs. We sat for hours, eating, drinking wine that Paul had brought, and only when we stood up to pay the cheque did I realise that Nick was with us, that he in fact *had* been with us for the entire meal.

None of which would mean very much if his music weren't extraordinary. In the course of a very short life (he out-lived John Keats by about a year, which, with his slightly morbid sensibility and devotion to the whole Romantic ethos, would have both amused and irritated him – in certain ways, he was very competitive), Nick Drake recorded three albums of unmatched beauty and power that have touched people in ways that few records ever do. In concert and on record, his songs, his voice, and his arrangements seem so fragile and delicate that you'd think the slightest breeze or sound from the street would blow them away or obliterate them; but five years after his death, the songs seem stronger, more full-bodied and more fully-rooted than they sounded six, seven, eight, or nine years ago. Like operas made of stone, they sing and they are quiet.

In his best work (and none of his recorded songs are less than good), there are moments of true feeling and pure vision which easily transcend the influences – Van Morrison's *Astral Weeks*, Tim Buckley's jazz-inflected vocals, Jim Webb's melodic patterns, the sambas of João Gilberto, John Martyn's rolling, percussive guitar style – turning them into extended moments that are purely cinematic, dense with images of every sort. The songs are hypnotic, narcotic, black holes that it is possible to fall into and lose yourself in.

The songs are adolescent, but adolescent in the same way that Rimbaud is, in a way that magnifies adolescence. There is little self pity and no anger whatsoever; the songs vacillate in mood between wonder and dismay. These are songs of barely remembered grace, of accumulated loss, of a shadow world where emotions are impossible (or unreachable – the singing of the cuckoo that's locked inside the clock), change is unlikely, and failure is the price already agreed upon; the songs of a man who is afraid of angels, but who does not want to bother with anything less.

Five Leaves Left, Nick's first album (released in 1969, when he was 21), remains his most seductive record, probably the best introduction to his music; the arrangements are sparse but elegant, and the songs are haunting without having the desperate edge of *Pink Moon*.

49

Bryter Layter, recorded and released a year later, contains some of Nick's most beautiful songs ('Northern Sky', 'At The Chime Of A City Clock', 'Hazey Jane I'), but was the album he was least satisfied with. To compensate for *Five Leaves Left*'s lack of success, *Bryter Layter* was slicker, more polished, more 'commercial'. Individually, the songs are wonderful; more varied in tone and style, and if possible, more cryptic than the songs on *Five Leaves Left*. Still, the album feels slightly askew, off-centre; the arrangements are sometimes too pretty, and the sense of desolation (which is deeper here, more rooted) is glossed over by the production, as if it were no more than a light breeze blowing through the record.

By the time of *Pink Moon* two years later, what may have started as a light breeze had become a full-scale tempest. It's a record best left for midnight. Recorded in two days, most of the songs recorded in one take, it is completely bare and unproduced, just Nick and his guitar with no other instruments, no overdubs except for several notes of a piano that punctuate the title song.

And then there's the songs themselves, which seem almost like messages from the beyond:

> *Know that I love you*
> *Know that I don't care*
> *Know that I see you*
> *Know I'm not there*

And all too soon, he really wasn't there.

Nick Drake could literally disappear from rooms, from people, from situations, just as he eventually disappeared from his own life. One minute he is there, huddled in the corner, smoking a cigarette and staring out the window at the shadows falling over Hampstead Heath. A bird flies overhead. A car honks in the distance. And then even the smoke is gone.

His songs, however, refuse to disappear.

(The original version of this article was published in *Musician* magazine, in 1979. It was revised and updated by Brian, in 2010, for this book.)

Gabrielle, Rodney and Molly Drake and John Wood interview Walhalla, a Dutch radio broadcast, 1979

Gabrielle: We had an exceptionally happy childhood. We were a very close family and we had parents who were everything that children should have as parents; they were wonderful. We used to have ... I mean, they were also quite strict, you know, we were brought up quite strictly. They always made clear for us that although our parents expected us to work hard and everything, that ultimately decisions in life about what we wanted to do would remain with us. And whatever we wanted to do, provided we really wanted to do it, they would help us.

He was a bright boy; he went to Cambridge University, but his heart was always in music. And when that became obvious to my parents, to my father, they did everything they could to encourage him and certainly never put any bars in his way.

Rodney: He didn't seem to be interested in what most boys are interested in, somehow, although he was very good at things. Molly just said that he didn't really want to be head of things, but the fact of the matter was that when he went to preparatory school, he became head boy – although he didn't really want to be. He was a boy of very good physique – he had a fine figure – and he was captain of various things when he was at his first school. When he went to his next school, he became head boy of the first house, but it didn't really seem to mean much to him. There was something else going on in his mind all the time. And I remember in one of his reports towards the end of the time at his first school, the headmaster gave him a very good report, but said at the end that none of us seemed to know him very well. And I think that was it; all the way through with Nick, people didn't know him very much. He seemed to be so very interested in music, and he did once say to me, much later in life, 'There's music running through my head all the time.' And I think in a way it started when he was very young, don't you?

Molly: Oh yes, I think it did.

Gabrielle: Nick was very obstinate as a little boy. He knew absolutely what he wanted, always. He was much quieter than I was in many ways. I think Nick was both a loner and a leader. I mean, certainly at school.

Whereas I would be a follower and seek friends, Nick would go off on his own and people would follow him. He'd definitely be a leader.

Nick never shouted. If Nick shouted it was really bad; he was deeply upset. I think it would take a lot to make Nick angry, and then when he was he wouldn't be able to get over it quickly. And I think he found it difficult in some ways to separate his aggression from his hostility.

Molly: He didn't sort of fit very much into the life of the university, but he did fairly well. He passed the first half of his exams and then *Five Leaves Left* came out, and also this booking at the Festival Hall, and he felt that he was on the verge of doing what he truly wanted to do. I mean, he wanted to go to Cambridge; he was quite happy there and worked very hard, but that wasn't the real thing in his life. And I think he decided, 'Well, I'm going to miss it, if I go on staying at Cambridge.' And then he only had another nine months to get his degree, but he felt, 'If I stay on and carry on with this and get my degree, I'm just going to miss my place in this other race.' And he felt he'd got to leave Cambridge now and concentrate on his music.

Rodney: As you can imagine, both of us were very keen on him staying at Cambridge. I remember writing him long letters, pointing out the disadvantages of going away from Cambridge. I remember one expression I used was that a degree was a safety net, and whatever else you do in life, if you manage to get a degree, at least you have something to fall back on. His reply to that was that a safety net was the one thing he did not want, so that kind of cut the ground from under my feet. We thought, good heavens, if he is as good as all that, his music, which obviously he was, perhaps we're wrong in putting too much pressure on him to stay at Cambridge. Perhaps his decision was the right one. It did however seem an awful pity to us and I'm not at all sure he didn't regret it in some ways afterwards. He used to look back on the Cambridge days with a certain amount of nostalgia. But anyway, that's another story.

Molly: He just had one pair of shoes which were completely worn out. He wouldn't have anything different. He wanted to be totally without material possessions at all, I think. This was a very bad time. He once said to me that everything started to go wrong from the Hampstead time on, and I think that was when things started to go wrong.

John: *Bryter Layter*, for me, I think, in a lot of ways is the most satisfactory record I've ever worked on. Usually when you make a record there's something you think, well, I'd like to go back, I'd like to remix that or it's a shame we didn't use such and such a musician or, it's a shame this wasn't better ... And there's nothing on *Bryter Layter* that I'll ever want to do again or replace; and that is the only record I think I've ever worked on, that I feel like that about.

When you make records and you expect people to see you and go to your concerts, or to buy records really – once you commit yourself to making records, then you commit yourself to appear in public. And on the basis of three records, Nick had an enormous reputation. Although he's not being 'famous', he's very much a cult hero, and the records that he made have had an enormous following, out of proportion to what they should have. For somebody who didn't really want to know the rest of the job of being a performer, I think he's had an incredible amount of recognition. Most people, to have the recognition that he has, would have to go out and work day after day, week after week, go on the road – and he never did any of that. So I think he's had more than his fair share of recognition really. I think basically, he just was shy.

Molly: I don't think he wanted to be a star and I don't honestly think he was the least interested in money. But, I think he had this feeling that he'd got something to say, to people of his own generation. He desperately wanted to communicate with them, feeling that he could make them happier, that he could make things better for them – and he didn't feel that he did that.

Rodney: I'm sure that's right.

Molly: He said to me once, 'I've failed in everything I've tried to do.' I said, 'Oh Nick, how can you ...' And then I stated all the things that he had so plainly done. It didn't make a difference. He had failed to get through to the people that he wanted to talk to.

He said once, 'I don't like it at home, but I can't bear it anywhere else.' That's the sort of state he was in. I think he felt it was a kind of refuge; he had to come back here. He tried many times to go away, often, and used to stay away sometimes for several nights and we never knew where he was. We used to ring up his friends and wonder if they'd seen Nick, in case he was in trouble, you know. I think he had rejected the world. Nothing made him happy.

John: The most startling conversation I ever had with him was when we were making *Pink Moon*. And as you've probably read we made the record in, I think, two evenings. Nick was determined to make a record that was very stark, that would have all the texture and cotton wool and tinsel that had been on the other two, pulled away – so it was only just him. And he would sit in the control room and sort of blankly look at the wall and say, 'Well, I really don't want to hear anything else; I really think people should only just be aware of me and how I am. And the record shouldn't have any sort of... tinsel.' That wasn't the word he used – I can't remember exactly how he described it. He was very determined to make this very stark, bare record and he definitely wanted it to be more him than anything. And I think, in some ways, *Pink Moon* is probably more like Nick is, than the other two records.

Rodney: He went to John Wood and spent a day or two with him in the recording studio, and this tape of *Pink Moon* was produced. And he found it very difficult to communicate with people by this time. Apparently he went along to Island and just went to the girl at the desk and said, 'Oh, this is my thing, I'm Nick Drake,' you know, and shoved the tape down; and I think she put it in a drawer or something, and they didn't realise what it was for a time, and a week later she said to somebody, 'Oh, a fellow called Nick Drake came,' and produced this thing, and they said, 'Good heavens, let's have a look at it,' and it was *Pink Moon*. He didn't stop to see that it got into the right hands or anything else about it. And they didn't know where he was or how to get in touch with him. All they had was that tape and they produced the record.

Molly: He went up to bed rather early. I remember him standing at that door, and I said to him, 'Are you off to bed, Nick?' I can just see him now, because that's the last time I ever saw him alive. And that was it. And the next morning... He often didn't get up at all early; he sometimes had very bad nights, and I never used to disturb him at all, but it was about 12 o'clock, and I went in, because really it seemed it was time he got up, and he was lying across the bed. The first thing I saw was his long, long legs...

Rodney: Apparently he'd been down during the night – he'd been downstairs during the night – and had some cornflakes or something like that. And he often did that as a matter of fact, when he couldn't sleep; he often used to go downstairs. More often than not, Molly would hear him passing our bedroom door and she'd get up, put a dressing gown on, go down and talk to him. This occasion, she didn't hear him, and he went back to bed and he took an extra strong dose of these pills that had been prescribed for him, called Tryptizol, which we thought were antidepressants. He told us he was supposed to take three a day or something. We were always worried about Nick being so depressed; we used to hide away the aspirin and pills and things like that. These particular things we didn't think were in any way dangerous.

Molly: He was just having a rotten night.

Rodney: A rotten night and he said, 'To hell with it,' and he took the whole lot of them. And I'm told now that they're dangerous to the heart and so on. Obviously, it was more than he could take, and it killed him. But there were many times before, that we would have been much more worried about Nick, doing something of that sort, than we were at this particular time; that's the extraordinary thing about it.

Joe Boyd interview
Rob O'Dempsey, *Musin' Music*, 17/02/86

Rob O'Dempsey: Can we talk about one of the artists involved with Witchseason. How did you come to be involved with Nick Drake?

Joe Boyd: Ashley Hutchings went to a benefit concert, I think it was an anti-Vietnam peace benefit at the Roundhouse, and there were a lot of groups on including Fairport; and Ashley, in typical Ashley fashion, was the one who stayed longest to listen to most people and really was interested and wanted to hear everyone else who was on and what they sounded like etc, etc. And he came in the next day to the office and gave me a telephone number and said there was a kid who sang and played the guitar and did a short set and was very interesting, and you should have a listen to him, here's his number – and that was Nick. And so I rang him up and he brought me in a demo tape and I took it home and listened to it and I just thought it was great. I thought he was just really a unique talent. So I summoned him in to the office and he came in, and we agreed to do a record. As I recall it 'Time Has Told Me' was on the demo and there was a song called 'I Was Made To Love Magic', which is one of the songs we're going to put on this new record.

The way that I worked with Nick was very different from the way that I worked with the other artists, in the sense that he worked slowly, we worked together slowly: there was no self-contained group around Nick. With the other groups of artists we tended to go in and do a record in a concentrated period of time, with Nick we just went in, did a couple of tracks, listened to them, thought about it, thought what we wanted to do with them, worked on them a bit, put down a few more tracks, wait a month, wait six weeks, think about it some more, perhaps work with an arranger ... So it was very different, and it was very reflective, and I think in a way the records reflect that, because they were much more carefully made than some of the other records I did at the time. It was a very good dialogue. I think I threw a lot of suggestions at Nick, but he didn't accept them by any means. I just kept throwing ideas at him or throwing him in the studio with various different people, and sometimes he would respond and sometimes he wouldn't. There were some things that happened and he'd say, 'I don't like that,' and we'd just drop it. And there were other things where he said, 'Oh, that sounds all right.' It was a very enjoyable process for me. I really enjoyed making those records for Nick.

Rob: Would he just come in and put down the vocal and the guitar track and then you'd add everything else?

Joe: Not always – particularly on *Five Leaves Left*, with most of those Robert Kirby arrangements, those were done live. We had the string players in the studio and Nick in the middle of the room playing and singing. It depends; some of them were worked on rather carefully. I think 'Man In A Shed', I put the piano on in New York. I just felt that Paul Harris would be a good piano player and I took the tape for Paul to track over to New York and found a studio and brought it back and played it to Nick, and he said, 'Oh yeah, that's nice.' But other things he was much more involved in. I mean, we had a different arranger at first for some of those tracks on *Five Leaves Left*, and we actually did a whole session with someone else who did the string charts on the Apple James Taylor record, I can't remember who it was, I heard about him from Pete Asher, so we got him in to do some charts, and Nick didn't like them, and

I agreed, they were a bit too corny. And when we were trying to think what to do, Nick kind of said rather timidly, 'Well, I have this friend, from Cambridge, who might be quite good,' and I said, 'Oh, sure, has he ever done anything? Has he ever done any work?' and he said, 'No, but I think he'd be quite good.' And there was something about the way Nick said it, you know. Nick was very definite when he knew he was on firm ground and you could tell it was a firm idea that he had. I said, 'Let's give it a try,' and I think I went up to Cambridge and met Robert to see what he was all about before I spent the money hiring a bunch of string players to come in, and I was impressed with him. And I really do vividly remember sitting up in the control room at Sound Techniques with John Wood, and the people tuning up and running through the parts, without the guitar, and John was getting the individual sounds out of the different instruments, and we didn't actually hear the whole thing together, and then they said, 'OK, let's run it through,' and he had all the faders up and we heard the arrangement, and John and I looked at each other and said, 'What! This is great!' and we were quite stunned.

I'd been doing a session on a jazz record, with Chris McGregor – and Chris is this wonderful eccentric white South African, who'd grown up living and spending most of his time with the black people of the Transkie, and a great smoker of the very strong South African Daga, and wearer of wildly coloured clothes etc... He always smoked his grass in a pipe. And it was during one of those 'assembly line' days when I had one session in the afternoon and another in the evening, and we had finished the Chris McGregor session and everybody was off out, and Nick showed up with the drummer and bass player, to do the track for 'Poor Boy', and Chris was just sitting in the studio, smoking and saying, 'You don't mind if I stay and listen do you?' So he was sitting there and I was listening to the track and looking at Chris, and I suddenly had this inspiration and said, 'Why don't you go on down and play on this, you just can't hang around. I'm gonna put you to work,' and so he said, 'I dunno ... sure, why not!' He was just stoned and ready for anything, and he just wandered in and that was the first take, the take that we used. And I think his piano really makes the track work. That was one of those lucky little accidents, it turned out very well.

Rob: What about the non-vocal tracks, like *Bryter Layter*?

Nick Drake: The Pink Moon Files

Joe: Well, he would go and meet with the arranger; that was something he and Robert would go off together and cook up. And I was very sceptical about the idea, and I mean, to me, at the time I was very resistant; I said well, we can record them but only at the tail end of the session where we're doing a proper arrangement of a song, because the idea of having instrumental tracks seemed to me to be sort of Chinese for 'Nick couldn't think of any lyrics'. And I was putting him under a lot of pressure to come up with lyrics for them, and again he was very adamant; he said, 'No, these are not songs, these are instrumental pieces, and I want one at the beginning and one at the end, and that's the way this album's going to be.'

And I gave him a real hard time about it, but he stuck by his guns and did it and I think it works fine.

Rob: Then he returned to a completely solo format for the last record, *Pink Moon*.

Joe: Well, it was again one of those things that was happening, as I was telling you before; my feeling that I had fulfilled a function and the function was no longer as important... The way that arose with Nick was that Nick came to me before we'd even released *Bryter Layter*, as soon as we'd finished the record, before the cover was done or anything, and said to me, 'The next record is just going to be me and guitar.' I think he may have found *Bryter Layter* a little full or elaborate. I know he liked it, but he did feel, 'OK, we've done this, now we're going to do something completely different.' I wasn't going to argue with him about it, because I knew Nick wasn't really someone you argued with; but again, he could do that with John Wood, he didn't need me to do a record with just him and guitar. It wasn't really going to make much difference to the way the record sounded. And so, that was yet another example that it wasn't that important that I stick around.

Rob: Do you think *Pink Moon* works as an album?

Joe: I haven't listened to it as much as I listened to the others. I don't know it as well. It's very hard to be objective about it. Yes, it is a good album. The last four songs he recorded, to me, are in a way more powerful songs than the stuff on *Pink Moon*. 'Things Behind The Sun' is one of his best songs; he did that live at the Festival Hall, when he opened for Fairport Convention, and it's a great song.

Rob: So what's the fourth disc going to comprise, will it be the four unreleased tracks plus ...?

Joe: No, they will stay on the end of *Pink Moon*. We've got a full disc without those. There are four tracks from the *Five Leaves Left* sessions. One is 'I Was Made To Love Magic', and the other is 'Mayfair', which Millie Small covered, and another is ... I can't remember the names because I think there's some controversy, they weren't actually titled. We've figured out what the titles are, and then there are some demos of the later recordings, some of the things he did for *Bryter Layter*. So there's a 'Poor Boy' without the overdubs, and simpler versions of things on *Bryter Layter*, and then some early demos from home; again some early songs of his and a couple of songs by other people.

I owe a great debt to Frank Kornelussen, who puts out a little magazine on Richard Thompson called *Flypaper*, who was over here for Cropredy, and asked to come along when Trevor Lucas and I were going into the Island vaults to dig out stuff for Sandy's boxed set, and he was the one who kept rooting around and saying, 'Let's look through everything.' And we were in the studio playing back some of the Sandy tapes, making notes and rough mixes and copies, and Frank would sort of wander in and say, 'What's this tape? Look at this,' and it'd be a four-track of Nick Drake with 'Untitled' or 'Song No. 1' and I'd say, 'I don't know what that is,' and it would be 'I Was Made To Love Magic' or 'Mayfair' or something like that. And then the demos that Nick's parents had, I'd had a copy of for some time, but the quality was really unusable, with a lot of wow and flutter and static. And I've never really wanted to put something out that wouldn't be commensurate with what people know of as Nick. I know once someone achieves a certain status in people's minds, there would be people who'd be interested in anything Nick did, even the most primitive demo sung out of tune. People would want to hear it because it would be interesting, because it would be Nick, and I don't blame them for wanting to hear it, but I wouldn't participate in making anything like that available, because I think the whole process of creating music is partly a process in which elimination is as important as what you present. You can find out-takes of any artist which would be embarrassing or fascinating but not something which you can listen to in the same way as you'd listen to normal finished results by that artist; that's why I've always resisted the idea and said when anybody asked me, 'No, there's nothing else,' because all I knew of were these demos. I just felt that the finished results that exist are enough. That's what he was happy with. And then Frank played these tapes and they're great, they're wonderful. And the demo from home we took it down to London and played it back on a proper machine, because the machine they made copies for me on was not a very good machine and a lot of the wow and flutter came from the playback rather than the original tape; so again you could hear on the demo the quality of the voice, the quality of the guitar playing, and it suddenly became something that was historically interesting and really good to listen to, so it seemed then that it would be nice to put it out.

John Martyn interview
Richard Skinner, *Saturday Live*, Radio 1, May 25, 1986

Richard Skinner: That was 'Fruit Tree', Nick Drake, originally recorded on the album *Five Leaves Left*, in 1968, and now out on a compilation that has been put together by Island Records. John Martyn, contemporary and fellow recording artist in those days, yes?

John Martyn: This is true. This is true.

Richard: Did you know the man well?

John: I did, yes. We lived very close to each other. He lived in one part of Hampstead and I lived just up the road. Erm, very quiet, very quiet lad. Extremely personable and charming when necessary; handsome to a devastating effect.

Richard: Yes, the pictures: quite stunning pictures. I mean, there's almost a touch of, erm … Cor, dear me, I can't think.

John: Pre-Raphaelite, and all that kind of stuff.

Richard: Yes, the word I wasn't thinking of, but a very good way of describing it. Why do you think Nick Drake has become the legend that exists today?

John: I would imagine because of the quality of the music and his writing. It's just very good music. It's very British, isn't it? And that's one of the things I like about it. I think Dream Academy have quoted him as being one of their influences.

Richard: They dedicated a hit to him.

John: That's right, to the memory of Nick, and I think it's because he's British. That's its secret for me anyway.

Richard: It does seem to have a perennial appeal, because it's hitting new generations. People who are what, 15 years younger than Nick, are now saying that the man is important.

John: Yes, well, it's just incredibly good. You can't really say that it's bad music, and therefore it has a certain strength.

Richard: What sort of man was he though?

John: When I first met him he was rather more urbane than he became. He was always charming, delicately witty, but he just became more and more withdrawn as time went by. In the three or four years that I knew him, he became more and more withdrawn. I think he just suffered from some sort of depression. They called it melancholia in the Victorian days.

Richard: You were saying about him being eminently British. I mean, he went to Marlborough and Cambridge and all that sort of thing.

John: (Laughter) I didn't quite say that he was eminently British. The music's eminently British.

Richard: But he seems to be a product of the English middle class.

John: That's undoubtedly true. I think that reflects very well in his music. I mean, what you see is what you get. It's erudite, it's refined. I like it.

Richard: Was he a typical singer-songwriter of his period?

John: No, I have to say that... The thing that set him apart, again, is his implicit, innate Britishness. Everyone else on the Island roster who was contemporary with himself, including myself, were having flirtations with American-based sounds, in the same way Elton John was with his very first record, all very American-based sounds. You know, the whole idea was to try and sound like The Band if you could, possibly. He was just very quietly going his own way and producing, as I say, very British sounds.

Richard: He played very few live performances, John?

John: Two, to my knowledge. One was a Christmas affair, given by the Quality Climax Apprentices. I suppose it was their Christmas ball.

That really destroyed him because I think they would have rather listened to the Troggs.

Richard: Amen Corner or something, yeah?

John: That's right, that's right. So I think that was a major blow to his confidence. I remember him being defensive about that for days and days. And then he did another one at the Festival Hall supporting Sandy Denny.

Richard: That sounds a bit more like him.

John: It was a good place for him but he was cripplingly nervous. I mean, he was distraught before the gig. It was rather embarrassing in fact to see him. He was distinctly uncomfortable onstage. I mean, the music was fine, but he just didn't like being there at all.

Richard: So this is the reason that the man didn't play many more gigs, it was just destroying him?

John: I get the impression it was just costing him too much to go onstage. It was just like no amount of applause or anything else would ever have paid him back the mental effort and energy he had to expend.

Richard: Did this get worse as time went by, because you say the man changed?

John: Unfortunately it did, yeah. He just slipped and slipped further away into himself and divorced himself from the mundane – very sad really. And it wasn't from a lack of trying. I mean, all sorts of people tried to be friendly and went out of their way to be nice but, you know, I suppose he'd see through that, being very bright and intelligent. He'd go: 'Mmm, yes, what's in it for you?'

Richard: The image of a troubled artist in a sense.

John: Oh, absolutely, classic case. Byronic stuff; heroic stuff.

Richard: Do you think he could have been helped, that the end might not have happened as it did?

John: It's very easy to look back and think that. You know, you look at your own behaviour. I look at mine and think, well, perhaps I should have done more. I think that everyone who knew him felt exactly the same way, because he was immensely loveable and a great loss and stuff. But, no, I think he had his sights set and that was that. Once he decided on his course of action he just took it.

Richard: Yes, he was prepared not to go on much longer, do you feel?

John: I think he found the place was just not quite good enough for him, in all honesty. I mean, whereas a lot of people just harden themselves to the whole nonsense and say, 'Well, all right, the world isn't exactly perfect, but I'll get on with it,' I think the weight of responsibility and the social ... I suppose in every other way just overpowered him. He didn't enjoy life very much.

Richard: Did he not try going places, being in other areas?

John: He certainly did. He went to Paris and spent a lot of time there, he went to the country, he came and lived with me in various locations, and he was just distinctly unhappy in all of them. I think he distrusted the world. He thought it not quite lived up to his expectations.

Richard: He is now undergoing a revival, or whatever, of popularity. Do you think that there is anybody since him that has touched the genius that he had?

John: There's no one covering that particular area, especially in the last seven or eight years. I mean, a certain coarsening of music in general has been apparent, to me anyway, and the acoustic guitar that was, I suppose, his medium, has fallen from favour. You know, the demise of the folk boom and all that sort of stuff, it's more and more difficult for acoustic instrument players, and people who are based around that, to break through. But there is no one who is doing that, not that I'm aware of.

Richard: Remarkable, the appeal of the man, because it says there on the sleeve notes (*Heaven In A Wild Flower*), it says that his parents still get letters from all the way around the world, wanting to know about his inspirations, about the way he played his guitar. And I dare say it's going to be around for a few years as well. John, thank you for talking to us.

The Leave Taking
Kris Kirk, *Melody Maker*, July 4, 1987

Best known to the British public as Nicola Freeman, recently ousted manageress of *Crossroads*, Gabrielle Drake is currently acting in a West End farce. Kris Kirk met her backstage to discuss her brother, the legendary Nick Drake, whose untimely and mysterious death in 1974 has added a lingering poignancy to his unbearably personal songs.

"I personally prefer to think Nick committed suicide, in the sense that I'd rather he died because he wanted to end it than it to be the result of a tragic mistake. That would seem to me to be terrible: for it to be a plea for help that nobody hears."

Currently on leave from *Crossroads* to play a man-eating Moulin Rouge chanteuse in a frenzied West End French farce called *Court In The Act*, the vivacious Gabrielle is a woman who normally twinkles her way through life. Today she's naturally subdued while recalling the life and early death of her younger brother Nick, a brilliant musician and songwriter whose music was virtually ignored throughout his life, which ended when he overdosed on antidepressants in 1974.

Nowadays, Nick Drake is a legendary figure to musicians as diverse as Tom Verlaine and Shelleyan Orphan – who cite him as a spiritual and musical mentor – and to his increasingly large body of latterday fans, an astonishing 10,000 of whom have purchased the recently issued box set *Fruit Tree*. This contains the three albums issued during Drake's lifetime (*Five Leaves Left, Bryter Layter* and *Pink Moon*) plus a posthumous collection of early work and privately recorded later songs.

Among the latter is 'Black Eyed Dog', a song which in the context of Drake's life is almost unbearably painful. The inner vision of a mind so completely alienated from the world that it has lost any will to live. It's a track his sister feels is a musical summation of the final tortured years of Nick Drake.

"In some ways 'Black Eyed Dog' is an absolute rounding-off of his work. One can hypothesise how the artist in him would have progressed if he hadn't had that illness, but a destiny is a destiny. His manger Joe Boyd said that, in a sense, Nick sacrificed his life to the music, and I think that, in a way, he did give up his life for his songs."

During the final years of her brother's withdrawal from life, the outgoing Gabrielle could not get as close to Nick as she'd have liked: "I suppose the real insularity started five or six years before his death, though change is never an instant thing and, if you look through anybody's life, it's like a detective story – you can see the clues have been laid right away along the line. But gradually his depressions – his, for want of a better word, schizophrenia – set in more and more and he went into his shell completely, and began being unable to communicate with anybody.

"At first, my parents and I thought it was just us he wasn't communicating with, and I remember it being a great shock to discover it was the same with his friends and record company, Island. When he was in this very down state he just couldn't talk at all, and it was only during those rare moments that he did open up that you could get him to clarify a little what he was feeling. Often one couldn't get the flow of what he was saying, and if you tried too often to say, 'What do you mean by that, Nick?' he'd clam up again. Even though I still felt very close to him, I'm not sure I knew him very well in those years."

It wasn't always the way; not during the 'upper middle-class-ish' childhood that Gaye, as Nick called her, remembers as being full of happiness for them both. The young Drakes spent their early years out East, where their father was an engineer. Gabrielle was born in Pakistan, Nick a couple of years later in 1948 in Burma; they moved to England in the mid-Fifties.

"Though he was younger than me, Nick was always a leader and I was always a follower – I was always rather ordinary, he was extraordinary. Even as a little boy he was a very elegant figure. I was the one with scraggy hair all over the place and buck teeth; he was a neat, beautiful little boy with his broad shoulders and elegant waist. We fought terribly as children, but we were very close as a family."

It was when Nick was sent to public school that he and Gaye began drifting apart: "To be honest, I don't know if he hated Marlborough or not because, by then, I was leaving school and concentrating on my own life, which was becoming very exciting; I lost touch a little with his problems and dilemmas. And at the time he seemed to be doing quite well; he was wonderful at sports, though he hated them, and was the kind of person who was quite capable of being Head Boy. He went up to university whereas I, like a fool, left school before my A-levels and had to try four times to get into RADA before I was accepted."

It was at school that he took up sax and then guitar.

"I remember him being very easy to embarrass. I went to visit him at school with a friend of mine, a really wild girl I was working with in Liverpool, and we took Nick and his friends out to supper and got them very drunk and they had to creep into school breathing liqueurs and cigars over everyone. The next day we both insisted on going to his sax rehearsal and he was very deeply embarrassed, he hated having his sister there.

"Looking back, I think, in a funny way, Nick always had to keep his worlds apart. I remember at his funeral being surprised that so many of his friends didn't know each other. Surprised – but I understood because I think both of us shared, in our various ways, that thing of being different people when we were with different groups. I feel that, but so many people come up with different theories about Nick that we all make of him what we will in a way.

"I have to keep reminding myself, because it's only true and fair to Nick, that he's been dead now for over 10 years and the tendency is to remember him in a rosy glow. The memory blurs things over and one has to try to hang on to the truth – it's the only way of being true to him."

It was at Cambridge that Drake began writing the fragile, melancholy yet never self-indulgent musical confessions which still sound fresh and unspoilt even today. And it was there, in 1968, that his sensitive, jazzy voice was first heard by American Joe Boyd – now best-known perhaps as producer of R.E.M.'s *Fables Of The Reconstruction* or owner of the excellent Hannibal label, but then a hot producer/manager responsible for Fairport Convention and the Incredible String Band among many others. A good friend as well as a good manager, Boyd signed Drake to Witchseason through Island, convinced that the 20 year old would make it big. But despite critical admiration for his three extraordinary albums, he never did.

There are those who feel that, had he had some measure of commercial success, Drake might have survived. His sister isn't so sure.

"Who can say? I know that both of us faced a similar kind of problem in the beginning in that it was difficult at that time to get accepted in both the music and acting worlds if you came from the background we came from – my accent was held against me from the word go – and so it's even harder to make your mark when you're against the fashion, and I'm sure Nick was very frustrated by that.

"I know that, for a long time, we felt that Nick was in a depression because his records weren't doing better. And then, one day, he disappeared again and we were worried because he was ill, so I finally rang up Island Records for the first time and I remember them telling me to my amazement that not only didn't they know where he was either, but they could get him any engagement he wanted – they'd had lots of offers for this, that and the other but he didn't want to do them. That came as a shock to me, because I thought he'd gone into depression because there were no offers, but it wasn't anywhere near that simple.

"It's like I've read reports of his concerts where the audience was sup-posedly bemused at this person who shuffled onstage, did his songs and shuffled off apologetically. That was never my impression. I feel he had an absolute charisma and that his audience were spellbound, and I think I know a little about when an audience is spellbound or not.

"I know he had a reputation for loathing playing live and I'm not sure I knew him well enough at that stage to know whether he did or he did not – it's very easy when someone is dead to take them over, and I wouldn't like to do that, so I can't say. But my feeling was that, for a creative artist, he had one skin too few. Because, to preserve that inner sensitivity, you need to have a very tough outer skin that is going to take terrible knocks from the public and, perhaps worse, indifference. And Nick just didn't have it."

Instead Nick Drake retreated so far into his mind that he couldn't find the way back out, lost that fine line between the two fictitious realms we call madness and sanity. That terrible inner fear that we all get occasionally – of being completely alone, of having to face up to the inevitability of death – Nick Drake appears to have experienced, towards the end, 24 hours a day. According to friends, he spent hours staring out of the window or looking at his shoes. After a short burst of happiness which took him to France, Drake returned to the home of his parents who, according to Gabrielle, made looking after him 'their mission in life'. After a short spell in a psychiatric hospital, Nick Drake returned home and, on November 25, 1974, his mother found him dead in bed.

"I may be wrong, I may be maligning him," says Gabrielle, "but I don't think there was any one incident that was so life-shattering it made Nick the way he was. To me it's more a question of how, if you fail too deeply in this world, it becomes unbearable.

"He used to do this thing of just sitting there, lost. The most truthful photo I've ever seen of him is in the record booklet where he is sitting on a park bench. Everyone, no matter how bad they are feeling, will try to pose when they are having their photograph taken, but here all Nick's desire to pose has gone – he's not even aware of the camera. I found it unbearably painful to be standing outside him and not be able to reach into his mind to help him."

Gabrielle has heard speculation that her brother was a repressed homosexual.

"To me it doesn't matter whether he was or he wasn't, it's not the relevant point about Nick. A lot of people, in order to identify with him, make him into whatever they want him to be; that doesn't matter – the point is that his music exists. I don't care what his sexuality was, all I care about is that he didn't find happiness with someone.

"The point is that Nick will always remain an enigma because there is no great mystery to be solved. What is there is in his songs, and will remain there."

Of Brilliance and Darkness,
the Bittersweet Saga of Nick Drake
Charles O'Meara (aka C.W. Vrtacek),
Fairfield County Advocate, November 21, 1988

Nick Drake ought to be selling lots of records these days. His music fits handsomely into the slot marked 'sensitive' that's been established for artists like Suzanne Vega and Tracy Chapman. His songs are intensely introspective, remarkably evocative, non-sexist and beautiful to listen to, pure poetry set to music. But he can't pose for *Rolling Stone*, he can't make videos and he can't tour or do any of the other things necessary for success in the Eighties. In 1974, Nick Drake died at the age of 26, leaving behind a dark, enigmatic personal life and three brilliant albums.

Though he's not well-known, myths and folklore about Drake are easier to find than the truth. Room-mates would find him sitting alone in a room, staring down at his shoes, or perhaps looking out a window in silence for hours. He was melancholy, quiet, solitary and dressed in black. He might or might not have committed suicide. Nearly 15 years after his death, he remains a man whose life is an unsolved – and unsolvable – puzzle, even for those who knew him. Haunted by a private depression yet capable of communicating his feelings through music, Nick Drake enjoys the dubious distinction of being a permanent enigma, a contemporary Sphinx.

Existing photos of him reinforce comparisons to that ancient Egyptian statue. He is shown alone, often looking away from the camera and hunched over, as if trying to disappear within himself, a slight Mona Lisa smile on his lips. When he does face the camera, his countenance is strikingly cherubic and innocent. As for his songs, they weren't political or even topical. Nick stuck to emotions, though he remained non-specific. Almost any Nick Drake song could be sung by a woman to a man, a man to a woman, a woman to a woman, a father to a son, or by one friend to another.

He assumed many roles in his songs; an understanding companion in 'Time Has Told Me', a seeker of things spiritual in 'River Man', a hopeful lover in 'Which Will', a prophet in 'Pink Moon'. If there is a common thread to his musical legacy, a central theme to his work, it seems to be one of alienation. Nick Drake's curse was the ability to see life around him with pristine clarity while being unable to take part in it. He was in the world but not of it.

Joe Boyd spent as much time with him as anyone. Now 46, Boyd was one of the hippest producers in London during the Sixties, working with Fairport Convention, Richard Thompson, Sandy Denny, the Incredible String Band, and these days with R.E.M., Billy Bragg and 10,000 Maniacs. Boyd produced all three of Nick's albums, *Five Leaves Left*, *Bryter Layter* and *Pink Moon* and the posthumous collection, *Time Of No Reply*. "I never balk at descriptions of reality," he states when asked about Drake. "Nick was not a cheerful guy. But if people led totally placid existences, I don't know how much art there would be. It's a way of expressing things that are blocked and otherwise wouldn't be expressed."

Nick Drake was definitely blocked, at least in his ability to merge with the world around him. Yet he was not as catatonic as stories about him might indicate. Boyd remembers him as "a lot of fun to work with in the studio. He was withdrawn, but cheerful most of the time. I remember one time calling him and telling him John Cale was outside hailing a cab to come over to his house. Cale had just heard his music and said, 'I've gotta meet this guy,' and demanded Nick's address," recalls Boyd. "Later, the two of them showed up at the studio as happy as clams." Cale, a founding member of the Velvet Underground, contributed to two cuts on *Bryter Layter*, an album Joe Boyd says, "shows Nick at the height of all his powers".

"There was a friend of mine," Boyd continues, "who seemed to be able to get Nick out of himself and enjoying life. He was a sort of cockney criminal type, very different from Nick's background. We would go round to this guy's house and play poker. One of the most vivid memories I have of Nick is him staring happily at his poker dice. This guy was not about to take Nick's introspection lying down, you see," Boyd explains. "He'd say, 'C'mon mate, what's wrong? Have a cuppa tea.' He just ignored Nick's moods and Nick loved that." Boyd agrees that perhaps what Nick needed most was more of this treatment, a climate that would discourage rather than tolerate his despondency. Left to himself, he only grew worse. But hands-on support "was not the English way", says Boyd. In a culture known for its stiff upper lip and carrying on in the face of adversity, no one was about to bend over backward to help one lost soul, including Nick himself. "In a way, I'd sort of say Nick was trapped by his Englishness," offers Boyd, himself an American.

And Nick Drake was thoroughly British, indeed. He was born in Burma on June 19, 1948, while his father was stationed there, but returned to England as a child, to a pastoral brick home with well-kept grounds in a tiny village. He appears to have led a normal childhood and adolescence. It was somewhere around the time he entered Cambridge that things began to change. Swept up in the mood of the times, he read poetry, hung out with an intellectual crowd, smoked hash and wrote songs on his guitar.

His first album, *Five Leaves Left*, was recorded in 1968 when Nick was only 20 and is surprisingly coherent and mature. It won comparisons to Van Morrison's *Astral Weeks*, a close contemporary. Nick was a resounding success when he played the Royal Festival Hall in London with Fairport Convention soon afterwards, but he returned from a tour of rural folk clubs bruised and beaten. Nobody listened. Nick didn't want to tour and Joe Boyd didn't push him.

Instead, Nick became reclusive, working on the music for *Bryter Layter*, a jazzy album Joe Boyd calls "Nick's most mature, most balanced, most complete work". Critics responded favourably again but the public passed it by and Nick was crushed. He went into a deep, dark place within himself for the next three years, finally emerging to record *Pink Moon*. This time it was only Nick and his guitar, and while the songs are as varied and lovely as any he wrote, the sound and mood are stark and skeletal, a musical line-drawing in black and white. He shyly dropped off the unmarked tapes of the record at his company's office without announcing himself. Days later someone discovered them.

Nick went from bad to worse. He checked into and out of a psychiatric hospital for five weeks, considered a career in computers or the army, and grew more detached. The last straw was the fact that his records didn't sell. Everyone around him was convinced of his talent, yet the public snubbed him. He was incensed. "Something happened with Nick that happens for many artists," says Boyd. "Though he always said commercial success didn't matter, the farther he got from it the more of an obsession it became." But without warning, Nick's mood brightened a short time later.

He talked of moving to France, of starting over, but it was not to be. Around noontime on November 25, 1974, Nick's mother found him lying in bed, dead. He was officially listed as a suicide, the cause as an overdose of an antidepressant drug he'd been prescribed, but friends doubted it. "Suicide is a very black and white word," comments Boyd, who seems to indicate that the truth might lie somewhere between intent and accident. "I think he always did have this feeling that he was his own executioner."

If Nick Drake did kill himself, he went about it in his own characteristically low-key way – alone, quietly and without a note or any clear message about what he was up to.

"I thought people would cover his songs more, that someone like Roberta Flack would do 'Time Has Told Me'," says Joe Boyd when asked to contemplate Nick's place in the world today. It's unlikely there will ever be a Nick Drake revival. Still, each year a few more listeners find his records. He will never be hounded for autographs, but his music seems destined not to be lost, either. "I'd like to think," says Joe Boyd, "that the more people discover him, the more it pleases his ghost."

If you'd like to discover Nick Drake's music, check for any of his albums, which seem to go in and out of print, but are always around. They are, in order: *Five Leaves Left, Bryter Layter, Pink Moon* and *Time Of No Reply*. The last is really a souvenir for fans only, and *Bryter Layter* is probably the best introduction to Nick's work. While Boyd speaks highly of the CD versions of the albums, he does not recommend the Nick Drake compilation album, *Heaven In A Wild Flower*, because of inferior sound. All four albums are available in the boxed set, *Fruit Tree, The Complete Recorded Works*.

Robert Kirby interview
Swedish radio, Eighties

Interviewer: And he came into the room and that was the first time you saw him?

Robert Kirby: Yes.

Int: And you didn't know each other before, you hadn't heard of him?

Robert: No.

Int: And what did he ask you to do?

Robert: He asked me if I would write arrangements for 'Way To Blue', 'The Thoughts Of Mary Jane' and 'Day Is Done', and one song which isn't on any of the LPs, but which we used to do live, called 'Time Of No Reply'. I think I have a tape of it somewhere, but not here. But we used to do that live, the four songs. We used to do concerts, about one a week, one a fortnight: college balls and dances and things. We would be the act between the rock groups, and we would do four songs with the orchestra. Then the orchestra would do one or two classical pieces, and then Nick would do four or five pieces on his own.

Int: How did Nick get along with his audience?

Robert: He was always very, very quiet, very shy. I wouldn't say nervous, because he always performed well; and usually if people are nervous they perform badly. It was more ... he was just quite retiring you know, shy; but he got on well with them, yes. I mean, he quite enjoyed what we were doing, enjoyed playing. Those were small audiences; maybe 150–200, something like that.

Int: There's written a lot of the bad communication between Nick and his audience, and how much it really bothered him.

Robert: Yes, I think things like the Queen Elizabeth Hall concert – I was at that one – and I think he was nervous of a big audience. But, again, I didn't really see much lack of communication in that he performed very well, and the audience liked what he did. OK, he didn't sort of tell jokes and talk between songs, but he got down to the job and played and sung his songs well.

Int: And then he asked you to arrange *Five Leaves Left*?

Robert: This was later in the year when Tyger Hutchings, who was in the Fairport Convention as bass player, had heard Nick playing and recommended him to Joe Boyd. So Joe got together making an album, and I think they had already been in with another arranger, and it didn't work out. So Nick said, 'Why don't we try these arrangements that we've already got, from this friend of mine.' So I went up to London from Cambridge, and we recorded them.

Int: I heard there was some trouble with the arrangements.

Robert: Well this was the first arranger. I think they'd got another person, and those arrangements didn't work out; so they didn't use his and redid it again with my arrangements; and it worked, I think.

Int: Yeah. When he titled the album, how did that happen?

Robert: Well, he was pressured. They needed the title quickly, you know, the LP was finished, and the artwork was done. In little packets of cigarette papers, when you get towards the end of the packet, it says 'five leaves left' – five leaves of paper – and Nick chose that as a title.

Int: Why?

Robert: I think because it has a sort of autumnal ring about it; leaves, and the end of autumn. But, at the same time, a certain kind of person who used those cigarette papers would know what it was about. It was a bit of an in-joke. And the same as the second album, *Bryter Layter* – Nick again couldn't think of a title – and in England, the shipping forecast, or the weather forecast, on the radio, they always say, 'Stormy with rain, but brighter later.' And that's how the title came about. It's just a phrase which is always on the weather forecast, brighter later, but Nick spelt it differently, with the Ys.

Int: Why?

Robert: I don't really know actually why. It looks a bit more old English, a bit more poetic; that's possibly why.

Int: You were the arranger on the numbers on *Bryter Layter*.

Robert: Yes, not all the numbers. I did four numbers, and the overture; the orchestral overture at the beginning of one side; and John Cale did 'Northern Sky'.

Int: You used one year to produce it. Was it difficult?

Robert: Well, I didn't really see much of that. I was called in when they'd got all of the rhythm tracks done, and this was one of the last things to be done, the putting on of strings, and the flutes. And the girls on 'Poor Boy', I did that, and the backing brass on 'Poor Boy'; but this was all towards the end. There's a misprint on the sleeve, it says, 'All string and bass arrangements by Robert Kirby,' and it should be, 'string and brass arrangements'. That's always upset me that, because Dave Pegg, the bass player, is perfectly capable of playing on his own. But I was called in at the end; I didn't know they'd been doing this album for quite a few months before. I really was just called in at the end to put on those arrangements on those tracks that I did.

Int: Yes. How was it, working with Nick?

Robert: I always found him easy to work with. I've done about 40 or 50 LPs now, in the last 10 years, and still I've not met anyone whose music I respect as much as Nick's. I still think he was the greatest acoustic guitarist to come out of England, and the greatest lyric writer. OK, some people might say his voice was weak, but, there again, his songs didn't need to be sung by a 'singer'. They need to be sung like someone reading poetry, and that's how he does it. I think he was the most all-round, perfect artist I've ever worked with, and I found him very easy to work with. He gave me quite a free hand. He gave me a song like, say, 'Fruit Tree', on the first LP; he came round one day, played it, and I taped it onto my tape recorder. He said that he possibly heard oboes on it, and strings, and that was about it. I used to then sit with him and go through exactly how he played his chords, because he always detuned his guitar. He used strange tunings, not proper guitar tunings, and not the ones like people use in D tunings. He had very complicated tunings, very complicated: sometimes a low string would be higher than the string above. And so it would be very important for me to write down exactly how he played each chord, and every bar; and I would do that with him. That sometimes annoyed him I think, because it took a long time; but I had to do it. And then he'd go away and leave me to do the arrangement how I wanted it; and he was very easy to work with.

Int: And the strange tunings is an explanation that it's so difficult to play his songs?

Robert: Yes. But I think *Pink Moon*, the last album — which is in fact my favourite, as far as the songs are concerned — if you listen to the guitar playing on some of those songs, I'd challenge anyone to play them, because you've got to crack what the tuning is to start with.

Int: Yes. When you travelled together with him at first, you got an impression of him as a person, was he a lot depressed at that time?

Robert: He was always quiet and he was frequently depressed. But I think a lot of us are depressed quite frequently. I think, quite often, too much is made of this by a lot of people; or it is as far as I'm concerned, because I saw Nick quite happy many times. You know, we would go to pubs, we would go out and enjoy ourselves. But, there again, sometimes he would come round and not say anything; but I just took this as he didn't have anything to say. Maybe he was depressed. Yes, of course he was depressed; but a lot of people have an image of him as being somehow abnormal, distant. He wasn't; he was perfectly easy to be friends with. One could talk to him, have a conversation; do what you would with anybody else.

Int: The last year too?

Robert: I didn't see much of him the last year. The news of his death came as a shock. I hadn't seen him for about eight months. I think he had spent a lot of time at home with his parents, and in France. I hadn't seen much of him, and it did come as a shock, because when I'd seen him about eight or nine months before his death he'd been a lot better than he'd been say three or four years before that. I think maybe his worst period, of depression, that I saw, was maybe two years after Cambridge; some time before he died.

Int: He wrote the music to *Bryter Layter* in a village? I think it was Hampstead.

Robert: He was living in a flat on Haverstock Hill then, which is gone now; it's been demolished – a very big, gothic, Victorian house. Yes, I went round there quite often and visited him. Yes, in Hampstead it was.

Int: Did you see how he worked with his songs? Did he work very intensely?

Robert: I never saw him in the process of actually writing a song. Whenever I heard a song it was finished. But I think it probably took him a long time to write, yes I do. I think he would probably come up with a tuning and a mood on the guitar first; or maybe at the same time as he had an idea as to what the lyric was to be about. This is the way I would think he wrote them, but it's just merely guess work. And then I would think once he got the support pattern on the guitar, he would then know what kind of lyric he could write.

Int: How seriously did he take it? Did he talk about his songs?

Robert: What do you mean? About what the songs were about? Yes – never in great depth, in fact, no. He seemed to leave it to yourself to work out what you thought they meant. This is another thing, on *Pink Moon*, a lot of people think this is a very depressing, down LP; yet I find it's got some of the most optimistic songs of his, such as 'Harvest Breed'. It's very depressing: 'Falling fast and falling free, you look to find a friend, falling fast and falling free, this could just be the end,' and then he says, 'but you're ready now for the harvest breed...' Which could possibly be about death, but you're ready now for it. It means one is ready for one's environment; one knows what is coming.

Int: What is 'Pink Moon'?

Robert: I don't know. I don't actually know what 'Pink Moon' means.

Int: I can think of one explanation: death. It's a kind of symbol for death. 'Pink Moon's gonna get ye all.' The only thing that's gonna get us all is death. But it's experienced as something not entirely negative.

Robert: Right. That's how I see it. It's quite a positive interpretation of it.

Int: But I read something about that; he was deeply depressed those two days when he recorded that album. Do you know something about that?

Robert: No, I don't in fact. The only person who would know something about that is John Wood, because I think Nick just turned up, said, 'I've got an album to do,' and did it in two days. I wasn't there. I knew nothing of it. I'd heard 'Things Behind The Sun'; he had that written for some time. That was written before *Bryter Layter*, because he performed that at the Queen Elizabeth Hall, in his set; and which is strange when you think that that's possibly the high-spot of the *Pink Moon* album, I think.

Int: The love songs that came before, do you know anything about that?

Robert: Yes, there were several love songs that weren't ever recorded. There's one called 'Blossom', that I remember we used to do at Cambridge, and that was really a very nice, happy love song: 'Black days of winter all are through/ spring has come and it brought you/ trees came alive and the bees left their hive/ they made way for you and the blossom.'

It was just a very happy song about, you know, how pleased he was about a girl, I think. There were a lot of these songs that weren't recorded in fact.

Int: And they were uncomplicated?

Robert: Very simple, very simple.

Int: But why didn't Nick record them?

Robert: I don't know.

Int: Did he say anything about it?

Robert: I think possibly not. I think he probably didn't even play those to Joe and John for selection. I don't think it would have fitted in with any of the albums, that song, in fact. I mean, concept album is a stupid word, but Nick's albums, I find, you have to listen to the whole LP; you can't really just listen to one track. They all follow on from each other, and I don't really see where a song like 'Blossom' would have fitted in. It might have fitted into *Five Leaves Left* somewhere or other, after 'Man In A Shed' or something like that.

Int: He could have done a whole LP with the songs 'My Love Left With The Rain' and 'Joey' and some others.

Robert: 'Joey'? I've never heard that one.

Int: But Rodney and Molly said that he said, about those songs, that they were very childish.

Robert: Yes, I can see him saying that. I didn't think so. I like simple love songs, you know?

Int: But it didn't fit in with his moods?

Robert: No, it didn't really.

Int: So that could be the explanation.

Robert: Yes. They wouldn't have fitted with the albums; that's quite true. There was another song of his called 'Mayfair', which...Do you remember 'My Boy Lollipop', by Millie? Well, Millie recorded 'Mayfair', because I was doing an LP with her. That's the only time I think where someone has recorded another one of Nick's songs. And that, at first appearance, it seemed like a simple song but, in fact, when you looked into the lyrics it was a very cynical song about the rich people of 'Mayfair', about rich people generally I think.

Int: Was he an upper-class sort of type, Nick?

Robert: He struck one as that, yes. When I met him at Cambridge, I came from a working-class background and had got to Cambridge, well, by luck, by passing exams; I didn't have to pay to go there. Nick did as well obviously, he'd passed exams, but Nick came from Marlborough, which is, you know, a very posh public school. I remember when I first went up to his house; it stands in large grounds, with a small crest over the door, and I think they had a Malayan maid or cook at the time. And I knew his sister was a famous actress at the time as well.

Int: She is?

Robert: Oh yes, she's on television at the moment, in a new series of an American comedian, and she was in *The Brothers*, which was very popular on the continent I think. It was shown in Holland. Gabrielle Drake, she's a famous actress.

Yes, he struck me as, he was out of his time; he was in the wrong time. If he had lived in the time of William Bird and the English Elizabethan composers, he would have fitted perfectly. He struck me as a very Elizabethan person.

Int: But you say he would talk normally in a conversation?

Robert: Yes. He didn't talk a lot. I mean, he was always quiet; but we went, as I say, out to pubs, drinking, and to parties.

Int: How did he get along with other people he'd just met? Could he fall in a talk with somebody, just...?

Robert: Yes, I have seen him do, sometimes, yes. But, other times, no. Other times he would not say anything at all, and people who would meet him for the first time could think he was strange because he would not say anything at all.

Int: But he would talk to you?

Robert: Not particularly; but, yes, he would talk sometimes, when he wanted to, when he had something to say. People also think that, if Nick spoke, the words he said would somehow be like the words of Mohammed or the words of Jesus Christ, that everything would have meaning. But he'd say, 'Terrible weather we're having,' just like anybody else would, or, 'God, I fancy a hamburger.'

So, you know, Nick was like that. One could talk of normal things. And, in fact, very seldom did I talk about what you would call 'deep' things with him. I think when we were at Cambridge we occasionally talked of poetry, because, his first year, his room was full of books; absolutely packed with books.

Int: Which ones?

Robert: As I remember then, particularly 19th-century French poetry there was a lot of, which I was interested in a bit at the time as well, because I was interested in the songs of Debussy and Ravel; and so we would talk a bit about impressionism. And in some of the arrangements I tried to get a bit of an impressionist feel. But, there again, say on 'Way To Blue', I tried to handle it completely as a baroque song, like Handel or Bach, and that's why we dispensed with the guitar and just had the orchestra and Nick singing. It seemed to suit the mood of the song. It seemed to me...It was almost like a Bach chorale; it was a religious song, I thought, a spiritual song. So we treated it a bit as a chorale.

Int: What about the other songs? When you arranged them, how much did you look at the lyric?

Robert: A lot, a lot.

Int: What about 'Cello Song', did you arrange that?

Robert: 'Cello Song', no. I'd come up with a cello line, but that was really Nick's line as well; he used to sing that. But, no, there's a lady cellist in England called Clare Lowther; she just came in and blew it, ad libbed it.

Int: But you looked at the lyrics?

Robert: Oh, yes.

Int: And then decided.

Robert: What mood to try and give the song.

Int: Did you talk with Nick about it?

Robert: A little. Again, as I say, he would leave you to interpret … I might have had an entirely wrong idea of the song, and he wouldn't have tried to put me right. He would be interested to hear what someone else thought the song meant, you know.

Int: You said before, you arranged 'Day Is Done'.

Robert: 'Day Is Done', yes, that's right.

Int: And that was one of his first songs?

Robert: Yes.

Int: And you travelled when you were on tour?

Robert: We didn't tour; all these concerts were in Cambridge. We never left Cambridge.

Int: You never left Cambridge?

Robert: No, not for those concerts. You know, there's 21 colleges in Cambridge, so …

Int: Did you sit in the background and play?

Robert: Well, I used to … Nick would sit in the middle of the stage, on a stool, in his jeans, with his guitar, and arranged behind him, in a semi-circle, would be the 12 girls with their violins, violas, cellos, and a flute we usually had as well. And I would usually sit in the front row of the audience, in the middle, and conduct the orchestra from there; sitting down, sort of thing.

Int: Was it difficult to do those numbers?

Robert: No. No, it wasn't. Nick always played perfectly in time, his guitar was always perfectly in tune; he always did them exactly the same way. So, no, there were no problems at all. The musicians were amateur, so the overall effect wasn't as good as on the record. They were all students. But I think it was quite popular at the time.

Int: It sounds like a really classical arrangement, in the baroque style.

Robert: Yes, it was. It had that effect.

Int: And did you practise with those a long time?

Robert: No, we would have two rehearsals before. Well, on the day of the concert, we would run through the act twice. But, on the record, all

the four string-arranged songs on *Five Leaves Left* we did in three hours – we just did them straight off with professional musicians.
Int: OK, I think I've taken enough of your time …

Joe Boyd and the Crazy Magic of Nick Drake
Kevin Ring, *Zip Code*, 1992

Joe Boyd was one of the first producers to be elevated out of the dark shadows of the studio to the point where he rivalled the fame of any particular band he happened to be producing at the time. His name first cropped up on a regular basis in the mid-Sixties, bands like Fairport Convention, Toots and the Maytals, Fotheringay, Richard and Linda Thompson, The Incredible String Band all bore his name on the production credits. He was a well-respected man. Joe Boyd worked with and assisted in the development of a group of prodigiously talented artists. It's a testament to Joe Boyd's own personal vision and creative spark that this music endures and transcends all fickle fashions. Not content with that side of things he ventured into owning his own record company, Hannibal. He built that record company into a leading outfit, largely in what is called a 'roots' music field, before selling to Americans Rykodisc. Now Boyd sits on the board and continues to bring good music, old and new, to the spotlight. His latest projects being the Sandy Denny and Nick Drake boxed sets on compact disc. Boyd was a personal friend of Nick Drake and produced his albums. Nick Drake seems to have had a profound and lasting impact upon many people. He released three near-perfect albums in his lifetime and rarely played live. He died tragically in 1974. We asked Joe Boyd to talk about this legendary figure and the thinking behind the release of Drake's records on CD and in a luxurious boxed set.

Kevin Ring: The thing I always remember about Joe Boyd is the fact that you insisted on Nick's records always being kept in the catalogue when you sold the (Witchseason) record label. Is that right?
Joe Boyd: Yeah, I guess at the time the records hadn't sold very well, but I was convinced that they would one day, and I wanted to make sure that they didn't disappear by default. They didn't sell initially

because Nick didn't have an in-person live performing career and it wasn't music exactly in keeping with the times. There were no singles, no hits, no in-person following. There was no real way to gain an audience, other than slowly by word of mouth. He was good friends with John Martyn and they did a couple of dates together.

Kevin: Nick was really shy?

Joe: Yeah. He couldn't deal...he had one very successful performance at the Festival Hall, opening for Fairport Convention, when they did their first performance after the car accident and the release of *Liege & Lief*. And so you had a very respectful, quiet audience and he went down a storm. Then he went out on the road and found himself playing student unions, with everybody clinking beer bottles and talking in the back of the room. An introspective, quiet guy, playing the guitar and singing in a quiet voice, basically people just didn't bother paying attention, they kind of turned off. He was very demoralised and discouraged by it and couldn't get up much enthusiasm for going back on the road.

Kevin: When did you first come into contact with Nick?

Joe: I guess it was 1967. The Fairport Convention did an anti-war marathon at the Roundhouse. Ashley Hutchings, the bass player for the Fairports, stayed around to hear other artists. Nick got a 10-minute slot at two in the morning and Ashley heard him and was very impressed, and told me about him and gave me his phone number. I rang him up and invited him to come in and he brought a demo tape in. I was knocked out, I thought it was great.

Kevin: Was he living in London then?

Joe: He was going to Cambridge then actually. He decided to leave Cambridge and concentrate on music. I don't really remember what he was studying. I think it was English.

Kevin: Where were the photos on the cover of *Five Leaves Left* taken?

Joe: *Five Leaves Left* was at a friend's house in Hampstead, not the one he eventually lived in, but a different one. I think the one on the back of the album, where he's leaning against the wall, with somebody, a blurred figure, rushing past, that's right around the corner from our office, which was in Charlotte Street in the West End.

Kevin: Was Nick optimistic when *Five Leaves Left* came out?

Joe: I think he was always having difficulty reconciling the fact that he would get great reviews and so many people would come up to him and tell him how wonderful his records were, how much his music meant to them, but yet he wasn't rich or famous. I think that was difficult for him to understand, to know he could get great reviews and not sell records. I think it was a source of some frustration.

Kevin: There's stories that he lived very frugally, basically. There's a picture of him wrapped in a blanket…

Joe: The 'wrapped in a blanket' was not because he lived wrapped in a blanket; it was just a blanket the photographer happened to have with him. He didn't live like that. Nick, in later years, as he became more depressed, tended to neglect himself a bit, wear un-pressed, old clothes and look like he slept in them and things like that. But though he was very introverted, he had a good sense of humour. I think in his songs there's a kind of humour about his own condition. He has a slight ironic view of his own neurosis, so he wasn't without humour. But he was kind of… there's some of his lyrics, something like, 'If songs were lines in a conversation then everything would be fine…' If he could communicate with people in life as he did with his music, he would have been a lot happier. But he found it very difficult talking to people. He had a rather self-effacing, apologetic manner of an introverted public schoolboy.

Kevin: Why is he more popular than ever now?

Joe: Just the fact that over time people have come to appreciate the records, and once you make a convert, it's a convert for life. People, once they discover the music, they then appreciate it and tell other people about it. The circle spreads. There hasn't been that much promotion, we've done a little bit over the years, but not promotion that a new artist gets on a major label or anything like that. I think, in general, you could say that his records sell more every year.

Kevin: There was an album of Nick Drake cover versions by an American singer, did you ever hear that?

Joe: There is a guy in New Jersey, can't remember his name. He puts records out on cassette on his own label. He did a lot of guitar arrangements of Nick's songs. He's been kind of obsessed with Nick's songs for a long time. I don't think they were that much in keeping with the spirit.

Kevin: What about the band Dream Academy?

Joe: I know Nick, the lead singer, and he's always been a big Nick Drake fan, but I wouldn't say that the song reminds me of Nick Drake. Nick (Laird-Clowes) is very influenced by Nick in a way. It was nice to see the tribute, it's a nice song.

Kevin: Do you think Nick would have coped with a level of success?

Joe: Sure, I think he would have been delighted with it. It would have helped him a lot I imagine. Everybody likes to be appreciated; even Bon Jovi likes to be appreciated. But, while you're waiting for that, some nice fat royalty cheques would help pass the time. Nick was anxious for that to happen in a way. As I said, I think he was frustrated. He did get artistic acclaim in his lifetime, people wrote about him, very remarkable reviews, how great he was, how wonderful he was. But it was just critics, Nick Kent and *Melody Maker* and a few American magazines. John Peel thought he was great. So he did have the respect of his peers and I think musicians around him were all very respectful of him.

Kevin: Did Nick have his own influences and heroes?

Joe: He was always a powerful influence on other people, even outside a musical level. Sure, the obvious influences for someone of that era, like Dylan; he played some Dylan songs on his early demos...Just listening to his early things and talking to him at the time, a lot of guitar players were very influenced by blues players, a lot of people were very influenced by the electric guitar players, the kind of darker and harder blues players, the Chicago blues players, whereas Nick was very influenced by what you might call the 'folk hero blues players' like Brownie McGhee and Josh White, who had more of a clean, finger-picking style of country blues. He was very influenced by those two. I saw a lot of their records at his place and you can hear a lot of that in his playing. Other than that I would have thought that normal contemporary influences, Bert Jansch, John Renbourne, The Beatles and Dylan. Every songwriter was influenced by The Beatles.

Kevin: What about literary influences?

Joe: I'm not sure about that. I'm not sure what his poetic influences were. People talk a lot about Rimbaud, but I think his were more English; Tennyson and the 19th-century poets.

Kevin: What's your favourite Nick Drake record?

Joe: I think *Bryter Layter* is the one on the whole that I was happiest with. It's one I can sit down and listen to without ever thinking I wished we'd mixed that differently or we shouldn't have done that. It just seems to work as a record. I can appreciate it beyond worrying about any aspect of the production. It was a record where everything fell together pretty well. It ended up as a good reflection of Nick's music, what we tried to accomplish.

Kevin: How do you feel about Nick Drake being in a boxed set, a thing normally associated with big stars? People might say he never had any number one hits!

Joe: Well, it was out as a boxed set in vinyl and it sold well. Not spectacularly, but enough to justify the expense of the box and the booklets and everything. I think we've sold 20,000 of the boxed set in vinyl. Hopefully we'll do the same in CDs.

Kevin: Did he spend any time back in his home village of Tanworth-in-Arden?

Joe: Yes. Particularly after he became more and more depressed, he found it difficult to cope, living in London. He'd go back to live for long periods with his parents. It was his introversion and difficulty in making contact with people. A lot of the most interesting artists don't have the obvious outlets that other people have, sort of going down the pub on a Saturday night and talking easily with people. Some people don't find the normal forms of social intercourse easy, and all that drive to communicate and express yourself, comes out in music or painting or writing. I think an awful lot of creative people do have problems communicating; it makes their artistic communication all the more intense.

Kevin: Do you think there's an element of the romantic notion of dying young in the interest? How old was Nick, around 27?

Joe: I think there is to a certain degree, but that can only go so far. People can get interested in certain individuals as personalities, but not unless the music is of a substance to back up the interest. People might explore the records because they were interested in the story, but unless the music rewards repeated listening, you're not going to build up the kind of following Nick's records have built up.

Kevin: Nick's on a par with someone like Tim Buckley in that respect?

Joe: I think he's on the same level of renown, certainly in England and

France, maybe in America too. He's not as widely known in America, but he's getting there. Generally sales have been about on a par between England and America. Obviously America is a much bigger market; it represents a much smaller percentage of the market. But in terms of the number of people that know Nick, the figures are about the same. Having the box set on CD helps. We're having discussions with some people about a tribute album, other people doing his songs. It's tricky, his songs, you don't want to be too respectful when you're doing covers. The Imaginary label are doing a covers tribute album. We're happy that the interest is there.

Talking to David Sandison
Jason Creed, *Pink Moon 6*, April 24, 1996

Jason Creed: Why do you think Nick sold so few records?
David Sandison: Partly because he didn't...he wasn't capable of, or couldn't do, that promotion thing that you just have to do. You've got to be real about it, and the fact of the matter is, if you're not out there...even if he'd been doing small gigs with a manageable number of people, which probably would have doubled or tripled sales, and word of mouth would have done a bit more as well...But, you know, how many gigs did he play in his life? There weren't any radio stations that were going to play him. John Peel played some stuff, but where else was he going to get played? It was severely left field in commercial terms, so there was nothing really that Island...I mean, OK, Island could take out adverts, but adverts are only part of a jigsaw which includes live performance and interviews and radio play, and three out of four of those were missing. Because the one interview I persuaded him to do, with Jerry Gilbert, the fact that Jerry got two or three paragraphs out of him was amazing; a triumph of skill over reality. In the half-hour that we sat in that cafe, I would think Nick probably said a dozen words. We finished up like two idiots sort of blithering at him. Jerry would spend two minutes asking him a question that demanded an answer, and Nick would say 'Yes' or 'No', and then hum a bit and stir his tea, and maybe then sort of start a sentence and then kind of give up. Witchseason were

amazed that he agreed to do it, and I still don't know why he agreed. I think I passed a message to Anthea Joseph of Witchseason saying, would he do an interview; and she was amazed that he agreed. To be fair, Jerry had written a couple of nice reviews and positive things, and quoted him in context with other people in past features, so he knew who he was talking to.

I met him at the Queen Elizabeth Hall when he opened for John and Beverley Martyn, at a backstage party afterwards, and I said, you know, that the show was really nice, and he sort of said, 'Thank you,' and then wandered away. And I just thought, 'Well, OK,' because I'd seen the set and I'd heard the albums, so I didn't expect him to throw his arms around me and say, 'Thank you very much!' Because, again, during the show, I think, if he introduced one number he certainly didn't do any more than that, and he didn't even say, 'Thank you,' and, 'Goodnight.' But, you know, Gabrielle says, 'That's not the way I remember it…'

Jason: In your *Zig Zag* article, you said: 'At the time of *Bryter Layter* I got the impression from Nick that he didn't like the strings, or the way the album was presented.' Can you remember what Nick said or did to give you that impression?

David: It's quite funny actually, because this connects with a conversation I had with Tim Hardin, who had the same beef about his first album. Tim claimed that the strings had been put on after he'd left the studio, and the first time he heard it, he said, you know, 'What the fuck are these? Where did they come from?' And I could never understand it at the time because Robert Kirby was such a close friend and he had been brought in by Nick. Now whether he – I don't think it was the presence of the strings – he wasn't quite happy with the arrangements, or he would have preferred them to be done again, or if Robert had more time maybe, I don't know.

I think it was part of the pattern he had in his mind, and Robert was the person he thought could make sense of it, rather than get an outsider to arrange it. But I think it really just didn't meet his expectations, rather than he didn't like the strings being there.

Jason: Do you think that Nick felt that his music was the only thing in his life that was real or genuine?

David: I think he felt his music was the only real part of him. Whether he wouldn't or couldn't dress it up any more elaborately to make it more commercial, or whether that wasn't the point anyway, I don't know. I mean, he was incredibly lucky to have Joe, because he was prepared to invest money in him, and if that's what he got, then that's what he got, and it went out. Obviously with help from Joe and with help from John Wood they would enhance what they could and add what they could. But it was just that sort of contract, between times as well, with people who would normally be responsible for developing a career. I don't think the word 'career' ever occurred to Nick's mind's vocabulary. It was just what he did, and the next album wasn't going to lead anywhere, it was just going to be the next album.

But it's like the story John Martyn told me about the time that Nick came down to stay with him and Beverley in Hastings, and they were sitting, either watching TV or listening to something, and Nick got up and left the room. They'd been chatting before Nick left the room and John thought he'd gone for a pee or to make a cup of tea and, in fact, about an hour later, he realised Nick hadn't come back; and he opened the door and there was Nick sitting outside, hunched up against the wall with his knees up. John said, well, you know, 'What are you doing here?' and he didn't get any kind of answer that made any sense, and he just sort of got used to it. But John was one of the people who was prepared to give Nick that space, and to give him support by being a friend, as much as Nick wanted it; and you couldn't force it on Nick. He'd draw on it when he wanted to draw on it. I just think he was withdrawn into a world of his own for so long.

Jason: Why do you think he became so withdrawn?

David: I'm not a psychologist, so I couldn't tell you whether it was manic depression or what. He may have dropped some acid at some point, you know, some bad acid, and got locked inside himself. I don't know. I don't know enough about him before to know how normal he was at Marlborough, how outgoing he was before that. You know, was there a cut-off point? Was it the pressures of academic life? For a lot of people it is; they suddenly get overwhelmed.

Jason: Do you think he would have lived the 'rock star' life if he could have, or was it something he simply wasn't interested in?

David: I don't know if he harboured, in the early days, an ambition of stardom, but he certainly didn't display any willingness to follow the routes that you have to take to achieve it. Now, whether the first experience, when he did some folk clubs, was so horrific to him, because he discovered that he wasn't good enough for it, or ready for it, I don't know. He certainly shouldn't have been crushed by any reviews that *Bryter Layter* got because they were all very positive. But if he wasn't going to get himself involved in the other parts of it, either if he couldn't or wouldn't, then he didn't have the right to be disappointed.

Jason: When Robert Kirby talks about the early gigs, the folk clubs and college appearances, he says they were always enjoyable.

David: Yeah, in that case I suspect something happened to him either chemically or psychologically; because working at that level when you're first starting out was one thing, but when you're confronted with the reality of doing something grander or bigger or more sort of assertive, and you either don't want to do it or realise you can't do it, for whatever reasons, it can affect your confidence. But I don't get that impression with him. There was very definitely a wall that he did erect around himself; that very few people got over or through. John Martyn certainly did; obviously Joe Boyd and John Wood did; and there may have been some others, Robert Kirby, but apart from that...

Jason: What's the full story about the *Pink Moon* tapes? Did he really just leave them at (Island's) reception and disappear?

David: I saw him in reception after I came back from lunch. I was talking to somebody in reception and I saw a figure in the corner on the bench, and I suddenly realised it was Nick. He had this big, 15ips master-tape box under his arm, and I said, 'Have you had a cup of tea?' and he said, 'Erm, yes.' I said, 'Do you want to come upstairs?' and he said, 'Yes, OK.'

So we went upstairs into my office, which was on top of the landing – it was a landing that went into the big office with a huge round table where Chris Blackwell and everybody else worked – very democratic – and there was a big Reevox and sound system there – and he just sat in my office area for about half-an-hour. I think we got him another cup of tea, and I had a couple of phone calls to make and a couple came in and, I have to be honest, I didn't really relish trying to make conversation, because he wasn't offering any, and the interview with

Jerry Gilbert had proved to me that you couldn't force anything out of Nick. After about half-an-hour he said, 'I'd better be going,' and I said, 'OK, nice to see you,' and he left. Now, he went down the stairs and he still had the tapes under his arm, and about an hour later the girl who worked behind the front desk called up and said, 'Nick's left his tapes behind.' So I went down and it was the big 16-track master-tape box and it said 'Nick Drake Pink Moon', and I thought, 'That's not an album I know!'

Jason: Were you the first person to hear the album?

David: No. The first thing to do was get it into the studio to make a seven-and-a-half-inch safety copy, because that was the master. So we ran off a safety copy to actually play; and I think, 24 hours later, or so, it was put on the Reevox in the main room and we heard *Pink Moon*. And I think Chris Blackwell or Muff Winwood called John Wood and said, 'What is this?' And, well, you know, we knew it was Nick's new album, but, thanks for telling us folks!

Jason: Did Nick have anything to do with the artwork for the album?

David: I don't think so.

Jason: Was Michael Trevithick an artist Nick admired?

David: I assume he was given approval. Someone must have liaised with him. I told you about finding the original artwork. Chris Blackwell bought the house next door to Island to extend the offices, and there was a load of debris in the basement, and they said, 'This is going to be your office,' and I said, 'Thanks a lot,' because there were desks piled up and everything, and part of the debris was the framed, original *Pink Moon* painting. It didn't have any of the credits on it or any of the tracks or anything, it just had the Island logo and the spread. So I took it upstairs and said, 'Does anybody want this?' and they said, 'No.' So I said, 'Can I hang it in my office?' and they said, 'Yes, if you like.' And I meant to put it up but didn't because it didn't work with what we had in the office, and eventually I said, 'Look, I'm going to take this home, does anybody mind?' And they said, 'No.' And it hung in my house in North London for about two years, and then I moved to Hertfordshire and took it with me and hung it there. And then I moved back to London, and I was working for a company called Caribiner, a conference production company, and one of the women who worked there, on the theatrical side, mentioned that she'd just done a TV thing with Gabrielle, so I said, 'Look, can you get in touch with her and ask her if her parents would like the painting?' And a message came back: 'Yes, please!' And I wrapped it up and got it delivered to her agent, and I had a very sweet letter from Molly thanking me for it. I saw Gabrielle about 18 months ago and introduced myself, because I'd never met her, and reminded her and she said, 'Thank you for that, my parents were very happy.'

I don't honestly know whether Nick would have had sight of it. I can't believe they wouldn't have tried to show him. So I don't know how they would have done it. We didn't know where he was half the time.

Jason: Do you know where he was living when he recorded *Pink Moon*, because he moved back to his parents' after *Bryter Layter*? Was he living in London at the time or did he just come down to make the record?

David: Around the time of *Pink Moon* he definitely had another place in Hampstead. On one occasion I tried to get hold of him, because if you don't ask you don't get. I think John Wood gave me a number in Hampstead where he said he thought he was, but they said he was in Paris, that he wasn't there, he'd left anyway. But that was about the third call, the first two people I spoke to didn't know who he was, so it must have been a bunch of flats. I mean, there was a bank account into which money was paid, and withdrawals were made from it; so Joe looked after him incredibly well with that deal. I mean, he sold Witchseason to Island for about £1, I think it was, and the condition was, look after everybody, but especially Nick. Nick especially was to be persevered with. But nobody ever tried to pressure him because they knew it was impossible, because he just functioned at his own pace.

Jason: Did you see Nick again after he left the tapes at Island?

David: No, that was it.

Jason: Is there any one thing in particular, from your meetings with Nick, that still sticks in your mind today?

David: (Laughter) Three words, in no particular order: extracting, blood and stone. Erm, no, I suppose you could call it hard work. I was mortified because I think I can get on with most people and I can get most people to open up...

I was just reliving the moment of the advert we ran, you know, the weird smile. It was an embarrassed smile, it was really strange.

Jason: A nervous smile?

David: No, it was embarrassed not nervous. It was almost like he was embarrassed to be the subject of attention. It's like when people say, 'If you really want to know about me, listen to my songs.' I mean, most of that is bullshit; just somebody plugging their new album who can't be bothered to do an interview. But I think with Nick it was possibly true. I think the songs were the closest he was able to come, certainly for many years, to articulating anything about himself and how he was feeling, and what turned him on, what excited him, you know, what took him, what moved him. I do think that when you listen to Nick Drake, you're hearing Nick Drake. I think you are hearing a very gifted songwriter. But I don't think there was a lot of 'artiness', if you like, in those songs, apart from the difficulty of rhyming or whatever. I think whatever was going on in Nick's mind is there in the songs.

Jason: Do you know if Island ever collected any live footage or recordings of Nick? Perhaps if somebody recorded the Fairports or John and Beverley, Nick's set may have been included.

David: There is a possibility that whoever worked the sound desk at those gigs might have. The chances are they might have let it roll during Nick's set, but Nick was such a mystery and such an unknown quantity that I'm not sure if anybody had been bootlegging that night, as a John and Bev fan, they would have recorded Nick. If somebody was recording off the desk, which did happen, they might have recorded Nick's songs. But I would be very surprised, simply because they haven't already appeared. Because I think rarity value alone would make them a wonderful part of a compilation, with extra live tracks added to the CD or whatever. But I suspect that... No, you know, I think we can safely assume that, had anything been recorded, it would have appeared by now.

Jason: How do you feel about the distribution of the various bootlegs? Joe Boyd is obviously down on them, and Gabrielle is too.

David: Well, certainly when they're mass-produced by sharks it's bad news, but when members of a fan club or appreciation society swap them I don't think there's any harm. But it's a big industry, like all the

Springsteen and Dylan bootlegs that have appeared through the years, somebody's making an awful lot of money out of those and they're ripping the artist off. But I think when somebody's got an iffy cassette recording from a hand-held mic, two-thirds of the way back at a folk club, I think it's perfectly acceptable because it's a manifestation of love and admiration. But I think the fact that people are still finding ways of getting Nick Drake out is wonderful.

Jason: Do you think Nick's illness was something he struggled to overcome or something that he accepted?

David: I think he worked at it to some degree. The fact that he did see a psychiatrist, he did take medication, albeit unwillingly. I think he had to accept it. I noticed your next question is whether the songs were an escape, and I don't think they were; I think the songs were an articulation of it. Back to what I said, that Nick's songs were an expression of the person. OK, some are fantasies, some are whimsies, some are allegories, but I think they are all Nick, and they were his way of expressing really what he was all about. In that regard maybe they were a kind of release of pressure; but they weren't an escape. I mean, sadly, I don't think he ever escaped. That's the problem; we're talking about a dead person, because he didn't escape it – which is not to say he committed suicide. No, if Nick had been in Amsterdam or Paris or somewhere like that, after six months of doing whatever he did in exile, you could maybe say, 'OK' – but he was at home; he was back with people who loved him. He was safe where he was, there were no threats or pressures, because his parents wouldn't apply any pressures.

Jason: Nick once said, 'I don't like it at home, but I can't bear it anywhere else.'

David: Well, everywhere else posed too many problems. I just have this horrible suspicion that Nick dropped something sometime and it was bad stuff and it tipped him over – something he couldn't get out of. It's pure guess work, but there was definitely a point at which Nick retreated. Why did he retreat? Who knows? I don't know. There was definitely a pull back from *Bryter Layter*, or *Five Leaves Left* in fact, and I don't know whether he had a look at what was involved and what it entailed and decided he didn't want it. You can theorise and theorise and at the end of the day the only person who can tell us is Nick, and he's not here. It was so marked that I just think that there was some event, rather than an accumulation of events; and whether it was a chemical event, or whether it was an emotional event; he pulled back and decided to do it at his own pace, and he was very lucky to have Joe Boyd because nobody else I can think of would have persevered with that state of affairs. It made no commercial sense. It made artistic sense to very few people. It's like Van Gogh, you know, during his lifetime he sold one picture – and maybe Nick was 10 years ahead of his time in some ways.

The romantic, dead poet is a wonderful attraction for a lot of people. It doesn't matter how they got into him, as long as they get into him, and they discover him. As far as I'm concerned, he's a kind of little island of tranquillity, which is very nice to visit now and again.

The Sad Ballad of Nick Drake
Mick Brown, *The Daily Telegraph*, 1997

Towards the end of his life, when his reserves of self-belief – his very will to live – had run almost to empty, Nick Drake returned to his parents' home in the Midlands village of Tanworth-in-Arden.

The depression that had plagued him for the previous four years had now settled on him like a shroud. The talent that had shaped three consummately beautiful albums – among the most beautiful ever to emerge from British pop music – could find no greater expression than strumming the same chords over and over again on his Gibson acoustic guitar. His parents came to see it as a sign. At some point in the long afternoon, he would stand up, put the guitar to one side, leave the room and, without a word, set off in his car. Two, three or four hours later the telephone call would come. Unable to face the ordeal of stopping and buying petrol, he had run to a standstill. His father would patiently drive the 40, 60 or 80 miles to collect him.

When Nick Drake died in 1974, at the age of 26, from an overdose of antidepressants, it was a tragedy that passed largely unnoticed. The three albums which he had made in his short lifetime were all, by any strictly commercial criterion, failures.

Nor was there anything about his death to arouse the interest of any but his friends, family and a small band of loyal fans: no histrionics, no spectacular burn-out. The coroner's verdict was suicide, but even that is disputed by some of his friends. According to one of them, it was as if Nick Drake 'simply faded away', a victim not of excess, but of 'some profound, deep-seated unhappiness'.

Not long before his death, Drake went into a recording studio. Such was his condition, his lack of equilibrium, that he was able to record only four songs. Heard now, they have the ethereal quality of the last breath of a dying person captured on glass. Among them is a song called Black Eyed Dog:

'A black eyed dog he called at my door/A black eyed dog he called for more/A black eyed dog he knew my name ...'

It is a clear metaphor for death. Nick Drake was writing his own obituary. This air of fragility and foreboding hangs over all Drake's work.

Among the tracks on his first album, *Five Leaves Left* – recorded in 1969, five years before his death, when times were good – is a song called 'Fruit Tree'. It is a caution on the subject of fame; a prophecy of the belated recognition that would come for his own work. 'Safe in your place deep in the earth,' Drake sings, 'That's when they'll know what you were really worth ...'

Last year, Island Records released an anthology of Drake's work, *Way To Blue*. Drake recorded only 31 songs, and during his lifetime none of his records ever sold more than 10,000 copies. *Way To Blue* has sold five times as much – just one example of how the Drake legend has grown since his death. For in a manner as quiet and unobtrusive as his records, Nick Drake has become a cult, his records revered, his life a subject of endless scrutiny and speculation.

Performers as various as Peter Buck of R.E.M., Ben Watt of Everything But The Girl, Paul Weller and Kate Bush have all paid tribute to Drake's songs and his influence on their own work. Among a new generation of even younger musicians – young enough in some cases not to have been born when Drake was recording – he has achieved the status of an icon. There are Nick Drake fanzines and websites, endlessly recycling the scant details of his life. A tribute album is planned, and so too is a television documentary – despite the fact that no 'live' footage of Drake has been found.

By any standards, Drake was an unusual candidate for a pop music icon. At a time when middle-class boys like Mick Jagger felt obliged to adopt faux-cockney accents and manufacture street-credible roots, Drake came from an affluent, middle-class, ex-colonial family. He went from public school to Cambridge. In an age when the prevalent musical influences were American, Drake's music had an unmistakably English quality. His songs, melodies and open-tuned guitar playing owed as much to his love of Vaughan Williams and Delius as to Dylan and The Band; his lyrics were as much influenced by the vernacular and sensibility of the 19th-century Romantic poets, as by the locutions of blues and folk, lending his themes of love, yearning and self-identity a particular literacy.

In the years since his death, Drake has come to personify a particular idea of ill-starred romanticism. Taken together, his early death and the fragile, elegiac beauty of his music – steeped in a melancholia that suggests an infinity of autumns – present a picture of a poetic and tortured young man, who left behind him a legacy of wistful, evanescent beauty.

But the life of Nick Drake is more complex than that. He was an artist constantly frustrated by the lack of recognition. A man with scores of friends, none of whom seemed really to have known him at all. A writer of achingly romantic love songs, who appears never to have enjoyed a single intimate relationship. Trying to shape a picture of Nick Drake is like watching a figure behind a screen of smoke. Sometimes he is there. Sometimes he seems hardly to have existed at all.

Pop music has its places of pilgrimage: the Dakota building in New York, where John Lennon was shot. Père Lachaise in Paris where Jim Morrison is buried. Tanworth-in-Arden is hardly among the most famous, but in the years since Nick Drake's death a steady stream of fans have made their way to the graveyard of the village church where he is buried.

Until the death of Drake's mother, Molly, in 1993, the more intrepid visitors would also visit the large Queen Anne house in the village, where the Drake family had lived. Molly Drake grew accustomed to people from America, Scandinavia and Australia turning up on her doorstep, eager for her version of her son's life.

"They used to have tea-parties, which was quite fun," says her daughter, the actress Gabrielle Drake. "I always got quite anxious with her being on her own, but the fans who turned up were always very sweet young people, and I think she felt obliged."

Molly Drake was a talented musician herself. She played the piano and wrote songs – lullabies for the children, love songs to amuse friends. Heard on her scratchy home tape recordings, they echo an England that had begun to vanish in the Fifties. The crystal middle-class diction suggests a certain innocence; an image of French windows opening on to manicured lawns; of balmy summer afternoons, civilised conversation, the splash of tonic on gin. This was the world Nick Drake grew up in.

He was born in 1948 in Burma, where his father, Rodney, an engineer, worked for the Burma-India Trading Company. When Drake was three, the family moved back to England and Rodney took a job as managing director of a Birmingham engineering company. The family moved into their large, comfortable house in the picture-postcard village of Tanworth-in-Arden.

At the age of eight, Nick was sent away to the Eagle House prep school in Surrey. He developed into an outstanding athlete and was, in time, made head boy. But as his father (who died in 1988) once recalled, 'it didn't really seem to mean anything to him. It was as if there was something else going on in his mind all the time. A headmaster's report said that "none of us seemed to know him very well". And I think that was it, all the way through with Nick. People didn't know him very much.'

Following the family tradition, Drake went on to Marlborough, where he distinguished himself at athletics and rugby (playing alongside Mark Phillips in the first XV), and began to develop his interest in music. He studied cello, piano and clarinet, fell in love with the music of Bob Dylan and Josh White, and began to write his own songs.

He won a place at Fitzwilliam College, Cambridge, to study English, but delayed for a year. He made the almost obligatory excursion on the hippie trail to Morocco, and then returned to London, sharing a flat with his elder sister Gabrielle, whose career as an actress had begun to flourish. In London he made a new group of friends, centred on Chelsea and Fulham, mostly ex-public school, with connections to the landed gentry – Astors and Ormsby-Gores.

They were united by the common enthusiasms of the day: rock music, the poets Romantic and maudits, getting, as a Rolling Stones record of the day had it, 'out of their heads'. A friend, Julian Lloyd, describes 'a life centred on scoring black hash at eight quid an ounce, buying 20 Embassy and a packet of Rizla papers, then getting terribly stoned and laughing a lot, followed by a companionable silence.'

In this company, Drake's tendency to introversion was hardly noticed. Friends remember him as shy, but with a droll sense of humour, 'a very sympathetic person, with a charming smile,' remembers Lloyd. 'He was always ready to laugh, quick to get the joke, without being loud or noisy.' Sometimes he would get out his guitar and play his songs for his friends, 'but even among people he knew well he would never face you; he'd be singing to his guitar.'

His friends recognised that Drake was a precociously talented song-writer and musician. But if he had ambitions towards a career in music he never mentioned them. Ambition was uncool. In one other respect, Drake stuck out. Most of his friends were couples. Drake was always alone.

There is a photograph taken in 1967, of Drake on a visit to Hatley Park, the home of the Astor family in Cambridgeshire. The Hon. J.J. Astor, Mrs Astor and friends ride in a horse-drawn cart, their faces turned to the camera in broad smiles. Drake sits in the front seat, his face turned away, as if he is not quite part of the group.

'Nick was a watcher,' says Victoria Lloyd, née Ormsby-Gore. 'He was always just there, floating along on the fringe observing it all. And he had an ethereal quality to him; he was incredibly sensitive about how things were, the beauty of things: he was very gentle and looking to higher things.'

In October 1967, Drake went up to Fitzwilliam College, Cambridge, to read English. 'He was profoundly disappointed by it,' Victoria adds. 'He had this wonderful vision of going up to Cambridge – the dreaming spires, the wonderful, erudite people. We went up to visit and he was in this grim, redbrick building, sitting in this tiny motel-like bedroom. He was completely crushed. He just sat there saying "it's so awful." It was anathema to him. Torture.'

In fact, Drake had fallen into a circle in Cambridge not dissimilar to

the one he had left behind in London – 'long-haired, cooler and hip-
per, or thinking we were', remembers one of his college friends, Brian
Wells – with much the same rituals: sitting around with guitars, listening
to Dylan and Van Morrison records, smoking copious amounts of dope.

Wells describes Drake as 'a slightly isolated figure who lived in his
own head a lot. He was the guy who would just get up in the middle of
an evening and leave, and everybody would say, where's Nick going?
He was probably just going back to his room, but it made him mysterious to people.'

Drake was mostly indifferent to his studies, but his music began to
blossom. In 1968 he performed at a benefit concert at the Roundhouse
in London, where he was spotted by the bass-player of Fairport
Convention, Ashley Hutchings, who referred him to the record producer Joe Boyd.

Boyd remembers Drake coming into his office in Charlotte Street,
London, to deliver a demo tape, 'very bashful and apologetic' and leaving as suddenly as he had arrived. Boyd played the tape that evening,
and the next morning offered Drake a contract. 'The songs were just
wonderful,' says Boyd, 'and the guitar-playing was astonishing.

'Nick was 6ft 3in, but he was very apologetic about himself physically. He kinda slunk into a room. Everything about him seemed slightly
smaller than it was. But then he'd put his hands on the table, and there
were these immense, powerful hands – always with dirty fingernails.
And he'd start playing the guitar, and every note would ring out clear
and true.'

Between lectures, Drake travelled down from Cambridge to record
his first album, *Five Leaves Left*, which was released in 1969. The title
was a whimsical reference to the slip found near the bottom of a packet
of Rizla cigarette papers – instant code for dope smokers.

'He made no fuss about the record at all,' remembers Gabrielle. 'I
knew he was doing it, but he'd hardly mention it. Then one day he just
came into my bedroom and tossed a copy of it on to my bed and said,
"There y'are." I think he was enormously proud of it, but in this very
quiet, self-deprecating, quite ironical way.'

With the record completed, Drake abandoned Cambridge to follow a path in music – 'career' would be too strong a word to describe

his aspirations. 'It was not really a word in his vocabulary,' one friend remembers.

'It's hard to imagine a situation today where an artist wouldn't ask any questions, or wouldn't have something to say, or would have no clear position regarding his career, but Nick really didn't,' recalls Joe Boyd. 'He was very clear about his music, but almost totally indifferent about everything else.'

Five Leaves Left received encouraging reviews, and early in 1970 Drake made his first major appearance, at the Royal Festival Hall supporting Fairport Convention. Boyd was exultant. 'People loved him live; they were saying they loved the record. And I thought at that point, everything is working out according to plan.'

Boyd instructed his office to book Drake on a tour of clubs and student unions and set off to America with Fairport Convention, whom he managed and produced, confident that his new protégé career was under way. After only a few days he received a phone call. 'Nick had played just three or four dates, and he said, "I can't do this any more: I'm going home."' At one concert, at Warwick University, Drake had come on stage and fought a losing battle against people clinking glasses at the bar and talking. 'It was very depressing for him, very dispiriting,' says Boyd. 'He just didn't have a personality that would say, shut up at the back, I'm trying to play.'

Drake was too diffident even to agree to interviews for the music press. 'The only way was through record sales,' says Boyd, who put him on a retainer of £25 a week, set against royalties. He moved into a bedsit in Hampstead, where he wrote songs for what would be his next album, *Bryter Layter*. The room was barely furnished and so cold that he would drag his mattress off the bed closer to the gas fire to keep warm.

Living alone, Drake became an increasingly withdrawn figure. Boyd had introduced him to the singer-songwriter John Martyn, who lived nearby in Hampstead. Occasionally, Drake would turn up at Martyn's house. Martyn's wife Beverley would cook them dinner; Drake and Martyn would smoke and play guitars. Another one of Boyd's friends was a second-hand car, stolen goods and sometime hashish dealer – a character – who would host evenings in his kitchen playing liar-dice and kaluki. 'He could always jolly Nick up,' says Boyd. 'Not many people could.'

The most common description that his friends offer of Drake's life is 'compartmentalised'. A wraith-like presence who would simply appear, and then just as quickly vanish, never causing the circles he moved in to overlap.

At a party thronging with London's *jeunesse dorée*, Boyd was astonished to discover that Drake had been close friends with the Orsmby-Gores and the Astors. 'I'd known Nick for three years and had no idea he knew these people.'

Nor can anyone recall Drake ever having a girlfriend. 'There were girls at Cambridge who were crazy about him,' Brian Wells remembers. 'They'd worry about him, make him cushions and so on. But nothing ever happened, as far as I know.' For all the aching romanticism in his music, it seems that Drake was never able to express it in his life. In one of the songs on *Bryter Layter*, 'Hazey Jane', he sang, 'If songs were lines in a conversation, the situation would be fine ...' When there were no songs, increasingly, there was only silence.

It was at this point that Nick Drake's life seemed to take some turn away from troubled reserve to a deeper and more alienating sense of isolation. On one occasion he simply vanished from his Hampstead flat for three to four weeks, without telling his family or friends where he was going. Shortly afterwards, a Cambridge friend called at the flat on the off-chance. After ringing the doorbell to no avail, he peered through the window to see Drake simply sitting, staring at the wall. He was so disconcerted by the sight that he left. Always indifferently dressed, Drake began to look more and more shabby, not washing his hair or cleaning his fingernails.

Among the early songs which Drake recorded as a Cambridge student was a traditional blues about marijuana, 'Been Smokin' Too Long':

'Nightmare made of hash dreams/Got the devil in my shoes/Tell me tell me what have I done wrong/Ain't nothing go right with me/Must be I've been smoking too long.'

Drake renders the song as a flip homage, but it's tempting to speculate the song had begun to assume a measure of truth.

Introversion is one of the consequences of smoking hashish over a sustained period. The initial feelings of giggling elation give way to reflection and then often to mild paranoia – the sense of hearing what you say even before you say it, deciding it's foolish and thinking it better to say nothing at all. 'Nick was an extremely sensitive guy,' says Julian Lloyd. 'I think communication was difficult for him anyway, and smoking didn't make it any easier. He had such incredibly high standards and ideals, and he found it hard to get across, to connect.'

'It was as if he slipped into this terrible inertia,' says Brian Wells. 'People often get into that situation and snap out of it. But Nick didn't have the inner resources to do that.' More than that, Wells believes, in some peculiar way Drake was increasingly becoming the prisoner of an image which his reticence and self-consciousness had created for him. 'People saw Nick as being this remote, fragile, slightly romantic, neglected figure. I think he was quite conscious of that, and he became more and more like it.'

Bryter Layter was released in 1970. It is Drake's most beautiful album, couched in deceptively luxuriant, almost exuberant arrangements. 'Everybody involved with it thought this is the one,' says Boyd. But while the album received good reviews, its sales were negligible. Drake could not hide his disappointment. He told Joe Boyd that he wanted his next record to be radically different; no plush arrangements, no other musicians – just him and his acoustic guitar. 'I said, "Fine,"' says Boyd. '"If that's what you want." You couldn't force anything with Nick.'

Boyd's attempts to foster Drake's career were going nowhere. He had given Drake's two albums to the French singer, Francoise Hardy. She loved them and expressed an interest in Drake writing songs for her, so Boyd took him to Paris to meet Hardy at her apartment on the Isle St Louis.

'It was excruciating. Nick sat there, head down, drinking his tea and didn't say a word the whole time; and I had to fill in the awkward silences.' Nonetheless, the meeting ended with a resolution for Drake to write some songs. But somehow he never got round to it.

In 1971, Boyd sold his company to Island Records and moved to California to pursue a new career developing film soundtracks. Drake's records had never been released in America – his music was regarded as too particular, too English, for American tastes, but he had his fans. David Geffen, who has now become one of the most powerful men in the American entertainment industry, loved his records and wanted to manage him but, like so much to do with Drake's career, it came to nothing.

Eventually, Boyd negotiated the release of an album combining tracks from Drake's two English releases. It was unveiled at a party at the Troubador club in Los Angeles, with a cardboard cut-out of Drake on stage. But, without performances or interviews to support it, the record failed to catch fire. With Boyd absent in America, Drake became ever more rudderless. Unable to bear his own company in the Hampstead flat, he moved back into his parents' home. 'Home was both a sanctuary and a prison,' says Gabrielle. 'Somewhere he couldn't escape from, and somewhere he needed to be.'

'It wasn't the old Nick,' says Ben Lacock, an old friend. 'It was a different Nick. I can't explain it; I've never been able to. I would ask him, why he was so down. Things seemed to be going well, his records were beautiful. And he wouldn't say, or couldn't say. And in the end it really became a struggle to talk to him.' On one occasion Drake opened up enough to tell Lacock that he thought he had 'a hell hound on my trail', quoting the song by the tormented blues singer Robert Johnson, who died at the age of 26. 'A little shiver ran down my back,' says Lacock.

At a loss how to cope with their son, Drake's parents telephoned Joe Boyd in America. 'They felt he needed help,' says Boyd. 'He sort of agreed, but felt it would be shameful; that people would think ill of him. A typical English point of view.' In the end Drake agreed to see a doctor, and he was prescribed the antidepressant Tryptizol. It was the drug that would eventually kill him.

Chris Blackwell, the head of Island Records, offered Drake the loan of his villa in Spain, to have time by himself. Drake spent a couple of weeks in the sun, and returned apparently refreshed. He contacted his recording engineer, John Wood, and told him he was ready to make another record. Recorded over just two evenings, *Pink Moon* is Drake's music at its starkest and most uncompromising: no other musicians; no arrangements, just Drake and his guitar. The album has an unsettling simplicity. He delivered the tapes to Island himself, arriving unannounced and simply leaving them on the reception desk. *Pink Moon* received good reviews, but its intimations of darkness left people feeling uncomfortable. It was hopelessly uncommercial, and it sold next to nothing.

Drake's depression deepened. He checked himself into a psychiatric hospital for five weeks, then checked out. Sometimes he didn't bother to take the medication he was on. He seemed to lose interest in music altogether. His father arranged a place on a computer-programming course, but Drake walked out after a day. Bizarrely, he even made inquiries at an Army recruitment centre.

It is always hard to measure the degree to which any artist creates solely for himself, or needs the affirmation of his audience. Late in 1973, Boyd returned to London on a visit and Drake turned up at his Notting Hill flat. 'He looked terrible. He was thin, his hair was very dirty. And he kind of lashed out. "I don't understand... people say I'm great and I've got nothing to show for it. I don't have any money. The records don't sell..." I was really taken aback, because I'd never heard any of this kind of line from him before.' His sister Gabrielle says, 'I think Nick both wanted to be left alone, and at the same time he desperately wanted to communicate and be recognised. But I have never known anyone do less about actually courting recognition.'

To appease Drake, and in the hope of reversing the tide, Boyd booked some studio time to record more songs. But Drake was in such a parlous state that he was unable to record his guitar and vocal parts at the same time. 'I can't think of words,' he told the engineer John Wood. 'I feel no emotion about anything. I don't want to laugh or cry. I'm numb – dead inside.'

He was able to complete just four songs, the last recordings he ever made. Among them was one song, 'Hanging On A Star', which seemed to sum up all the disenchantment which Drake felt about the music business, about his life:

'Why leave me hanging on a star/When you deem me so high...'

Late in 1973, an old friend, Alex Henderson, threw a party in London. Drake arrived, wrapped in an old overcoat. His friends, some of whom hadn't seen him for two years or more, were appalled at his state of deterioration.

'He came and stood just inside the door, against the wall, just holding on to himself, looking at his feet and saying nothing,' remembers Victoria Lloyd. 'It was agony. He just stood there for an hour, two hours. It's been such a haunting image of him ever since.'

Gabrielle had taken a lead role in a new TV series, *The Brothers*. She invited Nick to visit her at the BBC rehearsal studios and they sat in the canteen with some other members of the cast. 'He was this stony presence, not saying a word, and very quickly everybody else just left the table. It was a positive negative presence. It was almost impressive in a peculiar way.'

On another occasion, Gabrielle received a telephone call from the police. They had found Drake at a zebra crossing, where he had been standing for an hour, unable to cross.

His condition had so deteriorated that his parents felt unable to leave him on his own. He told his mother, 'I have failed in everything I have tried to do.'

But then, quite suddenly, his spirits lifted, and he began to smile again. His family could hardly believe it. He set off for Paris and rented a houseboat on the Seine. But after only a few weeks he was back. He told a friend that while in Paris, it had occurred to him that he could renew the contact with Francoise Hardy, perhaps write the songs he'd promised her. He went to the apartment on the Isle St Louis and rang the bell. But he didn't recognise the voice on the intercom. He didn't say who he was, just turned and walked away.

On November 5, 1974, Julian Ormsby-Gore, the son and heir of Lord Harlech, the elder brother of Victoria Lloyd, killed himself with a single gunshot to the brain. He was 35. The coroner was told that for the past 10 years Ormsby-Gore had been leading an increasingly reclusive life and receiving treatment for chronic depression. Though Drake had met Julian Ormsby-Gore only in passing, Julian's sister Victoria was among his closest friends. According to Gabrielle, he was intensely depressed by the death.

At home, Drake kept his own hours, so his mother Molly thought there was nothing unusual when, on the night of November 24, she heard her son pad past her bedroom door and downstairs to fix himself some cereal.

105

The next morning, she entered his room to find her son's body sprawled across his bed. He had swallowed some 30 Tryptizol tablets. On the turntable in his room was a recording of Bach's Brandenburg Concertos.

The coroner's verdict was suicide. But among Drake's friends there is the belief that it was an accident. 'The week before he died he was euphoric, full of energy and optimism,' says Boyd. 'But the sorts of doses he was taking, you rollercoaster – you're up, then you're down. And when you go down you think, I'd better take extra ...'

But for Gabrielle Drake, the belief that her brother had decided to take his own life has always been more consoling to her than the possibility that it was all a terrible mistake. 'I can just see him now pouring a whole lot into his hands and taking them at one swallow, and thinking, "What the hell, either I live or I die, but one way or the other something will change." But I somehow don't believe the pills would have killed him if he hadn't taken some kind of interior decision to die. I think the life force is so strong that unless somewhere deep inside you, you really want to commit suicide, I don't believe you succeed.'

Two years ago, Drake's old friend Ben Lacock and his wife Rosie stopped by an off-licence in Edinburgh. To his surprise, Lacock realised that they were playing one of Drake's songs, 'Time Has Told Me'.

'I said to Rosie, gosh, it's Nick! And the little girl behind the counter – she was only 19 or so – said, "Do you know his music?" I said, he was a friend of mine. And she said, "I'm privileged to have met you." I thought then, gosh, what would Nick have thought ...?'

Singing for Nick
Robin Frederick

In the winter of 1966–67, I was a 19-year-old American girl living in Aix-en-Provence, France. I was (and still am) a singer and songwriter. At that time I was singing folk songs and originals in a cabaret in Aix with a partner. Nick Drake came to see us at the Club De La Tartane, a venue that was part basement, part cave with a small stage at one end.

Nick and a friend introduced themselves after my set and asked if I'd like to get together to play some songs. So, one evening we met up in the room where Nick was living in Aix. We sang late into the night as friends dropped by to listen. Among the songs I played for him was one called 'Been Smokin' Too Long' which I had written. He played several blues songs in a fluid guitar style that seemed totally effortless. He also played a Dylan song with a very different rhythmic feel than the one I was used to; it sounded odd to me. I wasn't sure I liked it and it certainly wasn't the kind of let's-all-sing-along sort of thing that most people did. He was already different. I do remember his beautiful voice – intense, quiet, and honest. I fell in love with him that night but was too insecure to let it show.

Watching him that evening, I got the feeling Nick was absorbing everything around him – music, lyrics, sights, sounds, people – quietly taking it all in. I wasn't doing anything on guitar he didn't already know, I'm sure, but he still soaked it up in an instant. He asked me for the lyrics to 'Been Smoking Too Long' but never asked for the chords. Those he probably had five seconds after he heard the song, along with his own arrangement. I also saw the way he drew people to him. The room where we were playing was small and I remember being completely encircled by his friends who listened intently as he played and sang.

After that, he would sometimes come by my flat late in the evening and we would sing for each other. I don't recall him singing any original songs at all. He may have been writing then but he didn't share any with me. I was singing mostly my own songs so I think he would have shown off his if he'd had them. Maybe he was just starting to write and didn't feel confident yet. He was doing songs by Bob Dylan, Bert Jansch, Jackson C. Frank and other contemporary songwriters. I remember singing a song for him called 'Changes', written by Phil Ochs, that he liked a lot.

Certainly he was physically beautiful, younger than I was and a little awkward still, and that plus his natural quietness, made it easy to embroider a tapestry of fantasies around him. Baudelaire, Rimbaud, that whole 'poètes maudits' thing. This was the south of France, after all, and we were writers and singers roaming ancient streets where Cézanne painted and Rimbaud died. I was already quite good at imagining myself to be all kinds of people I wasn't. So it was a simple matter to envelop Nick in the dark halo of Baudelaire. I'm not sure how much he himself played this role. More than a little, as I recall.

He didn't seem to care about clothes or money or even his physical well-being. I remember Nick showing up at my door late on a cold winter night (which can be *very* cold in Aix). He was dressed the same way he is on the cover of the *Five Leaves Left* album: jeans, a black sport jacket, and white shirt open at the neck. I remember thinking how cold he must be and wondering whether he even owned a coat. I invited him in and gave him a glass of red wine to warm him up. I had a little gas fire; I remember the room was lit just by the fire. After that, he came by a few times, always late in the evening. He brought his guitar with him or he played mine. We played songs back and forth but didn't sing together. He often fooled around with the rhythm of the songs I knew, making it hard to sing them the usual way. I would just listen.

The real 'poètes maudits' were exquisite writers but they had miserable relationships! So I was expecting the worst. (That's my excuse, anyway.) One evening, Nick asked me to meet him at a cafe and then never showed up. I was furious. And hurt. I wrote a song that was one part anger and two parts victim. It was called 'Sandy Grey'. Then I left and went to Greece. Maybe I over-reacted just a bit.

That summer I hitchhiked to London with Bridget St John, and soon afterwards I met John Martyn. He recorded 'Sandy Grey' on his first album, *London Conversation*. I don't think John had met Nick yet, or if he had I wasn't aware of it. I never told John who the song was written for so I'm sure Nick never knew.

Nick did turn up in my life one more time after that. In 1992, someone gave me a copy of the *Time Of No Reply* album with 'Been Smoking Too Long' on it. I had completely forgotten the song but as I listened to Nick's voice I felt sure it was in some way connected to me. It wasn't until he got to a line where he had changed the words that I realised it was my own song. He sang 'Got no other life to choose', a line that was very much him, not me. As I listened to Nick singing my song that day, I was aware he had recorded it in 1967 and I was hearing it 25 years later. But somehow the years had turned into hours, or a short distance I could almost reach across. As if Time had twisted a little and become Space, and I was standing on a bridge between 'then' and 'now'. There must be some law of physics that covers this, maybe Einstein's lost Theory of Emotional Relativity.

When I listen to Nick's music, especially the *Pink Moon* album, I wish I could really cross that bridge, the one between then and now. I wish I could go back and sing for him one more time. I want to play him the songs I write now. Some I've written for him because that's how I deal with things I can't go back and change. And I want to thank him for writing 'From The Morning', and that really nice key change into the chorus of 'Things Behind The Sun', and all the other amazing ideas and innovations he left behind in his songs. And, although I know it wouldn't have made a difference in how things turned out, I want to tell him I loved him. Somehow, in some way, I know this can happen. Love is never really lost, and, if we let go, all things come back to us again someday, someday our ocean will find its shore.

(*Singing For Nick* was first published on Mikael Ledin's internet site, The Nick Drake Files (www.algonet.se/~iguana/DRAKE/) before appearing in *Pink Moon* in 1997, and was updated by Robin in 2010 for inclusion in this book. The February 1999 issue of *MOJO* magazine featured an article by Robin – called TRULY. MADLY. DEEPLY. – which was in part developed from *Singing For Nick*.)

Beyond Tunings and Techniques
Scott Appel, *Pink Moon 13*, 1998

There have been many articles written about the enigmatic life of Nick Drake, the best of which is included in a booklet contained in the reissue of the *Fruit Tree* box, a four-record set that chronicles an extraordinary life-work. That article, by Arthur Lubow, first published in *New Times* magazine, offers a searing explanation as to why Drake's musicianship should be so unique. Yet nothing has ever been printed regarding the technical aspect of his enormous abilities as a guitarist – I will attempt to shed some light on one of the most baffling, unconventional guitarists to emerge from his era.

Nick Drake didn't begin playing the guitar until his 16th year, but progressed so rapidly that he was signed to Island Records by Joe Boyd at the age of 20. His first influences were his contemporaries: Bert Jansch, John Renbourn and, most importantly, John Martyn. His first focus, like those mentioned, was traditional blues, but he quickly began to transcend the form and its limitations. Within two years of having first picked up a guitar, he was composing his own songs. His earliest compositions were simple, plaintive songs in standard tuning. He would soon dismiss them as amateurish, and utilised conventional tunings rarely from that point on.

He never had the benefit of any formal instruction, and perhaps that contributed to an approach that would not recognise restrictions. The demo tape that caught the interest of Boyd consisted of several of the songs that would appear on his first album, *Five Leaves Left*. Boyd was initially struck by Nick's sense of melody, as most listeners would be later upon hearing the material for the first time. One quickly recognises the guitar accompaniments as peculiar gems that could not be reproduced in standard tuning, though they didn't sound decidedly non-standard. My first impression was that he was working in something close to a dropped D. Indeed, some of the compositions lend themselves to dropped D adaptations, but one soon discovers that the voicings are not quite right; in addition, the left hand is working awfully hard to achieve some of the unusual fingerings required.

Part of the mystique is how Nick arrived at the tunings. That he was familiar with open-chord tunings is evident, given his influences, but they could not quite provide him with the alternatives he was hearing. The material on *Pink Moon* is easiest to discuss, and work through, being devoid of the string arrangements that mask his guitar figures on the first two LPs. 'Place To Be' is a good place to start. The basic changes are simply D E – F#m. Gradually, the tuning he employed became D A D G A F#, a D Major tuning with a suspended fourth. Actually all of the tunings he utilised were suspensions of some sort (stemming from D Modal), where he could use the odd voice as a passing tone or add it to a minor block creating a four or five voiced minor seven or nine. The tunings were certainly a matter of convenience, further freeing his left hand for some of the linear playing that would have been extremely difficult to execute in a conventional open-tuning. He capoed for this song on the second fret, and, as you will immediately notice, the interval between the second and first strings is a major sixth. Elsewhere, he would tune the first string up a full step-and-a-half, to a G, as on 'Fly' (D A D G D G capo 1). On 'Hanging On A Star' he would tune the sixth string down to a C, four ledger lines below the staff: C G C F C E.

The havoc he created on the neck of his small-bodied Guild M-20 (the only steel-string he recorded with) must have been profound, due to the varying extremes of tension it was subject to. He finger-picked with a combination of flesh and nail; strummed with nail alone, never using picks of any kind. This combination of circumstances, coupled with the small acoustic, would normally yield a sound notoriously thin. That his sound was as full and pervasive as if he had worked with a dreadnought instrument, is partially due to John Wood and his micing techniques. Wood had, by this time, arrived at a system of using four mics, in the truest sense of ambience, placing one completely across the room. He engineered all of Drake's sessions, and had a wealth of experience with Britain's finest acoustic guitarists, among them Richard Thompson, John Martyn and Robin Williamson. But Drake himself, by the time of the recording of *Pink Moon*, had also arrived as a master of tone and timbre, gradually adjusting to the limitations of the smaller instrument. This becomes increasingly evident in listening to the home-recorded demo versions of the later material, circa 1971–72.

His right-hand technique merits particular attention on two of his compositions, the first being 'Things Behind The Sun'. He actually double picks the bass note with his thumb on the B section while maintaining a major triad with his first three fingers on the treble strings. What he accomplishes on 'Road' (D G D G A D capo IV) is an especially fascinating subject of discussion, in which he completely reverses the function of thumb and fingers. This obviously assigns the odd rhythmic responsibilities to the thumb in such a way that it can never settle into a clearly defined pattern, as it has in virtually every other finger-picked piece in the folk genre. (Normally, the thumb is accustomed to serving as an anchor, playing 1-5, 1-octave, in a regularly repeating manner; aka alternating bass.) The magic, in these instances, is the subtlety of the result.

Drake worked tirelessly toward the precision he attained. When a piece evolved to performance level, he rarely varied the reading or strayed very far from a rendition he deemed particularly effective. Robert Kirby, who provided the arrangements for the first two albums, remembered that Nick always performed a given piece precisely the same way. While he only appeared in support of the records a handful of times, he was an uncomfortable, albeit charismatic performer that rarely acknowledged the audience. The insularity he portrayed, a shield such as it was, and his habit of losing himself in mid-song, repeating a figure over and over again, made his persona and music even more difficult and inaccessible.

Nothing could have been further from his attention. He wanted to be recognised as a new, important voice; he was quite aware of the fact that he was breaking ground with the tunings and material. He even explored odd meter, as in the case of 'River Man' (in standard tuning), in 5/4, an essentially lopsided time signature that often feels askew. That it almost feels like four is a testament to an even picking pattern that hardly betrays the extra beat, softened somewhat by the string ensemble. As with the tunings, you get a real sense of the necessity of alternative, rather than a composer forcing himself within the odd framework for its own sake.

One critic referred to Drake's compositions as '3 a.m. introversions' – a more accurate observation than he realised. Nick was an insomniac who rarely retired before dawn. He utilised the stillness as a creative outlet and worked on most of his music between midnight and morning. No one ever witnessed the creative process of a composition in progress – except perhaps a tape recorder he used to flesh-out ideas, he never showed a piece to anyone until it had been completed. It seems almost as if he were concerned that the reaction of another to an unfinished idea may in some way colour his perception of it or influence his perspective. He guarded his material with the purpose of retaining complete authenticity.

His lyric portrayals of isolation and lost grace are recognisable enough; his guitar accompaniments had really become the emotional equivalent. He was no longer listening to anybody else for inspiration or ideas; he was listening very intently to the music within. The music on *Pink Moon* (recorded in two nights, again, sessions beginning at midnight) is so staggeringly unified and of one piece, you get the overwhelming feeling that the music ate its way out of him. In a sense it did, as he would never completely recover from the demands the material made of him. Two of the four 'last session' tracks (recorded in 1974) are horrifying listening for their resigned despair – but now he sounds as hopeless and weary as the songs he's singing. 'Hanging On A Star' asks just two painful questions over and over; his guitar, playing just a simple figure, has externalised the inner storm remarkably. If, as a critic opined, he once sounded as if he were playing on the moon, he now sounded as if he were playing from the centre of the cyclone.

Nick kept notebooks full of lyrics and lyric fragments, but never felt the need to spell out the tunings he used. He had developed his own language that revolved around six basic tunings, five already mentioned. His favourite one, in which he interpreted 'Which Will', 'Parasite', both 'Hazey Jane's, 'From The Morning', 'Pink Moon' and 'Northern Sky' (capoed at various positions) was D A D G D F#. It was in this tuning you would invariably hear that trademark minor seven/minor nine voicing that he was so fond of using, or, more obscurely, the odd major seven inversion he referred to in 'Parasite'. As I've implied, the tunings are the key to Nick Drake as a musician. What makes them difficult to establish is, that, because they are all suspensions, fretting is involved in arriving at the tonic. That is, to convert his last tuning to a D Major chord, you must raise the third string a whole step by adding the second finger, second fret. In a simple major tuning, the tonic is stated at the beginning and/or end of the song as an open chord, and this is much easier to hear. Furthermore, the open IV and V chord shapes are somewhat standard, while the closed chords are achieved by simply barring the index finger across the fretboard. Arriving at the tunings that Nick used is 90% of the battle. Anyone with any open-chord experience will find it quite easy to determine the shapes after the tuning has been established. Naturally, a good ear is an asset.

Nick Drake died in his sleep in the early morning hours of November 25, 1974, at the age of 26. It is important to consider that some of the music we're discussing was recorded 18 years ago, and some of the innovations he established were clearly unprecedented in any genre. He opened a door and shattered the boundaries for numerous acoustic guitarists to follow; for me, he is simply the most important and influential guitarist I've ever come across. His records sell better now than they ever have. A friend once remarked that the reason he kept coming back to the music of Nick Drake, over and over again, was that he believed it to be 'timeless.' A frequently hackneyed cliché, so often used inappropriately, it is, for once, thoroughly applicable. Perhaps his time has finally come.

Meeting & Listening To Nick
Iain Cameron, *Pink Moon 17*, September 1998

With all the current interest in Nick's work I have been looking back wondering about the paths that led me to meet and play with him. This article tells the story from my point of view. It's a bit of a tangled path but some of the nooks and crannies may be of interest to *PM* readers.

In my teens, in the mid-sixties, I became interested in the emerging blues-based acoustic folk guitar players and songwriters. I was stimulated by seeing John Renbourn in concert at the teachers' training college opposite my school in Isleworth, West London, when I was about 16. I wanted to find out more about this marvellous music. Les Cousins in Greek St, Soho, emerged as the best place to pick up on what was going on – also the club in the Horseshoe Hotel, Tottenham Court Road, which Pentangle started up, as I remember, in 1967.

I left school that year and I had just over a year to spend before going up to Cambridge to read philosophy, or Moral Sciences as philosophy was called then. I decided to use this 'year out' to explore the musical scene as far as possible within the constraints of trying to do a white-collar job in a factory on the Great West Road at the same time.

I was lucky enough to meet Linda Peters through her brother Brian that summer. We did a few floor spots in West London clubs which helped build up my confidence as a guitarist. But my main instrument was the flute which I wanted to use on the kind of interesting new songs that I was becoming aware of by listening to albums like Judy Collins' *In My Life*.

In September 1967, just as most of my friends were going to university, I took a number of related steps – I signed up at Chiswick Polytechnic for evening classes in jazz improvisation and arranging and I answered an ad in the musicians wanted column of *Melody Maker*. The band behind the ad was Tintagel, a student outfit based at Goldsmiths College in South East London (the college where John Cale studied music a few years earlier). Tintagel took two of us on board as a result of the ad – myself and Ian MacDonald who had just left the Army. Ian went on to be a founder member of King Crimson and Foreigner. Ian and I both lived in West London and Ian had a minivan which suited me rather well, saving me a two hour journey on the Greenline bus to get to rehearsals.

Tintagel specialised in playing versions of songs by West Coast bands – particularly Love (*Da Capo* era), The Byrds and The Doors plus one or two Donovan tunes. One of the members had a Danelectro electric 12-string and also played sitar amplified through a bug. So with the flute, the band was able to make quite a convincing 'flower power' sound which meant it was regularly booked into the Middle Earth in Covent Garden.

Indeed, exactly one week after auditioning with the band I found myself playing at the Middle Earth – on the same bill as an early version of Fairport Convention with Judy Dyble as lead singer. Richard Thompson's long guitar solo that night on 'Reno' made a big impression on me. It must have been the first time I heard a first-class guitarist let rip with a Les Paul in a style which combined the blues and West Coast music.

Ian soon left Tintagel, teaming up for a while with Judy Dyble after Sandy Denny took over in Fairport. Tintagel kept getting bookings at Middle Earth and so another ad went into *Melody Maker* and a guitarist called Geoff joined – a trainee quantity surveyor from Brighton with lots of equipment.

Tintagel's big chance came when the sitarist met Dorris Henderson – an American folk singer on the UK scene who had worked with John Renbourn. Dorris was on the bill for a folk concert at the Albert Hall together with Watersons, Al Stewart and Roy Harper in spring 1968. I think she was looking for something to make her stand out and

115

a six-piece acid-rock band seemed to fit the bill. I really enjoyed the Albert Hall and the review of our set in the *Financial Times* (which of course I have locked away) was quite favourable. I can remember our set included the Jackson Frank song 'Milk And Honey', which is also on Nick's Tanworth tape. With Dorris and Tintagel I also got to play at Les Cousins and the Horseshoe.

So by the time I got to Cambridge, I took myself rather seriously as a musician and spent the first term trying to find fellow-spirits. This wasn't easy at first, although on the same side of the quad of my college as my room there lived a rather mysterious medical student called Brian Wells who I eventually got to know through a certain third party. Then towards the end of the first term it all happened at once. A saxophonist and flute player from Islington, Steve Pheasant, suggested that he and I form a modal/free jazz quartet which we christened Horn. I also joined an acid-rock band called White Unicorn which was based partly in Cambridge and partly in Wimbledon led by John Cole. (I was recently surprised to discover that approximately 10 years later it was John who found Sandy Denny immediately after her tragic fall.)

The key event, though, took place at the Cambridge Union that winter. I can't remember who else was on the bill for that concert but the first or second spot was taken by a student called Paul Wheeler who played acoustic guitar and played his own songs. It was immediately obvious to me that he came from the 'right' background musically – I soon discovered that he had been hanging out with John Martyn before he came up to Cambridge. (It was curious how Paul, Nick and Robin Frederick linked up at this time.) Anyway, I just loved Paul's music and so (very uncharacteristically) I went up to him in the interval in the Union bar and told him exactly what I thought of his set.

Paul suggested that I come round to his rooms for a blow. This went well and we soon became firm friends. I got to know his repertoire and I just loved working with his tunes. They were linked to what I'd been playing and listening to before but were original and very evocative of certain moods. We played here and there, including a club in Amsterdam – we even got to blow at Cousins one night when John was on.

Two or three months later, one fine spring afternoon, I went round to Paul's. This time there were rather more people hanging out than

usual. Paul and I played a bit and then this rather quiet and very striking-looking young man played some of his songs. One of these was 'River Man' – which completely took my breath away. Readers might like to imagine what kind of impact this might have made, and all I can say is that you may well be right – it was extraordinary – the beauty, the invention, the meaning coming in and out of focus, the technical accomplishment, the timbres and sonorities. It was as if I had finally found something which up until that point I had only come across in various hints and suggestions – for me, like hearing Judy Collins sing 'Suzanne' for the first time, or hearing Jeff Buckley or Television out of the blue.

I can't remember all the tunes Nick played but when I got hold of *Time Of No Reply* – about seven years ago – and played it through for the first time I felt that I was hearing Nick do a lot of the material again – not the same experience as hearing the Tanworth-in-Arden tape first time a few months ago. The Tanworth material is interesting to me because it indicates how far there was some sort of common musical agenda around amongst that generation of musicians, but it is not the stuff that Nick was playing when I first met him.

One point I want to stress is that in those circumstances, although Nick was cool and somewhat aloof, he had no trouble in projecting himself and his work musically to the eight or 10 people in the room. Those readers who have tried it will know that playing your own material to a small group of friends and family is not the easiest of audiences to work with – you are acutely aware of their reactions and it involves a lot of personal exposure. Speaking for myself, I would much rather play the Albert Hall. But Nick genuinely wasn't bothered – he just did his stuff. His music fitted in with other aspects of his presence – how he looked, how he spoke, his own charisma – and in my imagination at least this literally filled the room.

I don't know whether any readers have heard the Davy Graham CD which has just been released which was made in a student's bedroom in 1967 or 68 – I can certainly recommend it. That recording, in my memory at least, has a similar ambience to that afternoon – warm and appreciative. The music is similar but by no means identical, but it is the 'vibe' that I am talking about.

Another important point is that Nick was very easy to get along with musically. I felt I could establish a rapport with him, fit in with what he was doing. He did give you something back when you played along with his music in those circumstances. The fact that it was Paul's place may have helped – Paul and Nick had a great deal in common in all sorts of ways – they were both English scholars with a similar way of looking at many issues.

The next episode that sticks out in my memory is the Caius May Ball. I had quite a good time that night – John Mayall topped the bill and Horn, White Unicorn, Paul and Nick were all booked for the event. Robert Kirby organised a set of Nick's songs with accompanying musicians, including Steve Pheasant and myself. I am pretty sure that 'Mary Jane' was one of the songs that we played. I also played on 'Mayfair' as a duo and I remember the girl I took with me to the Ball saying that she hadn't enjoyed me playing on that one! I have checked this recollection with her just this year and all she can now remember is that there was a big argument between the musicians and the Ball organisers about what food we were going to get – whether it would be the same as those who had paid for their tickets. Such is life.

After that Nick left Cambridge – at the end of his second year, the end of my first. That summer, I was debating whether to follow his example. Graham Bond, a musician both Nick and I had liked in the mid-Sixties, was reforming a band, based in Cambridge, which I auditioned for. We seemed to get on quite well but in the end I decided not to chance it and went off to the Edinburgh Festival for a gargantuan Steve Pheasant extravaganza called Stoney Ground (which also involved Paul and a neighbour of mine, Derek Ridgers, who has become a highly regarded rock photographer). Then we all pitched back into another academic year and a different set of musical projects.

I have to go back in time about six months now to explain the next step. At about the same time that I met Nick, White Unicorn played Wimbledon Town Hall on the same bill as Fairport Convention – they played first and we finished off the evening. We went down rather well with a local crowd and on the strength of this Fairport recommended us to Polydor. This led to some exploratory recording sessions. I had rather enjoyed the experience and I wrote to Geoff, the guitarist from

Tintagel, telling him what it was like to go into the studio – how much easier it was overdubbing the flute part than playing with a live rock band. These were the days before PAs came with monitors and fold-back.

In his reply, he invited me to come and meet the vocal harmony group he was working with called Design who were based in Kensington. It was at Design's flat that I first met Alec Reid, a radio producer at the BBC, who was taking an interest in this group.

In the autumn of 1969 Alec started booking me for sessions with various folk artists for the late night show he produced for Radio 2. It meant catching an early train from Cambridge, turning up at Broadcasting House in the morning and recording eight songs in a day, working with the artist and a session drummer and bass player – a busker's paradise which suited me quite well. I remember the bass player – a Welshman – who Alec often used, also played with the Dudley Moore trio. This was all quite good fun, got me through a BBC audition, supplemented my grant and did something for my credibility on the student music scene.

I got on well with Alec who has a very wide ranging and discerning taste in music and the arts, and at that time was writing poetry. I recommended *Five Leaves Left* to Alec because I thought Nick's combinations of talents should appeal to him. I was delighted when Alec booked Nick for *Nightride* and asked me to play on the session – no bass player or drummer.

To prepare for the session, I went to Nick's flat near Belsize Park tube station. (One little personal irony is that this flat is close to where I was married in November 1973.) In many ways this collaboration with Nick was quite a sharp contrast to playing with him in Cambridge. This was at the time when Nick was working on *Bryter Layter*. When I heard this album I was surprised at the extent to which the music was unlike the material which I remembered working on in his flat or indeed the material we'd done in Cambridge. I have yet to locate a tape of the radio session and so at this point I am relying purely on my memory.

My recollection is that Nick was working with a set of musical ideas then current amongst people who wanted to push out the boundaries of songwriting. A good example would be the McCartney song 'Martha

My Dear', from the 'White Album'. This may sound like another domestic Macca tune but in fact it is very artfully put together with bars of different lengths thrown in mainly to follow the logic of the tune rather than a standard eight-bar pattern. A similar thing happens in Bulgarian folk music and in the Grateful Dead's acoustic music which was emerging around then. My recollection is that Nick was doing this, which made his newer material much more demanding to accompany. Having created these intricate patterns, Nick rightly wanted them followed precisely.

The music on *Bryter Layter* is intricate in its way, but I have to say armed with the preconceptions from working with him, I was disappointed with the second album and it has taken me over 25 years to get round to buying it. Possibly it is an album which works better as a CD than on vinyl – in my view the opposite is true of *Five Leaves Left*.

I didn't see Nick after I left Cambridge. Indeed I only met up with Paul again in 1975. In November 1974 I was in Edinburgh and I think somehow the news of Nick's death filtered through as a shock but not a surprise. I came across *Pink Moon* in a record shop shortly afterwards in Islington. I bought it without even bothering to hear it. It was clear enough from the cover what it would be about, and the songs and the treatments were immediately accessible.

In 1975, I met Paul again. I was separated from my wife, and Paul had a raft of wonderful new songs which we have been working on here and there over the years. One in particular starts:

> *Waking up to confusion, it's so hard to face the day*
> *But you couldn't stop it coming, there must be fusion on the way*

When you read the story of Nick's last three years, there is a temptation to think, 'Oh, if only I'd been in touch, I am sure I could have made a difference.' Knowing some of the people who were closer and their assessment of how things were, I conclude this is an understandable misapprehension, but a misapprehension nonetheless.

Books

There has been a surprising amount written about Nick Drake over the years, and as time passes, more appears. The first book, that I'm aware of, called *Pink Moon*, by Danish writer Gorm Henrik Rasmussen, was published in 1986, by Hovedland. It was a biography of around a hundred pages, featured quotes from Nick's parents, a few photos, and lyrics to all of Nick's songs, released and unreleased. I corresponded with Gorm in the Nineties and he gave me permission to reproduce any part of his book for the fanzine, but the costs of having it translated into English prevented this.

Patrick Humphries wrote the first full length biography *Nick Drake: The Biography* (Bloomsbury, ISBN 978-0-7475-3503-4), which is still in print after 13 years, and has just been republished with a new cover. A review of the book, its launch, and an interview with Patrick Humphries, from *Pink Moon*, can be found below.

The second full length biography, *Darker Than The Deepest Sea: The Search For Nick Drake*, by Trevor Dann, was published by Portrait in 2006. This came out after the fanzine, so I've reproduced a review from *The Independent* below.

The most recent book about Nick is Peter Hogan's *Nick Drake: The Complete Guide To His Music* (Omnibus Press, 2009). Not a biography this one, but a nicely written guide, offering 'a thorough analysis of every officially released album by Drake, from the early albums that were overlooked at the time of their release, to posthumous collections.'

Also of interest is Joe Boyd's memoir, *White Bicycles: Making Music in the 1960s* (Serpent's Tail, 2007). Reviewing the book in 2007, Sylvia Majka wrote: "*White Bicycles*, by Joe Boyd, is a 'pick up and don't put down all weekend' type book. Boyd has great storytelling style, here telling us about his career and where it took him with various recording artists, his escapades and participation in London in the Sixties, and his professional development as a producer. I got the book primarily because I am a Nick Drake fan. The two existing Nick biographies, while diligently researched, and containing info based on many interviews, still have that degree of detachment that necessarily exists when the authors have never personally met their subject. I certainly wasn't disappointed, as Boyd's few chapters on Nick brought this departed artist to life for me more than the two existing bios. He conveys his interactions with the shy artist, and writes about him in a way that lets us see the person as well as the artist. Yes, it is very funny to read as Boyd describes how Nick answered his telephone (as if it had never rung before) and his first meeting with him after the intro by Ashley Hutchings of Fairport Convention, then moving on to the production of *Five Leaves* and *Bryter Layter*, and Nick's decision to take a new direction with *Pink Moon*, which Boyd did not produce ..."

Luca Ferrari's pocket-sized Italian/English book, *The Sweet Suggestions of the Pink Moon* (1999, ISBN: 88-7226-424-X), begins with an introduction by Lyn Dobson, written in 1999:

"The name of Nick Drake meant nothing to me when I arrived at the studio in King's Road, Chelsea, in 1969. But the quiet young singer whose album I was to play on, made me feel at ease immediately. He seemed shy and slightly withdrawn, unlike many of the extroverted performers I had previously recorded with.

"However, when he started to play and sing, there was a powerful emotional change in his songs which I responded to spontaneously.

"There was harmony between us and he was very happy with what I played on the song (the instrumental 'Bryter Layter'), without finding it necessary to give me any guidance. I found him to be a genuinely kind and compassionate person, able to communicate better in songs than in other social interaction. In retrospect, I treasure those few days I spent recording with him."

Sweet Suggestions... is an essay, commentating on what has been written about Nick since his death, in the music press, *The Biography*, *Pink Moon*, etc; and there is some discussion of musical influences and analysis of songs and lyrics.

This was Ferrari's second book about Nick. The first was called *Un'Anima Senza Impronte* (*A Soul With No Footprint*), written in Italian and published in 1987. More details at: www.lucaferrari.net

'Molto sexy' is how Nick is described on the cover of a biography, by Stefano Pistolini, titled *Le provenienze dell'amore*, which was released in Italy in 1998. It has over 200 pages, all in Italian, so I can't tell you anything about its contents. It's very nicely produced though, with a thick, glossy cover featuring the Julian Lloyd photo of Nick wrapped in a colourful blanket, although in the book the photo is credited to Keith Morris. The book is published by Fazi Editore.

The Nick Drake Estate will release the first official Nick Drake book in 2011. Described by the manager of Nick's estate, Cally, as a 'Companion Volume', it will include a collection of writings on Nick, new and old, previously unseen photographs, entries from Nick's notebooks and diaries, letters, and all of the lyrics, including unreleased songs. The book will be published by HarperCollins.

For more information go to www.brytermusic.com, the official website of the Estate of Nick Drake.

Frozenlight (Floating World, ISBN: 978-0-9565023-0-8) by Colin Betts is part one of the *Riversong Quartet*, four books covering the counterculture from 1962 onwards, and is essentially an autobiography of Colin's teenage years written in the style of a Beat novel. The book includes two chapters which describe Colin's meeting with Nick Drake and the time they spent together in Aix-en-Provence.

Joe Boyd has described the book as 'a vivid account of the Sixties underground; a compelling tale of life among the people who really made the era what it was – those who bought the great records, took the great dope and lived the life everyone was singing and writing about. I enjoyed it immensely.'

Robin Frederick, who was in Aix at the same time as Colin and Nick, wrote the following review of the book for www.nickdrake.com in 2007: "In January of this year, I received a letter from a man named Colin Betts. The name seemed familiar but I couldn't place it, and with good reason: it had been 40 years since I last saw him in Aix-en-Provence, France. He was a busker then, playing guitar and singing for whatever francs people threw his way. Though the same age as the rest of us, he seemed more experienced and worldly; he had already lived a troubled lifetime or two by the time he plunked down his guitar case on the cobbled streets of Aix.

"Colin's relentless drive to emulate his beat-era heroes — Kerouac, Cassady, and Ginsberg — had taken him to Morocco. On the ferry, heading back toward France, he met Nick Drake. After exchanging a couple of guitar tunings, Nick invited him back to Aix where Colin remained for five or six weeks at the Residence Sextius. Colin had already begun his lifelong habit of journal-keeping; he wrote a daily account of his experiences and the people he met, including conversations, names and dates. He recalls Nick much as I remember him and, thanks to his journals, brings him to life with the kind of detail you might find in the photos and film we wish we had of Nick from this period of his life. (And he's very kind to me on a couple of pages so I can't complain.)

"Colin's recollections of Nick are in two chapters of this book and the rest is well worth reading! The book is a remarkable, moving, entertaining, very well-written memoir of the Sixties stretching from the earliest days of The Rolling Stones (Colin roadied a couple of gigs) through the innocence and optimism of 1967 in France, London and California on into the dissolving of many of our most-beloved illusions in the student riots of Paris/May 1968. Along the way, friends died, lovers were lost, dreams dreamed and destroyed. If you want to know what the Sixties were like, you can live it here.

"This is a memoir; the dates and facts I'm aware of, or I was able to check, are all accurate. His memories of Nick strike me as true to the person I knew. With permission Colin used actual names; when he couldn't find the person to ask permission, he changed the name.

This is his first attempt at publishing a book based on his journals; he is a very good writer and I would like to see him continue. I hope you enjoy the book as much as I did!"

Part two of the quartet, *Burninglight*, is now complete. Once part three, *Shininglight*, is ready, all three books will be published together. Colin is also currently working on another book (or possibly screen play) about his time with Nick in the spring of 1967.

After spending 16 years of his life (1963–79) on the road, Colin, in his own words, 'spent five years acquiring degrees and diplomas to teach English in the war zones and refugee camps and universities of Asia, before retiring at 49, in 1997, to live in a cabin by the river's source in the deep woods of Scotland, rescuing dogs, feeding birds, writing books and music (and letters) for fun, without mains services or a decent phone signal, several miles from the nearest road, neighbour or phonebox, in one of the coldest, wettest places in Europe. Nick would have understood, he trusted nature to give it to you straight: life, love, death, all that stuff…'

I am very grateful to Colin for allowing me to reproduce the following chapter from his book *Frozenlight*, part one of the *Riversong Quartet*.

Chapter 11: Get Together
Colin Betts

It's not enough to be at the right place at the right time, you need to be the right age too. And to be eighteen in 1967 is perfect. If you realise that it can't last and will never come again, that's the spirit of '67 and you'll never forget it. But every moment must count: right here, right now. Trouble is, you need money to live and breathe, even at Moroccan prices. And right now you're broke in Tangier, the tourist season is starting and you need to get to Paris or somewhere fast. The busking season starts there in April. The American tourists love to hear some credible R&B, while the French are grateful for anything.

The only option is to hitchhike for three or four days through Spain again, then two more through France, and you've only got two pounds in francs left. So when you see a happy band of hippies in a battered car with GB plates you have to be interested. They board the ferry to

Algeciras too and head for the sundeck. The tall skinny one has a guitar and you gravitate towards them. There must be two hundred hippies on the boat, having a high old time, trailing a cloud of smoke in their wake. Everyone knows the Spanish fascists bust smugglers for six years and a day, so they're getting rid of their stashes. While the rock of Gibraltar glides by.

It's a brilliant, sparkling Mediterranean morning, cobalt blue and golden bright. The hippies are grooving away around little cassette players (the Americans) and guitars (mostly Brits). The latest vibe is Acid Rock from California, so the yanks are playing Big Brother, the Grateful Dead, Jefferson Airplane. Some English Beats are playing 'Cocaine' and Nick Drake's playing an arabesque instrumental in a tuning that leaves his long, hammerhead fingers free to improvise on the open chords, magic fingers that make you glad you didn't start playing first.

Nick's style has the clean, technical dexterity of the bearded folkie brigade, who can all play 'Angie' faultlessly. There are also bluegrass, clawhammer, jazz and classical elements, and a drone effect on the bass strings he can only have discovered in Morocco, where every radio blares out the music of Oum Khalsoum and other Egyptian divas all day long.

You found a vaguely Arabic tuning yourself, over a month in Tangier, and proudly unleash it. Should have known better. Nick promptly retunes two strings and it's twice as good. You sadly decline to sing a couple of songs for the moment and roll a joint instead, talk about music, trade credentials. He's a Gemini too: 10 days younger. Gets every allusion and laughs at your cynical jokes.

Nick says he'll be busking in Aix-en-Provence and it sounds like a cool place: thousands of students from all over Europe and the USA pretending to study French. He asks where *you're* going and you say: 'France.' A moment later he offers you a lift all the way up through Spain, non-stop, about six hundred miles. You'll write a song about it.

Can relax now, enjoy the trip, that's the biggest problem solved, just have to negotiate Spanish customs. But the English Boys on Tour breeze right through, like you just steamed past the Rock: full speed ahead and keep on trucking. Too many kids forget where they put their stash, or try to smuggle a lump of hash, and will spend the rest of the decade rotting in one of General Franco's jails.

You're crushed in the back of the Cortina, Julian and Richard to the right, buried under luggage and guitars. Nick and the other driver are up front and your job is to keep them awake while they're driving. You talk about the Stones first, not failing to mention your slight connection. But Nick met them down in Marrakech and actually played for them. The Stones were originally a beatnik group and although it's good to know the hippies like them too, it makes you feel old.

Nick wants to know your busking set list: 'Walkin' The Dog', 'House Of The Rising Sun', 'Get Together', 'San Francisco Bay Blues', 'Not Fade Away'. He nods. There is a mention of Leadbelly and Woody Guthrie, then a debate about Acid Rock versus pure acoustic folk. You maintain that the punters in 1967 want four or five chords and a chorus they can learn to play at home. Every skinny white boy's got a guitar these days, must have been a dozen of them on the boat. You're worried that in a year or so there'll be buskers everywhere and say so: 'You'll have to queue up to get a good pitch.'

'That's good,' says Nick. 'Music on every corner and lots of competition.'

You're not so sure. Apart from knowing only about 10 chords, you wouldn't want to try so hard. The songs you like best are simple. Most people are like that about music. They can't sing a note or even bang a tambourine in time, but they know what they like. And what they like at the moment is the next step up from twelve-bar blues: tuneful, folkie R&B, with a hook-line, guitar solo and a chorus. The Mamas and Papas are having the same idea, The Byrds and Spoonful.

'So if you want to make a living out of rock and pop,' you conclude, 'get a group together with acoustic guitars, vocal harmonies, a pretty girl, and Bob's your uncle. You can sing, right?' Nick nods that he can, comes in with 'Goodnight Irene' in D, and you supply a higher harmony. Then you switch over for a verse (he must have seen the Leadbelly songbook) and both forget the rest of the words at the same time. Then Nick says:

'Did you bring anything back?' And you say:

'Just a bit in my mouth, in case I had to swallow it. You?'

'Just a bit, but I'm driving, so we may as well smoke yours.'

His hunched shoulders quiver with mirth around the wheel. Every

127

part of everyone is scrunched and cramped in the tiny Cortina, but that's okay when you're young and spreading your wings of freedom ... is how it feels after a nice joint of zero-zero. And from where you're sitting Nick really does look like a watchful bony eagle in the Spanish sun, cruising at 50 mph, left hand on the wheel, right hand trailing smoke out of the open window. So the joint's burning too fast and if a bit drops off he might burn a hole in his jeans and crash the car.

'Don't let it go out,' you say.

Once you get over being jealous of Nick's guitar-picking, he's quite a cool guy. By early 1967 the hippie revolution might not have evolved a comprehensive philosophy as such, but everyone you met in Morocco smiled all the time and was ready for anything. There are unspoken rules that really matter: you don't play games, go on ego trips, rip people off or put them in danger. That's selfish. Otherwise you can pretty much do as you like, as long as no one gets hurt. Basically, if you can't do good, at least don't leave the planet worse than you found it. But above all never lose your cool. You've found some rules you can live by. Being a hippie is alright.

While Nick has a doze, you talk to Richard about his plans and hopes for the future. It seems they're all bound for university after the summer. Already the spring has been so good everyone is talking about the Movement by now. That'll be the American influence, and they're all over Europe with their Acid Rock music, five dollars a day and funny little joints with only one paper. They really believe we can stop the war and change the world for the better – that this will happen because it's right. The very idea is militant, liberating. Why settle for anything less? If everyone turns on and tunes in we'll all be fine, the earth can be protected and Mick and Keith won't have to go to jail. How could you not support a proposition like that? Say what you like about Americans, they think big.

There's a stop for a stretch and a breath of air. No food, just water in bottles and canteens, plenty of fags. Then the new banger groans as you all pile back in and knock up some more miles. Time doesn't matter: it was light, now it's dark. Bob Dylan's on the agenda, another Gemini – indeed Grand Master of the House of Gemini. Nick's caught every LP from the start. You don't mention you've had Fixin to Die tattooed on your arm since Approved School, and sing 'Blowing In The Wind' instead. It's a song borrowed permanently from his Bobness, on which you owe him busking royalties. Nick too, has obviously loved it since first setting eyes on Mary out of Peter, Paul and. You share every cultural reference since 1948, know all the Beatles and Dylan songs by heart, really dig Phil Spector. You do 'Be My Baby' way down low with vibrato.

'Three chords and a chorus!' you gloat.

'No four,' says Nick, and you both giggle like schoolboys who've pulled a stroke. The other guys are asleep, passively smoking, while two Geminis try to keep each other awake. Nick says it's easy to score in Aix, prompting you to roll another one. He asks where *exactly* you are going.

'Paris.' It's almost a question though. You're also ready for anything.

'You could come to Aix. There's always a place to sleep at Sextius.'

'Huh?' Sex what?

'Residence Sextius, it's a hall of residence without the supervision. And you can eat free at the university, everybody does. What do you think, Jules?'

But Jules had crashed out. So you say:

'Sounds great. "Follow your karma", this American Beat in Tangier used to say. Thanks a lot.'

Conversion is complete: from loner-tramp to flower-power evangelist. Just have to be nicer to everybody, try to love them. And it really does sound like the right place to busk for a while, with warm weather and thousands of wealthy students. Every student loves a singalong in English. If they also smoke you won't have to play crap tunes.

Could be the Pyrenees out there, judging by the rugged star-lit horizon. One of the headlights is wonky but the motor's running fine. Nick says it's 'rally-tuned', and you're a little surprised to learn that he takes Donovan seriously. Here's a hippie who gets by on two and a half chords and a chorus. To prove a point you do 'Don't Think Twice' and just know Nick plays it inside out, 'Wildwood Flower' all that stuff. It's been the standard Beat repertoire for several years now. Hippies haven't sprung from nowhere, perfectly-formed. They had to be Beats first;

dig Miles, Coltrane and Mingus; Woody Guthrie, Robert Johnson. It's essential. But:

'Acid Rock is all you need,' you blurt out. Dope's getting low and you held it down too long. 'I bet you a joint in Aix that your favourite track this year is Jorma's guitar-instrumental on the Jefferson Airplane LP. Pure Acid Rock.'

Got it in one, and you can tell he's thinking about it. You also know if you had ten percent of his talent and Nick had ten percent of your brass neck you would both be stars, the new Peter and Gordon, only better looking, with far better tunes.

'Why don't *you* get a group together, then?' says Nick.

'Because it would mean staying in one place, getting a pad, money for dope and food. And then organising people. Besides, I'd have to practise for years to be any good at the guitar or song-writing.'

Nick agrees that this is so.

'You've thought about it though,' he says.

Not really, and certainly not for a while. I'm trying to get to California, that's where it's at. I want to drop acid and peyote in Big Sur and Yosemite, see San Francisco before it's too late. How about you?'

'Oh I suspect I'm doomed to Cambridge.'

'How do you mean, doomed?'

'Well it's all organised from the moment you're born, whether it's suitable for you or not.'

'So drop out! If you change your mind you can always go back.'

'If only it were that simple.'

'If we can't afford to put off our lives for a year or two we're really in trouble.'

'Yes well, we'll see,' says Nick.

'I just don't think there'll be a better time than this. And if we don't do something, nobody will. It's all up to us. It's scary.'

Now suddenly you're an expert on revolution already, but all you hope is that these kids will remember the spirit of '67, that even if they become lawyers and politicians they'll still give hippies lifts. And this Aix place sounds better than Paris, where you'd have to sleep rough and sing Catch the bloody Wind on the Boulevard Montparnasse. In Aix there'll be lots of stoned bright hippies who know the words of 'We

Shall Overcome'. You might meet an heiress from Santa Barbara or
Nob Hill, maybe do a bit of busking with Nick. Those pretty little rich
girls will just love two good-looking, six-foot-three-inch guitar-pickers
who can really hold a tune.

The Biography, book launch and review
Jason Creed, *Pink Moon 13*, 1998

Patrick Humphries' long-awaited *Nick Drake, The Biography* is available
now. Reading the book it suddenly dawned on me what an enormous
responsibility it is to write someone's biography; to paint a picture of
someone which will be viewed by and remain with countless people —
but this is a picture well painted.

The only real shame for me is that a few key people — John Wood,
Joe Boyd, Gabrielle Drake and John Martyn — declined to be involved,
as I imagine a whole book could be written on their memories alone.

The biggest success of the book, I think, is the way Nick's earlier
years are documented. As Patrick wrote, he wanted to 'discover something about Nick's life and not just dwell on the last few years leading
up to his death'. So, with the help of Nick's old friends and acquaintances, vivid, colourful accounts of his early days are presented — especially those spent at Marlborough and Aix — bringing a whole new Nick
Drake to life.

Of course, a biography that focused solely on the movements of Nick
Drake would be a very slim volume, so here we have not only a detailed
and fascinating portrait of Nick, but also of the life and times that surrounded him and shaped his life; opening a welcome doorway into the
past.

The book is, perhaps surprisingly, frequently joyful — though, of
course, at times, painfully sad — and always revealing and engrossing.
As Patrick points out, more than once, misconceptions, mostly in the
form of what has been written about him since his death, have taken
Nick over; but now it's time to discard the myths and move on. Indeed,
Patrick felt he had a mission 'to give this young man his life back', but
whether that is possible, when, after all these years, and despite Patrick's

exhaustive research, parts of Nick's life are still shrouded in mystery, remains to be seen.

There are no real answers here, regarding the cause of Nick's illness, but, as such illnesses (despite Nick's seemingly normal and happy childhood) are usually linked like a long chain from past to present, from birth to death, and can't even be defined by the sufferer, there probably never will be.

What we do get though is a better understanding of what made Nick Drake, how he lived, and who he was.

On November 27, 1997, I was at Helter Skelter bookshop in Denmark Street, London, for the launch of *The Biography*, where Patrick Humphries gave a talk and answered some questions about the book.

When I arrived, I was surprised to find the shop packed to the doors with people, all sipping their complimentary drinks and talking enthusiastically about *The Biography* and, of course, its subject, Nick Drake. I later discovered that among the crowd were Robert Kirby, Richard Charkin, Iain Cameron and Keith Morris. David Sandison was there too, and we went outside for a cigarette and a chat. 'How's *Pink Moon* going?' he asked. 'I'm just putting the final issue together,' I replied. David laughed. 'You say that every issue,' he said.

Next we made our way to the downstairs bar, where by now even more people had gathered, and Patrick was there, seated on a small stage, surrounded by microphones. The following is an edited version of Patrick's talk, which was also aired on Radio 2's *Reading Music* programme, December 13, 1997.

Patrick Humphries: Writing is a very solitary business, so it's genuinely pleasing for me to see so many of you here tonight, who feel the same way as I do about Nick Drake. So much written about Nick over the years has been either misleading or inaccurate, serving only to fuel the many myths which surround his short life. In my book, I suppose I've attempted to debunk the myth. Along the way, as the myth began to peel away, like the layers of an onion, underneath a somewhat surprising real life began to emerge. For example, the best

known photos of Nick show him alone, a solitary figure; and that loneliness only enhances the myth of the outsider. So it was quite a shock
when I first saw pictures of Nick as a chubby, smiling schoolboy, in
the Marlborough House rugby 15. The mythmakers insist that Nick
came out of the womb dressed in black, that he never smiled, and he
only ever listened to records by Leonard Cohen. Now, when I put a
request in the magazine of Nick's old school, I had dozens of letters
and phone calls and requests from people who were at school with
Nick, at Marlborough, who wanted to communicate their memories
of the Nick they knew. So I did over 50 interviews for the book,
and exhaustive research; and over a two-year period all sorts of different impressions of Nick came to life, jarringly at odds with what had
already been written about him.

So, as a writer, it was terribly challenging. But, of course, the image
of Nick that you're left with is this one, frozen in aspic, of the beautiful
lost boy; of Peter Pan. So, people said – when they asked, you know,
what I was working on, and I said, 'It's a biography of Nick Drake,' –
'Gloomy,' you know. But, it wasn't. I mean, it was actually very uplift-
ing. There was sadness in it.

I was very lucky to get some tapes of interviews that an American, T.J.
McGrath, had conducted (with Nick's parents) in the Eighties. Listening
to those, you really got a feeling of his class. I mean, I think a lot of
people don't appreciate that Nick Drake was the product of an empire-
building, upper-middle class, English background. He made no attempts
to ever disguise that; and in one fragment of Nick talking, at the end
of the bootleg, the voice is what I would expect from a public school-
educated, upper-middle class, English schoolboy. He never denied who
he was or where he came from; and you listen to his singing voice, and
the Englishness comes through, absolutely inimitable.

What I tried to do in the book was put him in the context very
much of his class and his background, but also of the music industry of
the times; because, again, some people think, 'Oh, when he was alive,
the music press was full of Nick Drake features.' Well, actually, no; he
gave one interview in his life, to *Sounds*, which was unrevealing. The
original, contemporary reviews of the albums – I was quite surprised –
weren't as glowing as I thought they would be: as good as any accorded

to a singer-songwriter album on Island, and as good as any album produced by Joe Boyd, but rarely better.

There's a conspiracy theory that Island Records didn't appreciate Nick, didn't know what to do with him. Island were actually very supportive. Nick's albums were always well received inside Island, but there were always two questions: Where's the single? Is he on the road? The only way you could get people, in the late Sixties and early Seventies, to buy your records was to go out there and gig. He had a real problem with performing, I think. He didn't gig: nobody bought the records. It's as simple as that.

And yet, here we are a quarter of a century after his death, and his name is dropped by the great and the good, from R.E.M., to Elvis Costello, to Kate Bush, to Beth Orton, I mean, Nick's is the name. I talked to Peter Buck the week R.E.M. re-signed to Warner Brothers for $80m – you know, you'd think he might have a few other things to do, like go down the bank – but he spent an hour and a half on the phone to me talking about Nick Drake. He made this, I think, really interesting connection between Nick and Robert Johnson; particularly *Pink Moon*. Robert Johnson, similar age to Nick when he died, handful of recordings made in a hotel room, his back to the engineers, pouring, you know, heart and soul into voice and guitar – a hell hound on his trail. You would think that the connection between a black, illegitimate blues singer, in the Deep South of the Thirties, in the Great Depression, and an English, upper-middle class, public schoolboy from Tanworth-in-Arden, you'd think there was more than an ocean to cross to make that connection. But you listen to 'Black Eyed Dog', and Nick Drake had a hell hound on his trail. And Buck made that connection, and I thought it was very interesting. To me it was indicative of just how wide Nick's music... how far it's travelled.

The one good thing that came out posthumously is that his parents, Rodney and Molly, before they died, did appreciate that Nick's music was valued. You know, in his lifetime it made such a negligible impact. After he died people would come from all over the world; and they were quite used to, you know, opening the door, and people would turn up to say how much they loved Nick's music – and that meant a lot to them.

I found the contradictions in the life really interesting; that there was someone that put immense value in the quality and purity of his music, and yet was bitterly disappointed when it didn't sell more copies. He could communicate, but this corrosive shyness and whatever kept him from his audience while he was alive. But his ability to communicate was his music.

I tried to get rid of the myths. I tried to say it wasn't all gloom; it wasn't doom; there was sunshine. And it's important to see that about Nick, that it wasn't all this dark side. It was a terribly short life of only 26 years, but the bulk of those years were, by and large, happy ones. He enjoyed school and university, he made plenty of friends, he remained close to his family, and he was really happy to be recording and releasing records on Island. And only towards the end, in his mother's words, 'the shadows closed in'.

Nick's life was brief, but it was not all bleak. And there was something in it which is both timeless and enduring, which is his music. And of course that's the real reason we're all here tonight. I'd like to thank you all for coming. If there are any questions I'll do my best to answer them as best I can.

Audience question: I wonder if you could tell me, compared to your other music biographies – Richard Thompson, Fairport Convention, Bob Dylan – how do you rate this one?

Patrick Humphries: Well, definitive, naturally (laughter). They're all upstairs, so why not buy them all; get the set and compare them? No, I mean, I'm very, very pleased with this. I mean, I think, for all, being the shy, retiring, inscrutable character, Richard Thompson's given an awful lot of interviews in 30 years. When I was writing his biography, if he couldn't answer a question, I could go back to a bulging cuttings file. With Nick there was nothing to fall back on. So, as a writer, it was really challenging, you know, to start writing a book and to open it and the pages were completely blank. It's very challenging, but it's also very exciting. So, I rate it very highly.

Audience: I've read different accounts of what happened when he died. Was it suicide or was it an accident? Did you uncover anything?

Patrick: What struck me was that he was prescribed very powerful antidepressants; and I believe it was an accidental overdose of prescribed drugs. Someone I quote in the book is Brian Wells, who was a very close friend of Nick's, who met him at Cambridge, and went on to specialise in treatment of addiction. His belief is that, for it to be suicide, there has to be an intent to take your own life; and he doesn't believe that Nick intended. If he'd wanted to kill himself, there were so many other opportunities he could have taken. To have chosen to do it at home, so he knew his parents would discover him – he was very close to his parents – was too wilful to be deliberate. And also, by all accounts, he was happier than he had been for a long time. So I personally don't believe it.

Audience: You were talking about the myth-making, to do with Nick, and obviously a lot of that has to do with the fact that he died very young. Do you think that people want to sort of romanticise when that happens, they want to believe that side of stuff?

Patrick: Yes, I think there is the danger, of anyone who dies before their time – you know, if it's James Dean, or Michael Hutchence, or Nick Drake – to mythologise. I think with Nick it happened because you had this career arc of this incredibly promising debut, and this lustrous, rich second album, and this stark, solitary final album, and then the final four songs; you know, including 'Black Eyed Dog', which is chilling. So, you've got that arc of a career, and you've also got this really striking looking guy. So I think that's undoubtedly fuelled the myth. But Dave Pegg said that – you know, he played on Nick's records – and he said, 'No, it's the quality of the music. It's timeless.' And that was something Clive Gregson said – he worked with John Wood, who engineered Nick's records – so Clive said, you know, you listen to *Bryter Layter*, and to *Pink Moon* particularly, and you play that against what else was around at the time, the other stuff sounds so dated, whereas Nick's has a crispness and freshness and vitality still.

Patrick Humphries interview
Jason Creed, *Pink Moon 13*, January 1998

After the talk, we made our back up to the shop, where Patrick signed copies of his book, and I met some enthusiastic *Pink Moon* fans; one of whom even asked for my autograph! Then we made our way up to the

Angel pub for more drinks, and I found myself chatting with Robert Kirby, Richard Charkin and Patrick Humphries – three thoroughly delightful characters. So, needless to say, it was an incredibly enjoyable evening, albeit quite a surreal one!

I had been hoping to interview Patrick at the launch night, but he was extremely busy signing books and answering questions. However, he kindly agreed to do the interview over the phone, on January 12, 1998, and it went as follows:

Jason Creed: Your book's on a second print run, there was a crowd at Helter Skelter, and it seems that every radio station wants to talk to you; are you surprised that a Nick Drake biography is attracting so much attention?

Patrick Humphries: Well I am, yes. I mean, when I began writing the book, people said, you know, 'There's a cult about Nick Drake,' but you're just not sure how big a cult it is. You know, the records have always been on catalogue, so there's obviously an abiding interest in Nick and his music; but it's very difficult because record companies are very reluctant to let sales figures out. So, you're not absolutely certain just how many people would be interested in a book. But, yes, I was absolutely astounded and obviously delighted that when it came out you know, for a hardback book, I don't think it's overpriced, but it's still some money to spend … But, you know, touch wood, it seems to have sold, and keeps on selling.

Jason: Did you feel that, because Joe Boyd, Gabrielle Drake, John Martyn and John Wood declined to cooperate, you had any questions that were left unanswered?

Patrick: Well, obviously I would like to have spoken to them all in detail. I mean, to be honest, the one person that I'm really sorry that I didn't have a chance to interview is John Wood. Joe and Gabrielle and John Martyn, over the years, have spoken about Nick; but to my knowledge John Wood hasn't ever spoken in any real detail about Nick, and he was one of the people who was really closest to him. You know, he was recording Nick even when Joe was in the States, and he kept in close touch with Nick. So I would love to have had his impressions of Nick, and his experience of working with Nick in the studio. But, yes, it's obviously unfortunate that some people who were close to Nick didn't want to cooperate, but that's their prerogative. And, as I say, in the past, they have spoken about Nick, so I could draw on those existing interviews. And it did make me work harder to find people who knew Nick and had never spoken about him before.

Jason: Have you had any reaction from the above people since the book's been published?

Patrick: No.

Jason: Have you made any further discoveries, since the book was printed, which you wish you could have included? And, if so, will there be an updated edition?

Patrick: Erm, yes (laughter); but you'll have to wait for the paperback! There's an American woman who wrote 'Been Smokin' Too Long'; she's been in touch. A couple of people who I tried to interview for the book, who knew Nick, but for various reasons I never actually got to, they've seen the book and have written to me and said, you know, 'Sorry we didn't get an opportunity to talk. It would be nice to get together.' So, I've actually got quite a few people, quite a few letters like that. And then, some people who I did interview, seeing their comments in the book, in cold print, said, 'Oh, actually, that reminds me.'

So I think there's enough for an expansion. I probably wouldn't look to expand dramatically; I'm very happy with the structure of the book, you know; the way it begins, the three parts it falls into. I suppose I might look at maybe putting some more in for the paperback, which is due later in 1998.

Jason: 'Compartmentalised' seems to be a key word, regarding the way Nick organised his life; do you think this is something he did intentionally, or was it perhaps something he wasn't even aware of?

Patrick: Difficult question. Because there's a lot of aspects of Nick's life, it's very difficult to say. Because he never spoke about himself in public, he was never interviewed about that, it's very difficult to say. I think, certainly, talking to people who knew Nick at school, but more so at Cambridge, they had got the impression that he was cultivating that image, of the poetic outsider, of dressing in black, and not saying much. And a couple of people actually said they really felt he was cultivating that image, and I think he was quite shy and introspective, you know, long before the illness appeared. So I think he was always someone who kept his cards close to his chest, and I don't think that he gave much away anyway, even when he was being fairly communicative. So I think he was quite careful at keeping different groups of different friends. I mean, again, a couple of people said that the only time they ever saw other people from Nick's life was at his funeral; and Brian Wells told me that he didn't know about Nick's friends in London; you know, he'd hear about these names, but he'd never met them. So I think he was quite good at keeping different sets of friends apart; whether that was deliberate or not, we don't know.

Jason: I believe that, for some, the attraction of Nick Drake is the air of mystery that surrounds his life; do you think that books, fanzines, radio shows, or anything else which aims to separate the man from the myth, may actually lessen his appeal?

Patrick: That's a good question. Erm, I don't think so, because you've always got the music, and I think it's the music that draws people to Nick. I used to think, before I started the book, that a lot of the appeal of Nick Drake was in the premature death; that's what drew people. Since writing the book, and talking to people who knew Nick, and listening to the records very, very closely, I really began … you know, I really appreciate them a lot more and I think there is something timeless about that music. So I've really come round to the idea that it's the music that draws people to Nick, and continues to draw people.

Now, undeniably, a factor in the appeal is how he looked, and that 'air of mystery' about him; I mean, he was a very striking-looking person. And because so little, up till the book, was known about him, I think that added to the mystery of the cult. But I would hope that, with my book, it would, you know, alert people to this very distinctive, this very individual talent, and draw them back to the music.

Jason: John Martyn has said that Nick was very much a singer-songwriter, and not just a depressive who picked up a guitar, yet many people believe that Nick's story can be found in his songs; had you been given permission to use Nick's lyrics, would you have drawn parallels between his life and words, or do you think that his lyrics were more 'art' than anything else?

Patrick: Yeah, that's again a very interesting question. I don't know.

I suppose, because I couldn't draw on the lyrics, because that avenue was denied me, I suppose I would have been looking for connections between the life and work. I personally think that, because of his early death, there are certainly eerie premonitions, but I think that that's perhaps been overdone in the past; people have – because he died so tragically early – people have said, 'Now, this song, this album title, this reference refers to …' you know, 'he was always going to die.' I'm not altogether sure about that, and I think, as I say in the book, if Leonard Cohen had died after his third album, there's a very good case that a lot of his lyrics could have been taken as premonitions…

So, in a way, I was quite glad I couldn't actually use the lyrics, because I think I managed to resist that temptation. I think Nick was very careful and very scrupulous about his lyric writing – his mother said that his notebook was her most treasured possession – and it was something he obviously applied a great deal of thought and dedication to. So, I think, like most art, it springs from personal experience, but it then goes on and it develops, and it's embellished and amplified by the artist, which is what makes it great art I suppose. I think that he distanced himself from the music and the lyrics more than the commentators who have written about Nick do.

Jason: Nick never got the chance to grow old; had he matured more, do you think his music would have become more popular, or do you think it's his 'innocence' that makes it so appealing?

Patrick: It's certainly a factor. Of course, trying to isolate and identify the appeal of anyone is quite difficult. You know, why someone like Tim Hardin, who was a brilliant singer-songwriter, who died terribly young, is hardly known at all today, whereas Tim Buckley, who died a few years later, is still quite widely known. It's very difficult to say. I've always found it odd that Nick's songs aren't better known; I mean, it's not like they're unmelodic, or difficult to access. I've always found them very pleasant and very melodic and very enticing, and I would have thought they could have lent themselves to cover versions. But, you know, that hasn't happened. If he'd lived? Well, that's the great 'What if?' isn't it.

I think he found the whole business of the record industry very intimidating and off-putting. In the book, I make the case of, there were precedents with people like Keith Reed, who just wrote the lyrics for Procul Harum; or Pete Sinfield, who wrote the lyrics for King Crimson; Brian Wilson and Syd Barrett, for The Beach Boys and Pink Floyd – they were sort of writers in isolation. So I suppose it's feasible that Nick could have got some sort of job just as a songwriter. Although Robert Kirby thought that he would have been a very good publisher; he had a very great interest in literature and writing and writers. It's impossible to imagine Nick's life had he lived; really, very difficult to imagine what would have happened. I think he would have somehow stayed involved; I think music would have been a part of his life, whether he just played the guitar, for pleasure, or writing and submitting songs to publishers, and trying to get cover versions.

You know, people from Marlborough have very happy memories of Nick performing, and it seems that his stage-fright, and his antipathy to live performance, only came about when he had to go out and perform solo. So, maybe if he'd had some encouragement, in terms of sales or cover versions, maybe he could have been enticed back in front of an audience, with a small group, and that might have lessened his fear of live performance. So, I think he would have always been involved in music one way or another.

Jason: You said you felt you had a mission to give Nick his life back; do you think that can be achieved when some people prefer to create, or subscribe to, the myths that surround him?

Patrick: What I found, especially over two years researching and writing about Nick's life, is that he's almost like a blank canvas, so people can project whatever they want on him. If they want to cling to this myth, that he was gloomy and never smiled, and never spoke, and only ever listened to Leonard Cohen records, and only ever dressed in black, and was just, you know, doomed from the start, there's nothing I can write or say that's going to change their opinions. You know, I think I've written a book that goes some way to redressing that balance. I've spent nearly 300 pages getting, I think, as full and accurate a picture of Nick's life as is humanly possible. And I think in that book, in those 300 pages, a very different picture of Nick has emerged. A lot of people who knew him, at school particularly, were very unhappy with the way the myth has perpetrated this image of the doomed outsider, and a couple of them said to me, 'It makes me really angry that this is the image,' you know. 'That was only towards the end of his life. That's not the Nick that I knew.' A lot of people said that to me. This image of Nick has gone into print, and onto the internet, and into, you know, all the stuff that has been written about him since his death, and they're very unhappy with it.

So, I think I've managed to get a balance there. I think I've shown that he was very athletic, that he was a very good driver, you know, he could get from Tanworth to Ascot without asking directions. I mean, he would travel; he managed to make his own way to Paris and Spain. He wasn't this sort of fragile, frail creature; he was quite determined, quite able to do things. And I think when the illness came, that stopped that side of Nick; but it was undeniably part of his life up till the illness came in. If anything, I hope my book's given a more rounded picture of Nick. But if people want to cling to this myth, then, you know, I think it says more about them than it does about Nick Drake.

Poor Boy, So Sorry For Himself
Suzi Feay, *The Independent*, February 2006

It's easy to become expert in the works of the singer-songwriter Nick Drake: the canon comprises just three albums (the final one, *Pink Moon*, lasting a mere 28 minutes) and a handful of other songs and bootlegs. Of course, considerable musical expertise is required to fathom the complicated tunings and meticulous guitar technique that awe musicians even today, but the freshness and immediacy of the songs, now over 30 years old, still seem to draw the listener into what feels like an intimate relationship with 'Nick'.

He died in 1974 aged 26, burned out, like Keats, by illness even before his premature death. His decline is horribly charted in sessions with the photographer Keith Morris. In 1970, he's a tall, gangly, studenty type with an open, fresh face. Just over a year later, he's a hunched, dishevelled figure, staring vacantly at Morris, ignoring the overtures of a friendly labrador or gazing blankly over Hampstead Heath. He had three painful years left to live, and looking at him, you wonder that he lasted so long.

Patrick Humphries' excellent and fairly exhaustive *Nick Drake: The Biography* came out in 1997. Is there much left to say about so short a life? Actually, yes; and much of it is a question of tone and emphasis. In contrast to Humphries' mournful reverence, Dann presents a less ethereal figure, tracking down acquaintances prepared to talk in uncomplimentary terms. The result is a more realistic portrait. Muff Winwood, Island Records' A&R man, remembers with a distinct lack of enchantment: 'My job was to get him out of his stinky bed...He was a complete pain in the arse, drove me up the wall.' The conductor of the first and last published Nick Drake interview, journalist Jerry Gilbert, when asked whether he liked Nick, replies bluntly: 'Well, what's to like? There was nothing expressive about him...if you wanted to be uncharitable you could say he was just a spoilt boy with a silver spoon and went round feeling sorry for himself. Horrible thing to say, but...'

Where Humphries was reticent about drug use, Dann reveals that Drake was such a good customer that his Cockney heroin dealer bought him a car ('he's gotta 'av wheels'). Catastrophically, in terms of his mental health, he smoked 'industrial quantities of cannabis', and Dann unpicks the details of Drake's disputed 'suicide', pointing out that he could have taken only slightly more than double his customary dose of antidepressants; it's not hard to imagine someone in his state of mind doing that by accident.

Some vexed questions are unlikely ever to be settled. Drake compartmentalised his life and relationships so severely that several groups of friends only met at his funeral. Consequently, in interview irreconcilable views emerge, particularly on the question of his sexuality. Gay? School friends said no: 'We knew what gay boys were...but it never occurred to me that Nick was that way inclined.' The singer Linda Thompson had a 'romance' with Drake, but noted: 'It was very odd that it wasn't a full sexual thing...whatever he was, he wasn't what we'd call red-blooded, definitely not.' Brian Wells, a Cambridge friend turned psychologist, says: 'I can't really imagine Nick having sex with anyone because he would have to take his clothes off, and he was always much too shy to do that.' But another student friend remembers going round to his hall of residence: 'One Saturday or Sunday morning he hadn't got any clothes on and he clearly had company as well, female company, two females in fact, so it wasn't the time.'

This aura of mystery is what makes him so compelling, even decades after his death. His 'natural quietness…made it easy to weave a web of fantasies around him', observes another female friend. 'Falling in love with Nick was a no-brainer and I promptly did.'

On the practical side, Dann demonstrates amusing necro-stalker tendencies: 'If you walk confidently past the porters' lodge, you should be able to walk up to P Block. Go straight on across Tree Walk…' And his painstaking song-by-song analysis will send you back to the albums with fresh ears ('Finicky listeners may enjoy the little mistake by the session drummer at 2′50″'). This is a haunting tribute to this most passionately adored of musicians. As his own lyric (inscribed on his gravestone) has it: 'Now we rise / and we are everywhere'.

Poems by Will Stone

The following three poems were submitted to *Pink Moon* by Will Stone, who I guess you could say was the fanzine's resident poet. Will has gone on to have great success with his poetry, essays and translations. You can read more about his achievements below. The poems were revised by Will in 2010 for inclusion in this book.

Nick's Secret Garden

He lies beneath the perfect tree
safe in a suit of soil.
Where else?
On every lolling tongue of meadow,
down every dark blue shaded lane,
in every dip and pothole,
along the dappled bank.
He lies shivering for the bluebells.

Stooping faithfully under love,
they come from Holland, Germany, France,

to leave their notes
all sodden and smudged
under a simple stone.
Will he bother to read them all?
I don't know
but I'll leave my elegy before I go,
lean my heart into the tree,
trace his name through storm flavoured rain
help restring the lyre.

Footfalls on the gravel path.
Orpheus is coming.
No stranger to the singer appears
and touching glasses full of tears,
we become intoxicated.
Out of my depth in a shallow sky,
I am lead slowly away
by Icarus, by angels,
by wanting to stay.

Elegy To Nick Drake

Fame is but a fruit tree
Yes!
And the heavy boughs moan harvest.
Yours is long overdue,
a quarter century on ice.
Until now,
you never had a chance to look up.
Diligently hunched in lucid shadows
playing softly across your strings,
those elegant fingers
with immense effort unseen,
worked the seam of genius.
Through fast dwindling meadows
your awkward body wandered,

beneath an oak, the picture of you
detached from a galloping world.
You were the carrier
of the essence, the other,
a desperate weaver of worlds.
Spines shiver
at the melody command,
fatal purple petals plucked
from the startled lips
of the seasons.

Far Leys

At evening he came up for air
had been suffocated, stretched
left the rear of the house and walked
downhill, ambled to the very end
where rabbits tore a last sweet blade
and bolted madly in every direction.
The air was cooler there and growing moist,
under leaf greens darkening to black,
between silver branches, tomb cracks.
Last scuffles of wood pigeons made him turn
and listless survey the mute murk.
He stopped at the border, rolled and lit
a cigarette in the lee of a hedge, amber flash.
In the further field the sated fox returned.
But he remained hollowed out
bound roots burned beneath the scalp,
and heavy hands held him darkly there.
Then from the house a name was called,
but his own slow blood was all he heard
and nettle banks grew keenly over no reply.
He turned to face uphill again, stared
through the organ's mad sustain,
the worn window seat where one

slender blue sleeved wrist lunged out
like gorse from a crumbling cliff,
and knowing the funereal future
briefly cooled the body anchor
in a welling moon of grey veined white.
Crossed later when the crutch snapped,
the makeshift bridge flameless burned
and ash from unseen bonfires drifted down
flecking lips, turning the bone disc pink.
Hours after cold books unread
stacked in a corner, reached towards,
but the banal adventure
of four white walls was stronger,
the need to stitch sky and land together.
No horizon.
Instead blood on the weather,
the single white hair's confirmation,
he was the unseen incline,
the fastest falling,
the wrong path that dizzily plunged
down the human mountain.

Will Stone, born 1966, is a poet and literary translator who divides his time between England and Belgium. His first poetry collection, *Glaciation*, published by Salt, won the international Glen Dimplex Award for poetry in 2008. His published translations of poetry include *Les Chimères* – Gérard de Nerval (Menard Press, 1999) and *To The Silenced* – selected poems of Georg Trakl (Arc Publications, 2005). Two landmark collections of translations of the Belgian symbolist poets Emile Verhaeren and Georges Rodenbach will be published in November 2010. *Stefan Zweig – Journeys,* a first English translation of the reknowned Austrian writer's travel essays, will also appear in September 2010 from Hesperus Press. *Drawing in Ash*, a second collection of poems, will appear in 2011.

Rare Recordings

There have been a number of bootlegs available over the years and there are still a number of unreleased Nick Drake recordings out there. Among the first bootlegs to appear were those commonly known as the 'Home Recordings', which Nick made at his parents' house in the late Sixties on a home tape recorder. In one of the interviews in this book, Nick's father, Rodney, explains that he grabbed a handful of these tapes before Nick had the chance to erase them. Copies of these tapes were often given, in good faith, to devotees of Nick who visited Far Leys, after his death, and at some point made their way into the hands of a bootlegger, and soon after appeared on CD and even vinyl.

The two most common CDs around the time of the *PM* fanzine were *Tanworth-in-Arden 1967–68* and *The Complete Home Recordings*. The former featured 18 tracks, mostly cover versions of traditional blues, Bob Dylan, Jackson Frank and Bert Jansch songs. Also included were a couple of Drake originals listed as 'Rain' and 'Bird Flew By'.

The Complete Home Recordings had the same track listing but included a few extra Drake originals, titled as 'The Seasons', 'Joey Will Come', 'Princess Of The Sand' and 'The Reason For The Seasons', as well as a recording of Nick talking.

The quality of these recordings, however, was generally very poor; listenable and very interesting no doubt from a fan's point of view, but not really suitable for commercial release. These CDs were very widely circulated during the Nineties and were even available in some high street record shops. Most of the material from these tapes finally got an official release on the *Family Tree* album alongside the songs recorded by Nick's friend on a cassette-recorder in France (see below) and songs sung by Nick's mum, Molly. The recordings were of course cleaned up and the quality improved greatly for the CD.

Sometime in the late Nineties, I received a tape of unreleased Drake material from a *PM* reader – a homemade cassette recording, not a 'proper' bootleg. It contained some 22 tracks, which were mostly alternative versions of Nick's released songs, but also a selection of unfinished, instrumental pieces played on piano and guitar.

These tracks have also been available over the years on bootleg CD, and one recent one, titled *Time Has Told Me*, contains some information about the sources of the recordings. Four tracks are Island demos, recorded at Sound Techniques in 1968. They are 'Time Has Told Me', 'Saturday Sun', 'The Thoughts Of Mary Jane' and 'Day Is Done' – the last two featuring arrangements by Richard Hewson. The next five tracks: 'Fly', 'Place To Be', 'Hazey Jane I' and two versions of 'Parasite', were apparently recorded by Nick's friend Brian Wells in Hampstead, 1969. The remaining tracks are a selection of demo and/or instrumental versions of released songs, 'Poor Boy', 'Time Has Told Me', 'Voice From The Mountain', 'Black Eyed Dog' and 'Rider On The Wheel'.

Finally there are the seven unfinished 'work in progress' pieces – some of which have been titled 'Brittle Days' (parts 1-3), or 'Far Leys', but whether they were titled by Nick or someone else is not clear. It's suggested on the bootleg CD that the source of these recordings are the legendary 'work tapes' which were given to singer-songwriter Scott Appel by Nick's parents, in the hope that he would complete some of Nick's unfinished songs, such was his knowledge of Nick's unusual guitar technique.

In an interview with DJ Malcolm Barker, broadcast on Australian radio station PBS-FM, in 1995, Scott Appel explained how the unreleased material came to him: '…I had organised a tribute on WFMO, which was picked two years in a row as *Rolling Stone*'s best independent college radio station, so there's a lot of listeners, and I organised a tribute to Nick and involved, among others, people like Brian Cullman, Arthur Lubow, *Rolling Stone* and *Musician* magazine … And, long story short is, the tape made its way to Nick's parents and they responded to me by sending several hours of work tapes, and then followed several hours more; so in all I've got about four and a half hours of Nick fleshing out ideas in his bedroom on a reel-to-reel player, and Rodney, his father, had transcribed the quarter inch to cassette and just kept sending me more and more material. That's when the light went on and I said to myself that there's a number of compositions included in here, earlier compositions circa 1966-68, that I guess was, for him, school: going to school, learning his craft. But the songs were just too strong, because you've a guy like Nick: the throwaways are like some peoples' best songs. And there were a number of things that he'd never made attempts at in the studio; and I said, you know, there's enough interest out there to warrant my recording these early compositions, because these are beautiful; and we're talking about 'Bird Flew By', 'Blossom, Our Season', and things like that …'

Continuing the subject in 1999, Scott Appel wrote: '… In 1986, Nick Drake's parents, Rodney and Molly Drake, sent me several hours of reel-to-reel tape containing unfinished, unpublished Nick Drake compositions. Some of those work tapes caught Drake playing and singing at his very best. One included a brilliant finger-picked version of 'Place To Be', which Drake inexplicably chose to simply strum on the version he recorded for *Pink Moon*. I included this arrangement on my 1998 album *Nine Of Swords*, a collection of expanded versions of these songs I worked out with the blessings of Rodney and Molly. The Drakes also shared one of these tapes with another Drake disciple and were dismayed when it appeared shortly thereafter as a low-quality bootleg, *The Tanworth Years 67–68* …'

Appel mentions receiving 'about four and a half hours' of material from the Drakes. This presumably includes all of the material already mentioned above – whether there is anything else is unclear.

So, where are the 'work tapes' now? I interviewed Scott Appel in 1999: he had been very ill, wasn't expecting to live much longer, and told me that he was hoping to make the tapes available, through a friend, after he died: 'Arthur Lubow (he's the guy that wrote the liner notes for the *Fruit Tree* box set) is working on a book regarding Nick Drake, and we've met three times, doing interviews. He's gonna use a couple of things that I had to say about my work on Nick's material in the book. I told him that I would will him the material that is unknown, and it will be up to him to take it from there, because he's probably gonna be faced with a great many legal problems in making them available to the public. But that's where things stand with that. I mean, they're not gonna die with me, they're gonna be passed on, and I can only hope that he can find a way to either come to an agreement with Boyd or find a legal loophole through a lawyer that will let him or allow him to set up ... I suggested that he set up some kind of charity for any royalties that are made from the sales of the tapes, and some of the other things I have; the Island out-takes, the Hewson out-takes, things like that. And he (Lubow) would benefit in no way monetarily. I have suggested that maybe he talk to Gabrielle Drake about a charity that Nick may have been interested in, and hopefully they'll see the light of day under circumstances like that ...'

I was also in contact with Arthur Lubow and I asked him about the work tapes. For *PM19*, March 2000, he wrote: '... Scott Appel has talked about bequeathing me some material he owns, including the work tapes. His health has been pretty bad, but he is feeling much better. So I really haven't given much thought to what I would do with the tapes, but I suppose I would just do what Scott has done, which is take good care of them ...'

Scott Appel died in 2003. I contacted Arthur Lubow in 2010 and he told me that he had not received the work tapes after Scott had died and did not know who owned them now. It may be that they are with Scott's family or another friend. I have been unable to verify which relatives Scott has left behind; various sources have mentioned a wife or partner and a brother. It is believed that Scott was also in possession of some of Nick Drake's personal belongings, which were given to him by Rodney Drake. These include a blue Oxford shirt, dating from Nick's Cambridge days, or earlier, and a small purse with a coin in it.

In his recent book, *Nick Drake, The Complete Guide To His Music* (Omnibus Press), Peter Hogan notes that I am in possession of the

'Creed tape' featuring unreleased versions of four Nick Drake songs, and that the source of these recordings is unknown. As nice as it is to have a tape named after me, I feel I must set the record straight. In *Pink Moon* 7, I wrote: "...Thanks to a *PM* reader from Canada, I have a recording of four demo versions of Nick's songs which were featured on a Canadian radio programme. The first song, 'Place To Be', is played in a finger-picking style, different to that of the *Pink Moon* LP version, and is quite beautiful. Some people may even consider it to be better than the album version. The second song, 'Hazey Jane I', is similar to the *Bryter Layter* version, but there are no strings and the guitar sound is different. The third song is an instrumental of 'Black Eyed Dog', musically the same as the released version. The fourth song, 'Time Has Told Me', is again just Nick and his guitar, but this version is a little slower than the one on *Five Leaves Left*. The song is interrupted as soon as it starts and Nick apologises ('Sorry, I got the tempo wrong') before starting the song again."

The radio show was a Nick Drake special, which Scott Appel had been involved in, and the original source of the songs was the 'work tapes' mentioned above.

Interplay One is a teaching anthology, compiled by John Watts and published by Longman in 1972. It consists of a book ('Teacher's Notes') and two LPs, featuring renditions of old ballads, folk songs and poems, with contributions from Nick Drake and Robert Kirby. Nick plays guitar on three tracks and Robert sings on one.

'I Wish I Was A Single Girl Again' is sung by Vivian Fowler with Nick Drake on guitar. John Wilkins also plays banjo. The song is originally from the Appalachian Mountains of the eastern United States.

'With My Swag All On My Shoulder' is a traditional Australian pioneer song, sung by Robert Kirby with Nick Drake on guitar.

'Full Fathom Five' by William Shakespeare, is sung by Vivian Fowler with Nick Drake on guitar. This dirge is sung in the folk style.

Vivian Fowler, who sang on two of the tracks mentioned above, wrote the following in 2009: "I became involved because my husband worked in the Audio Visual Department at Longmans but he had left by the time we got married in 1969, so if the dating is right, they must have contacted him to get me involved. It was probably Robert Kirby's girlfriend who worked there who got in touch with him at the time. Longmans had moved to Harlow but I frankly don't recall going out there to do the recording – I had envisaged it in a studio in London as I don't think they had recording facilities in Harlow.

"The other thing I can't recall is who wrote the tune for 'Full Fathom Five'. I was setting a few things to music at the time and can't remember now whether that is a traditional tune or whether it was one of mine. The recording was definitely done with Nick Drake in the studio. I have a feeling that I was asked to come up with a suitably 'dirgy' tune to accompany those words, and having done that it wouldn't have taken someone like him very long to create an accompaniment – I could have done it myself but thought someone else would do it better. A very good decision as it turned out.

"'I Wish I Was a Single Girl Again' is of course a well-known song and lots of people have recorded it.

"I think we had an hour or so to pull it together and then do the recording – half a day in the studio.

"My recollection of Nick Drake is pretty much like everyone else's – he just seemed a quiet, nice sort of guy, absolutely no airs and graces, he was there to get a job done. My guitar playing simply wasn't good enough and I was very relieved not to have to play."

Vivian's reminiscences were first published on Michael Organ's website – www.michaelorgan.org.au/drake3.htm – which features a whole page dedicated to the Longman LP, and the chance to download the three rare recordings.

Not rare recordings this time, but rare arrangements. In an interview for *Pink Moon* 18, Robert Kirby revealed to the fanzine that he had recently discovered some long lost and forgotten arrangements for some of Nick's earliest songs. Two of these were eventually recorded and added to Nick's songs – 'Magic' and 'Time Of No Reply' – for the *Made To Love Magic* compilation album, released in 2004.

Robert Kirby: OK – I haven't told anyone else this yet – but earlier this year I was up at my mother's, and I was pottering around in the potting shed, where I actually found all the original scores to *Five Leaves Left*, not just of the record. I thought I had long lost these. I thought I lost them in the Seventies, because I was burgled and robbed a couple of times. But not only did I find the original scores, I also found the scores – which I'd forgotten too – from when we did the live concerts, before he even got me to do the album *Five Leaves Left*. We used to do them live for some time before we actually put them to record. I didn't realise that they went through changes. I found the original arrangement to 'Way To Blue' that we did, and the instrumental section in the middle was totally different, really bizarre. But also I found the running order for the first concert we ever did: I'd done five arrangements for that, and one arrangement for a song that I'd totally forgotten. The song was called 'My Love Left With The Rain', and I'd totally forgotten this song, never seen any mention of it since – and I have actually just written to Gabrielle to see if she's got any knowledge of this song. But it's so frustrating because I've got the string parts, the flute parts, and also the French horn, which we did live, and I've got it all worked out; but, of course, what I haven't got is the guitar part, the vocal and the melody. And I can just remember the last line.

(The song Robert refers to is the one on the 'home recordings' which has previously been known as 'Rain' or 'Our Season'. Robert, at this time, hadn't heard the home recordings and wasn't aware that the song still existed. I told Robert about the bootleg and offered to send him a copy.)

Robert: That would be interesting, because I've not heard what's on those recordings. Because when I found this (the music scores) it sort of came back to me; that I've got a funny recollection that we worked on other stuff, and shelved it. You know, I've got the arrangement that we did to 'Time Of No Reply'.

I've found – we started work on 'Blossom' – and I found I'd written down his guitar part. I used to keep everything of his in one big manuscript book, and I wrote down the guitar part to 'Blossom'. But then, for some reason, we shelved it and went on to something else.

155

But anything you have got, I would be curious to hear. But, I mean, particularly this 'Rain'; because, as I said, I nearly fell over backwards: I'd forgotten all about it. It was the third song we did in a set of five songs. I'll let you know the running order of the first live concert we did, with the orchestra. And I'd forgotten actually that we had two flutes; I knew we had strings, but two flutes, and the French horn and an organ as well. 'Time Of No Reply' and 'I Was Made To Love Magic' were both in it. 'My Love Left With The Rain', 'Day Is Done' – and I can't remember the fifth one. I think it was possibly 'Way To Blue'.

Jason: And were those last two done the same as the album versions?

Robert: 'Day Is Done' never changed; note for note, that was the same from when it was written, right the way through. 'Way To Blue', the instrumental changed. 'Fruit Tree' had some changes as well, particularly to the cor anglais/oboe bit. We'd do a live concert, and then find one bit that didn't sound too good, so we'd just change it slightly.

Scott Appel interview
Anne Leighton, *The Music Paper*, February 1987

Scott Appel is a New Jersey based guitarist who's spent much of his life crossing back and forth over various musical paths, from electric rock and jazz to his real love, acoustic folk guitar. In 1964 he, like many of us, was exposed to The Beatles and that opened him up to rock and roll. Two years later he began listening to contemporary folk and blues players and by 1969 he had formed an acoustic duo with fellow Jerseyite Chris McNally, playing area coffee houses. "Every third song was a Grateful Dead song, so we could get away with an esoteric Moby Grape, Incredible String Band or Paul Simon song – or even an original," Appel remembered of those days.

From 1972–74 he attended Berklee College of Music in Boston and played the subways every weekend. He fluctuated between rock bands and jazz outfits until 1979, when he became disgusted with the fact that he wasn't getting anywhere. Still eagerly playing guitar, but only folk guitar now, Scott gave up on pursuing the elusive dream of 'making it' and became a forklift operator.

He came back with a gung-ho vengeance in 1983, getting a job in a record store, scoring documentaries for *Time Life* and pursuing a proper recording deal. Finally, in 1985, Scott joined the roster of Kicking Mule Records. Scott's first release, *Glassfinger*, is an instrumental album focusing on his various acoustic guitar styles and techniques. One of these techniques involves the use of a glass tube, known as slide or bottleneck guitar. The album features all kinds of traditional and contemporary pieces, including a medley of Gordon Lightfoot tunes. Scott has taken a grass roots approach to marketing the record, including town newspaper reviews, college radio play and a simple video.

Scott is also involved with a second project now, concerning British-based, but Burma-born, Nick Drake, a songwriter/guitarist of the late Sixties/early Seventies. Born of middle class parents, he studied English Literature at Cambridge University and was signed to Island Records a year before his graduation. He left school and recorded three albums (*Five Leaves Left*, *Bryter Layter* and *Pink Moon*). Commercially they bombed, but he was acclaimed by critics everywhere. Sadly this story ends with Nick's untimely death from a drug overdose in 1974.

Scott Appel became a Drake fan about a year after Nick passed on. Scott had all his records, so it was only natural for him to work Drake's pieces into his repertoire. In 1986 Scott put together a Nick Drake audio special for WFMU, Upsala College, South Orange NJ. The station's owner, personality Jim Price, sent a copy of the show to Nick's parents in England. They subsequently wrote back to Scott, asking him if he would like to complete Nick's unfinished works. "Yes!" replied Scott, with more gusto than he had approached almost anything else in his life, and the project began. It is unfinished as of yet, but Scott was willing to talk about it in a recent interview.

Anne Leighton: How do you go about completing someone else's compositions? How do you know Nick and his music?
Scott Appel: I got so involved with his tunings; that's the key to Nick as a musician, the odd tunings he employed. I started working on his material and had to tune the guitar the way he did. They were tunings nobody else did. And that would lead me to what his songs were about. I did this for two or three years and got inside his head as far as what

he was trying to express with his music. These unfinished tunes, when I first heard them, melodies just flew through my mind. There were so many places to go with them. I just have no problem with his music at all and feel really qualified to be able to complete his skeletons.

Anne: Are Nick's tunings different for every song?

Scott: For most. Odd tuning is used because it facilitates old inversions that one wouldn't be able to get when the guitar is tuned standardly. When Nick arrived at a tuning, it became the song. And he wouldn't be able to do the song in another tuning; the song dictated the tunings. To arrive at the tunings takes hours. A standard guitar is E-A-D-G-B-E. On Nick's 'Place To Be', from the *Pink Moon* album, the tuning is D-A-D-G-A-F# with the capo on the fourth fret.

Anne: Would I be doing it right if I wrote a tune with the standard tuning and then actually got down with music paper to figure out how to make the playing easier by changing the tuning?

Scott: I think that's exactly what Nick would do. He'd write in standard tunings and when he started to hear different overtones he'd want to use, he would construct the tuning according to the song. But I think he would get a framework for the song, like 'Place To Be' is really Em, F#m and D; those are the basic changes. Then he created his tuning and you'd have a 4th happening throughout the entire song. You wouldn't have had that if you played the song in a standard tuning.

Anne: Do you work that way with your material?

Scott: I do, but not to such a great extent. I became familiar with open-chord tunings (G-D-C) and I would work out an idea in that tuning.

Anne: Do you in any way feel like you're invading something private by undertaking the Nick Drake project?

Scott: I wonder if people will feel that way, hearing this stuff; if they'll feel it's sacrilegious for me to tamper with what he was working on. I don't feel that way personally. I feel incredibly flattered that his parents would have trusted this material to me to work on. And I think I can bring a lot to it. I know exactly what he was doing and what he was after. I know I will do the material justice. People may feel like it's not right, like that Jimi Hendrix album, *Crash Landing*, where producers took all the Hendrix parts but wiped everything else out and dubbed in a new rhythm section underneath his guitar. People thought that it was horrendous to do that. I don't know what the reaction will be (to my project) but if it was me and I knew there were unfinished Nick Drake pieces that some guitarist was working on, I would pick up on the stuff because I would really need to hear the framework of these compositions, to hear what somebody else's interpretation was. It would interest me. Am I invading? I don't think so, but it's really up to whoever hears it and what they feel.

Anne: What of Nick is in you?

Scott: The guy really expressed feelings of displacement, irony, having a tough time connecting. I think a lot of people can identify with that. I certainly do. Initially, that's what it was. I became a big fan of his ability as a guitarist, but that was after I listened to what his songs were about. So he appeals to me on both levels. He's an incredible technician, guitar wise. I can't think of anybody that plays the guitar who would be capable of doing what he has done.

Anne: What of you is in Nick Drake?

Scott: I identify with the guy on so many different levels that I just feel a kinship. There's definitely some kind of tie, but I don't want to sound ethereal about it. Somehow we're connected. I've just fallen into this whole body of music that he created. It's become so easy for me to work through his music. I'm not the kind of person who can really woodshed and tear apart something. I'm kind of lazy in that sense. I don't like to put a record on and keep putting the needle back over and over trying to figure out what somebody is doing. But Nick's stuff, although it's more complex than anything I've worked with, it seems to come easily to me.

Anne: It interests you?

Scott: Oh yeah. So much! So, I stick with it.

Nick Drake Tape Find
Record Collector (www.recordcollectormag.com), November 1998

Late last year, after the publication of his biography of Nick Drake, author Patrick Humphries received a letter from someone who claimed to have a tape of the singer-songwriter in France in early 1967. "Initially, I was very wary," Humphries says, "but I went to hear the tape, expecting to be disappointed.

"Even when I saw the tape, I still expected the worst. This was an amateur recording, on a standard C90 cassette which by then had been knocking around for more than 30 years. But when I finally heard it, I was just stunned. Apart from the amazing clarity of the recording, there was a real quality of intimacy to the performance. Given that Nick had only been out of school for six months, he already sounded astonishingly confident and assured. It was completely at odds with this image of Drake as the permanently bruised and battered outsider."

Familiar with the poor quality bootleg of Nick's Tanworth home demos which were recorded later in 1967, Humphries was expecting something of a similar standard: "But the quality of the Aix tape was so extraordinarily clear that it was really quite eerie.

"This chap had one of the earliest Philips portable recorders, which he had taken down to France so he could listen to tapes of The Beatles and Stones. Apparently Nick was curious to hear how his voice would sound on tape, and asked if he could be recorded. The guy who made the recording reckoned that the quality was so good because the apartment had one of those French stone floors, which provided near-perfect acoustics."

The tape was recorded in Aix-en-Provence, sometime during February or March 1967, a good two-and-a-half years before Drake's official Island debut *Five Leaves Left*, not released until September 1969. Drake had gone down to the South of France, ostensibly to improve his language skills, though according to a number of friends in Humphries' book he spent most of the time drinking cheap red wine, smoking Disques Bleus and developing his guitar technique. It was whilst in France that Drake wrote his first original song, 'Princess Of The Sand', which is among the numbers he performs on the newly discovered tape.

All the other songs are covers, among them Bob Dylan's 'Tomorrow Is A Long Time', Bert Jansch's 'Strolling Down The Highway', and The Youngbloods' 'Get Together'. Evidently one of the few who bought a copy of Jackson C Frank's eponymous album in 1965, Nick also chose to record three songs by the American singer-songwriter: 'Here Come The Blues', 'Milk And Honey' and 'Kimbie'.

"What is so fascinating about the Aix tape," Humphries explains, "is that it offers an opportunity to hear Nick Drake at the very beginning. To my surprise, the 35-minute tape was very much a complete performance, interspersed with Drake's own comments on the songs. But he sounds completely relaxed, quietly confident. He plays, he sings, he even laughs!"

The last 10 minutes or so of the tape are much less clear, and were obviously recorded on a different occasion. But Humphries believes that even these fragments have a certain fly-on-the-wall charm: "The background noise suggests a party, and Nick – probably fuelled by vin ordinaire – can be heard playing to a boisterous crowd. Of course, it's not John Lennon at the Woolton Village Fete, but it is a priceless snapshot, which I'm sure Nick's fans would love the opportunity to hear. And in the light of what happened to him later, it's just so nice to hear the young Nick sounding relaxed and happy, and so full of hope for the future."

Strange Face
Michael Burdett, June 2010

In the late Seventies, I was working as a post boy at Island Records. One summer's afternoon I was asked to give a hand taking a huge pile of tapes out to a rubbish skip at the back of the building in British Grove, Chiswick. These were spools of quarter-inch tape and boxes of cassettes – demo tapes, old copies and recordings that weren't required any more.

I helped take the piles of tapes out to the skip, which was already half full of the sort of stuff that record companies regularly used to throw out. As I worked, I thought that some of the bigger spools of tape would be useful to me in the studio that I was starting to put together. There were also some cassettes and tapes by bands I liked.

I went to see my boss and asked if it would be all right if I took some of the tapes home. He replied that I was welcome to help myself to anything that was in the skip.

That evening after work I completely emptied that skip and went through the entire contents. Mainly, I was looking for large spooled quarter-inch tapes, especially ones that had no edits or leader tape between the tracks, as I could tape over these and re-use them easily. I remember that there were old copy tapes by Traffic and Andy Fraser of Free, which I took home and taped over.

Right at the bottom of the skip were a couple of tapes that grabbed my attention. One was a demo cassette by a friend's band. I took it with the intention of showing him what had happened to his beloved work (though in the end it felt too cruel). The other was a scruffy little five-inch spool of quarter-inch Emitape. Written on the orange box in black felt tip pen were the words 'Cello Song... Nick Drake 7.5ips copy... With love'.

I looked at the box and was close to leaving it, but it was the phrase 'With Love' that stopped me. I thought, that has to be Nick Drake's handwriting. And it was simply this belief that made me pick it up.

Nick had been dead for about five years but I knew his material relatively well. Through (Island's press officer) Rob Partridge's enthusiasm for Drake, a triple box set of all of his material and a few previously unavailable tracks had just been released.

I took the little orange box home, along with a huge armful of tapes and cassettes, because I could simply not let it go to the dump.

I have always been a bit of a hoarder – I still have my cub uniform, for crying out loud – and so the tape stayed with me. For a long while I didn't play it.

After leaving Island Records, I worked as an A&R man before doing some engineering and record production, and eventually ended up writing music for television, which is what I still do to this day.

In 2002, I moved to Mid-Wales to take a bit of a break from television composition and to record an album myself. I had a studio installed in a beautiful cottage on the bank of a powerful little river and wrote and recorded a number of tracks there over a year or so.

During the composition period, one of the pieces gave me quite a few problems. It was a track written for three pianos and I had a lot of trouble finishing it. I acted as every miserable composer does and busied myself with all kinds of distractions, including setting up an old Revox tape recorder and going through loads of quarter-inch tapes that I had accumulated over the years. It was interesting and nostalgic, but most of all, it was perfect displacement activity.

Nearly 25 years after retrieving it from the skip, for the first time I took the Nick Drake tape out of its box and threaded it on to a tape recorder. I settled back in a huge armchair with the sound of the river coming in through the opened window, and relaxed.

The track started. I thought something was wrong with the tape machine. The guitar sounded different. The percussion started and was busier. It felt...well...funkier. Then Nick began humming, and *two* cellos came in. They played a flourish I didn't recognise. And finally Nick started singing, beautifully recorded but different, ever so slightly different. The cellos played more aggressively. I loved it.

I suspected that I was listening to something that no-one had heard for many, many years and it felt like a very special moment indeed.

A while later I returned to London to continue writing music for television. I heard about the fanzine *Pink Moon* and got in touch with Jason Creed and told him of my discovery. He was really helpful and an excellent source of information.

Through Jason I got in touch with Cally who looks after Nick Drake's estate and played the recording to him. Cally confirmed that it was an unknown recording of 'Cello Song', and a lovely version at that, but also told me that the handwriting on the box was not Nick's. It is a mystery to this day as to whose it might be and who had sent the tape in or under what circumstances it had been recorded.

It was lined up for Nick's friend and string arranger Robert Kirby to come and listen to the recording. Although Robert was not responsible for the string arrangement on the version of 'Cello Song' on *Five Leaves Left*, he was incredibly knowledgeable about all of Nick's demo and early recordings. He was friendly and avuncular. I enjoyed meeting him.

He settled down in the studio and I put the recording on. When the guitar started, it was obvious from Robert's face that he did not recognise this particular version. Then as Nick's voice came in, his eyes moistened. It felt like a very personal moment and I remember thinking that his face would have made a telling photograph.

I was watching a man who, I got the impression, simply missed his friend. Robert had spent the last few years talking about Nick and being interviewed about him, but here he was hearing something from 35 years earlier, a time when so much life should have been ahead of them both. Sometimes it is easy to forget how young they were when they collaborated on such terrific work.

"What a wonderful recording," Robert said, and as he left he thanked me profusely for letting him hear it.

What a gentleman and what a nice guy. I would liked to have had the opportunity to have worked with him and was delighted that, in the last few years of his life, Robert was finally being recognised as a special string arranger and began getting work with some terrific artists once again.

I realised that it was not for me to copy or release the recording so I put the tape aside as a curiosity and didn't think much more about it until I heard about Robert's death a few months back.

Around about that time, I saw the documentary film *Grizzly Man*. Towards the end of the film, in an immensely disturbing scene, we see the director Werner Herzog listening on headphones to the sound of the real-life subject of the film, Timothy Treadwell, being killed by a grizzly bear. The audience is saved this misery, but maybe there is something even worse about watching somebody listening to something so obviously horrific than actually listening to it yourself.

This got me thinking: what *would* I enjoy watching people listening to? And in that moment the concept of *Strange Face* (The 'Cello Song' project) was born.

Despite not being a photographer, I decided I would go around Britain giving people the opportunity to be amongst the first 150 people to hear the lost recording in exchange for my photographing them listening.

At first I was apprehensive – it was a bizarre proposition, even for me – but the moment I stopped my first subject in the street and watched a smile appear on his face as he enthusiastically agreed to put on the headphones, listen and be photographed, I knew I wouldn't look back. This felt like a good thing to do.

I would go to their houses. I would stop them in the streets. I would accost them in fields or on the land, whatever their age, whatever their profession, and ask them whether they would like to hear the record-ing. I would ask them irrespective of whether they knew Nick Drake's music or not, and I would record their thoughts and reactions at being amongst the first people in nearly 40 years to hear Drake singing this unreleased version of one of his finest songs.

I have done few things as stimulating, rewarding, fun and pleasurable in my entire working life.

(Michael Burdett is a television composer and founder of Little Death Orchestra – www.littledeathorchestra.com. He kindly wrote the above article for inclusion in this book.)

Tribute Concerts

When *Pink Moon* was first published tribute concerts were not the common phenomenon they are today. The earliest ones that were reviewed in the fanzine tended to feature lesser-known artists and were held in small pubs, clubs or old chapels, with small audiences. Towards the end of the Nineties though, they began to appear more frequently, each time bigger and better, and with more popular artists. To bring this section up to date I've included a review of *Way To Blue: The Songs of Nick Drake*, a tribute concert from the Barbican, 2010.

Bryter Layter in Brooklyn, New York
Janet Davis, *Pink Moon 15*, November 1997

It has been well documented that in his lifetime, Nick Drake never fully comprehended the impact his music had upon those who heard it. Certainly, he could not have foreseen that nearly 25 years after his death, and a continent away, the gifts he left would bring together an audience of 600 people to celebrate his legacy, and to share in the words and music of a man whose importance has only increased in the past quarter century.

November 8 was a cold, rainy day in the New York area, as a group of musicians and performers gathered in the sanctuary of St Ann's Church in Brooklyn Heights. Rehearsals for the evening show began at 3 p.m., with the arrival of the string players. Set on a riser on the right side of the stage, they tuned and warmed up, with parts of 'Way To Blue', 'Fruit Tree' and 'I Was Made To Love Magic', bringing the dusty old vinyl records to colourful, moving life.

Around 4p.m. the performers began trickling in. Duncan Sheik was the first to rehearse his numbers; he sang 'Hazey Jane II', the first time kneeling by the side of the stage, quietly, then twice more with a microphone, followed by 'Which Will'. The sound director, David Schnirman, reminded the singers to be strong and loud with their vocals, even though the tendency of the music itself was low and whispery, 'because that's how he did it'. Sloan Wainwright performed an expressive 'One Of These Things First', and Richard Barone sang 'Cello Song', his voice slipping up and down the octaves quite unexpectedly. The Welsh singer Katell Keineg was next on stage, with an impossibly high, yet clear, 'River Man'. Syd Straw sang 'I Was Made To Love Magic', and the strings came to the forefront with Susan Cowsill's 'Way To Blue'. Rebecca Moore's 'Fruit Tree' was a straightforward version, though now bearing the inflection of hindsight. 'Poor Boy', one of the more atypical entries in the Drake canon, was a deliberate change of pace, as Terre Roche was joined by backing vocalists Richard Barone, the program director, and the assistant stage manager, still working on the lyrics during this final run-through, and enjoying the back-and-forth rhythms of the song. 'From The Morning' featured the chiming vocal harmonies and piano work of the Kletter sisters, and Mimi Goese continued with 'Black Eyed Dog'. The final rehearsal numbers were Peter Blegvad's 'Clothes Of Sand', Richard Davies' 'Fly', and Richard Barone's energetic finale, 'Northern Sky'.

The stage was then set up for the evening, with the piano on the left, two stools in the centre for Peter Holsapple and Chris Cunningham, and the string section riser on the right. The doors opened around 7.30 p.m. for a fairly mixed audience, many being season ticket holders at St Ann's. Syd Straw came out to welcome everyone, wearing a black dress and fluffy boa; she thanked Joe Boyd for his blessing of the event. Her animated interpretation of 'I Was Made To Love Magic' began the performances. While several vocalists presented unadorned versions of Drake compositions, many added their own distinctive touches to the songs. Sloan Wainwright's deep and sonorous vocal style brought the richness of poetry to her two numbers, Mimi Goese's bright red evening dress and quirky movements accompanied her fluctuating vocal range in 'Black Eyed Dog', and Peter Blegvad used a prop cigarette to amuse the audience in 'Been Smokin' Too Long'. The ethereal singing voice of Katell Keineg took 'Time Has Told Me' and 'River Man' way up into the stained-glass reaches of the church's ceiling. Duncan Sheik startled the audience with not only his boyish, delicate vocal deliveries, but also his physical appearance; he wore jeans, an open-collared shirt, and black jacket, looking strikingly like Nick Drake himself on the back cover of *Five Leaves Left*, right down to the large square belt buckle. The highlight of the evening, however, came right after the intermission, when a lone, dusky light fell on the solitary figure of Peter Holsapple, the organiser and musical director of the programme, as he played 'Horn'.

During the intermission, the tall, distinctive Joe Boyd was seen talking with the sound crew and mingling with the audience members who recognised him; and his unannounced presence certainly added to an atmosphere of appreciation and celebration.

Although the interpretations and performances were magical, it was slightly disappointing that there was hardly a mention of Nick Drake himself, the musician whose influence had so obviously touched a very diverse group of talents. Aside from thanks by Peter Holsapple during the curtain calls, for the 'great material' he and the others had to work with, there were no other references to add to Drake's presence that evening. However, the energy and reverence brought to the performances, and the appreciation shown as each artist brought a song to his or her own voice, made this an evening to remember; a rare and cherished opportunity to celebrate the life and many gifts of Nick Drake.

The Direction Home (If you know the Way to Blue)
John Stokes, *Pink Moon 19*, October 1999

Tonight Matthew, I'm going to be ... Nick Drake.

Actually it wasn't quite like that. There were no imitators here tonight. All fourteen of the performers did it their way; but, much more than this, they each displayed a reverence for the words and music contained in songs that have been around for many years but only now, it seems, have come of age. If Qoheleth, that wise old prophet whose reflections on life form the Old Testament book of Ecclesiastes, was right in his contention that for everything there is a season and time for every matter under heaven, then I sense some inexplicable perception that now, as the earth's axle creaks towards Y2K, is the season for the songs of Nick Drake. The seeds and the stalk of Nick's fruit tree have lain relatively dormant in the ground for such a long time but now the tree is in full blossom. Nick's art is reaping a full harvest and the artists performing here tonight were fully aware of their task in ensuring that all will be safely gathered in.

Over the weekend of Friday 24th to Sunday 26th September, 1999, the London Barbican Centre, a cultural oasis within earshot of the chimes of many city clocks, held a celebration of the English roots tradition under the collective banner 'English Originals'. Friday night was party night with a 60th anniversary concert for Topic Records, and if you've never heard of Topic Records you surely have no sense of history for British folk song and thus you could honestly disregard the following soundbite from *Mojo* magazine: 'The Barbican exposes the irrefutable diversity of English musical heritage with its long-standing bastion, Topic Records.' A bastion of the full pocket also prevailed on the Sunday as all entertainment, including a talk by the folk singer Shirley Collins, 'In Praise of English Folk Music', was entirely free of charge. Stuck in between these first and last days, there was a full chapter of song and chat which culminated, on Saturday 25th September at 7.30 p.m. in the Barbican's main hall, with a tribute to Nick Drake. If you want to attach importance to dates then it could be said that this tribute concert was held to commemorate the passing of thirty years since the release, in September 1969, of Nick's first album. And if you want to attach importance to profits then there were none because all the proceeds from the night's concert were graciously donated to Mind: The Mental Health Charity in order to help awareness of their work with young people in schools. Thus all the artists who performed agreed to do so without payment.

Nick Drake himself probably went without any substantial payment for his compositions during his lifetime. Not one of his three official albums sold more than a few thousand copies, so it can truly be said that no one loved Nick for his money. Since Nick's death however, many people have come to love Nick for his art. Those three official albums contained just 28 songs and four instrumentals. A poor boy's legacy you may consider, but not so; an entire universe can be found in each of Nick Drake's songs, so those 32 represent an immense starry, starry night. 23 of Nick's songs were on offer on the starry night of the 25th of September at the Barbican Centre. 23 songs performed by 14 different artists.

Driving through London is a nightmare these days. The push and shove of city streets not only happens between Monday and Friday: the snarl ups and scowls overlap into weekend pursuits as me and JPF, my travelling companion, found on that busy Saturday evening. I have a lot to thank JPF for; he dragged the corpse of Nick Drake before me and pointed to the green shoots of a fruit tree growing by the graveside. Nick's songs made the journey lighter but we wouldn't have fared any easier if we'd taken the train: apparently there was a body on the line at Liverpool St: real blood on the tracks. We left the car and took a cab, arriving as it happened with 10 minutes spare to sample the whiff of culture that pervades the Barbican Centre.

Both JPF and I know Nick's songs pretty well, but only as performed on record by Nick. As we sat in our comfortable bucket seats we really didn't know what to expect, and we certainly didn't expect the interpretation of 'Pink Moon' by Robyn Hitchcock. What Spielberg was to Private Ryan, so Hitchcock was to Nick Drake: loud electric guitar, noisy confusion, chords and bullets flying, taking no prisoners. JPF turned to me and said 'It's Punk Moon!' and so it was. Yet this was no bastardisation of Nick's song: this was taking it further: pushing it to the brink of apocalypse, menacingly warning us: 'I saw it written and I saw it say/Pink Moon is on its way/And none of you stand so tall/ Pink Moon gonna get ye all.' If we thought we were in for a pleasant ride of harmony through the English countryside, Hitchcock's guitar style and psychedelic outfit made us sit up and take notice: one day that pink moon could really get us all. The following version of 'River Man' wasn't quite so menacing though.

I suppose, possibly because it was so outrageous, Robyn Hitchcock's

171

artillery-led version of 'Pink Moon' was my favourite performance of the night, but there were some other quite stunning interpretations of Nick's songs. Eileen Rose, a young American singer, transformed 'Black Eyed Dog' into a freight train that gathered speed and momentum as it swept through us and the auditorium. She also performed 'Hazey Jane II' with not quite so much power. There were performances of 'Saturday Sun' and 'From The Morning' by Katherine Williams, a young and rather shy chainsmoker; Hank Dogs were given 'Place To Be'; David Gray chose 'Way To Blue' and Trashmonk impressed with venerable versions of 'At The Chime Of A City Clock' and 'Joey'. The eastern bloc gave us Boris Grebenshikov with 'Time Of No Reply' and 'Rider On The Wheel' and the Pete Vuckovic-performed 'Road' and 'Which Will'. It really was an international affair.

Talking of affairs, picture this somewhat strange one: on to the stage sauntered a pop star looking for all the world like Michael Hutchence before he met Paula Yates and became a rock star. There were squeals and screams from the pop star's travelling fan club who, like their idol, probably hadn't arrived on the planet before the day that Nick Drake had left the same place. Bernard Butler looked cool; a new direction had taken him away from the pop band Suede, them of suburban angst and Brett with the Bowie voice. That new direction, or perhaps it was the continuation of a well trod previously found path, had brought the pop star to the Barbican where he took up an acoustic guitar in the spotlight to perform a song that the *NME* had called 'The greatest English love song of modern times.' When the screams had died down I sensed a kind of hush all over the world as Butler started those wonderful lines: 'I never felt magic as crazy as this/I never saw moons knew the meaning of the sea/I never held emotion in the palm of my hand/Or felt sweet breezes in the top of a tree/But now you're here/Brighten my northern sky.' The performance was faultless. I could've screamed too like a spotty teenager blinded by aura and charisma and recovering from my first wet dream. But I didn't. Thank God though for pop stars who listen to Nick Drake.

The violinist Nigel Kennedy was due to perform but he couldn't make it – perhaps the Villa didn't have an away game in the Capital, but it didn't really matter as other performers entertained with their own interpretations: Ben & Jason performed 'Man In A Shed' and 'Voice From The Mountain'; a bare footed and very husky Jackie Dankworth, yes, yes, the daughter of Cleo and Johnny, added some jazz to 'Cello Song' and 'Fruit Tree', and Nikki Leighton Thomas stepped from the shadows to give us her versions of 'One Of These Things First' and 'Things Behind The Sun'. There was just one more artist to perform but before the mention of her familiar name, credit must be given to Kate St John who lived up to her title and orchestrated some wonderfully divine string arrangements, out of which the performers were able to breathe their new lives into Nick's songs. That familiar name? Beverley Martyn, the former wife of John Martyn who was Nick's close friend and artist in common. I won't be unkind but I think Beverley was a little out of practice. They should have given her songs ('Time Has Told Me') to Bernard Butler and ('I Was Made To Love Magic') to Robyn Hitchcock. We would then have completed the night with Nick's music ringing well and truly in our ears as we made our journey home.

Way to Blue: The Songs of Nick Drake, Barbican 23/01/10
Joe Muggs www.theartsdesk.com

The dominant look among all ages of the sell-out audience at the Barbican Hall last night was distinctly 'smart-Bohemian', with plenty of thick-rimmed specs, duffle coats and subtly outré hairdos visible as they took their seats and gave one another knowing nods on spotting the 'Fruit Tree' motif in the stage décor. For Nick Drake, the fragile Cambridge-born singer-songwriter who died of an overdose of antidepressants in 1974 aged 26, is perhaps the perfect cult artist: utterly singular, too intense and serious to be appreciated in his short lifetime, but increasingly influential on the mainstream with each passing year.

The musicians gathered to pay tribute to him, appropriately, were all singular artists too: the question of how returned-from-retirement folkie Vashti Bunyan, Eighties pop star Green Gartside of Scritti Politti, wordy psychedelic revivalist Robyn Hitchcock and jazz pianist Zoe Rahman would all work together provoked an air of intrigued anticipation.

What really set Drake apart in his own time was that, although seen as part of a folk idiom by his connections to John Martyn and the rest of super-producer Joe Boyd's Witchseason stable, he was as much a jazz and post-classical composer as anything else, closer to Dvořák and Debussy, Nina Simone and Charles Mingus than to Fairport Convention or The Incredible String Band. So it was fitting that the show was conceived and put together with the involvement of Boyd and Drake's friend and string arranger Robert Kirby, who died last October.

It was also good that the show began instrumentally, Rahman liquefying Drake's dense cluster chords in her elegant piano runs as original Drake sideman Danny Thompson's equally jazz-inflected stand-up bass-playing glid beneath the string melodies of 'Joey'. Rahman and Thompson would later duet on an even more startlingly lovely 'One Of These', this even starker arrangement showing even better just how brilliantly odd and affecting many of the changes in Drake's writing really were.

It's a shame that the singers, at first, were not able to show this off so well. Robyn Hitchcock, a man clearly possessed of no small ego (as well as a series of eye-molesting patterned satin shirts) clicked his Cuban heels and threw rockstar shapes as he spat out 'Parasite' in Lennon-like cynical tones, bringing Drake's intense poetry to the fore but trampling musical subtlety under those heels. Green Gartside's voice, conversely, is a subtle instrument, and he acquitted himself well on 'Fruit Tree'; his problem, however, was the extreme distinctiveness of his breathy pop-soul style, which made the song his own rather than submitting himself to the song.

A very similar problem afflicted Vashti Bunyan, whose flute-like voice on 'Which Will' was beautiful, but made it sound like a Vashti Bunyan song rather than bringing out its innate qualities. And West Midlands newcomer Scott Matthews over-emoted 'Place To Be' in that pained, slightly cod-Irish style that has proved so commercial in the hands of modern MOR singers like David Gray and James Morrison.

However, far more sensitive interpretations were provided by young Gibraltarian jazz singer Kirsty Almeida, the husky-voiced androgyne Krystle Warren, and Irish singer Lisa Hannigan. Almeida looked potentially annoyingly kooky in crop-top, patchwork gypsy skirt and bowler hat, but the cool directness of her interpretation of 'Cello Song' was a delight, while Warren's treatment of 'Time Has Told Me' as a straightforward soul ballad exposed the twists of Drake's songwriting and his compositional similarities to Nina Simone brilliantly, completely stunning the crowd.

All these last three came together with the event's musical director Kate St John to create a backing vocal group for Teddy Thompson. I wasn't familiar with Thompson before, having a natural suspicion for celebrity offspring (he is the son of Richard and Linda Thompson) but his vocal was a revelation – powerful, but again submitting all ego to the subtleties of 'Poor Boy', unequivocally allowing Drake to lead the way. With the joyous harmonies of the backing vocals buoying it up, this rendition ended the first half on an almighty high, a southern-states Al Green-style country/soul feel blending with English pastoralism to create a wonderfully fresh synthesis.

The second half managed to maintain momentum, with many of the singers that hadn't shone redeeming themselves. Gartside joined in a nicely low-key 'Way To Blue' with Thompson and Hannigan, Bunyan sang a very peculiar and intriguing song, 'I Remember', by Drake's mother Molly, and Matthews atoned for his earlier over-singing by, after a false start, delivering 'Day Is Done' with perfect understatement. When Boyd took the stage to deliver his appreciation of Robert Kirby, this too managed to be understated without dropping momentum from the show. Even when the singers were able to really let go, as on Warren's completely a capella 'Hanging On A Star' and Hannigan's astounding voodoo blues stomp take on 'Black Eyed Dog', the song came first and the treatment was there to support it.

Even Robyn Hitchcock came good in a solo encore, albeit on a song of his own. It's ironic that while he was unable to tone down his flouncing mannerisms on Drake's songs, he performed the deeply strange and quite gripping 'I Saw Nick Drake' dead straight, creating a hushed, even awestruck atmosphere in the auditorium. A final 'Voice From The Mountain' capitalised on this atmosphere, turning into something downright mystical as all the event's singers completely gave themselves up to the forlorn otherworldly gospel of Drake's singular songwriting. Although the evening had not been without flagging moments,

moments like this were a tribute to how much talent was gathered there, and what can be achieved when the demands of great talents are subsumed to a greater vision.

Psychology

There was plenty of psychological debate in the pages of *Pink Moon*. It wasn't everybody's cup of tea, but I always found it fascinating; and it was relevant because educating people about different types of mental illness could prevent someone like Nick being incorrectly labelled. The insights into depression and the types of medication Nick took are also of interest.

Donnah Anderson, who wrote most of these pieces, was a *Pink Moon* reader from Australia. At the time of writing these articles she was in the third year of a four year Bachelor of Psychology with Honours degree at the University of New England, NSW, Australia.

Depression, Manic Depression and Mr N.R. Drake
Donnah Anderson, *Pink Moon 11*, July 1997

I've noticed in my readings about Nick Drake he is sometimes referred to as a 'manic depressive'. My knowledge of psychology made me wary of this label. Everything I've read about Nick and listening to his music indicates to me that he was depressed, but not manically depressed. Many people use the term 'manic depression' to mean a severe or long lasting depression, not realising the mania side of it construes a different disorder.

It is a strange task to attempt to diagnose someone who has been dead for nearly a quarter of a century, and someone who I've never interviewed or given psychological tests. Instead, I'm basing my opinion on Nick's music (the lyrics mainly) and things he's been quoted as saying.

Firstly, to define depression and mania: depression is a sad, low and lethargic state in which life seems bleak and overwhelming. Mania is the opposite of depression and is a state of frenzied energy and euphoria. Usually, moods such as happiness or sadness are transient responses to life events. In people diagnosed as having a mood disorder the moods last a long time, colour all their interactions with the world and disrupt their normal functioning. There are two main types of mood disorders, depression and manic depression (now known as bipolar disorder). In depression the person suffers recurrent depression but has no history of mania. Bipolar disorder entails alternating periods of depression and mania, usually with intervening periods of normal mood. Most bipolar mood disorders begin with a manic episode.

The symptoms of depression include emotional sadness, loss of pleasure from anything, lack of affection for other people, lack of motivation, dramatic decreases in activity, slow, quiet speech and movements, reduced eye contact with others, thinking of oneself as a failure and physically unattractive, and blaming oneself for almost everything. Confusion is common, although no intellectual impairment seems to occur. Physical symptoms such as insomnia and changes in appetite may also appear. Because depressed people focus inwardly, they may also magnify physical aches and pains.

Just reading through this list I can tick almost every characteristic as applying to Nick. For example, he told his mother he had 'failed at everything...' The lyrics of 'Know', 'Hazey Jane I' and 'The Thoughts Of Mary Jane' illustrate Nick's difficulty in relating to other people. Nick didn't feel comfortable with his height and physique, suffered insomnia, seemed confused, withdrew from social and professional contact, and the 'Poor Boy' was so worried about his health (to name a few instances...).

In contrast, during a manic episode people feel euphoric and jovial, although the joy is out of all proportion to what is happening in their lives. They are driven, impulsive, extremely talkative, desire constant excitement and companionship, but do not realise they seem overwhelming to other people. Their behaviour is hyperactive, rushed, loud, and they make grandiose and impractical plans. Listening to Nick's music he certainly doesn't seem manic. The only evidence I can find that suggests anything like bipolar disorder are references to his last years as 'see-saw years' and 'dipping and soaring' with 'brief periods of elation overcompensated by plunges into despair' (Patrick Humphries, *Record Hunter*, March 1991; *Mojo*, Feb. 1997). I interpret the 'dipping' to refer to depression and the 'soaring' to times of a more normal, happier mood state. Also, often cited is Nick's sudden happiness during the later months of 1974 where he 'loved Paris and the Seine'. But, again, I see this as a return to a normal mood state rather than a manic episode. Indeed, at this time Nick realised he might be happier writing for others, which is probably a practical solution to his distaste for promotion and performing, rather than a grandiose manic plan. The quest to find an alternative occupation, such as attempting to enter the army and starting a computer programming career, do not, in themselves, constitute manic plans, especially when his motivation to write music was at a low ebb. I feel if Nick did have manic episodes we would probably have several more Drake CDs on our shelves! During manic episodes productivity skyrockets (but not necessarily quality!). Instead, we have a slim, yet slowly worked perfectionistic legacy.

Nick's stillness, quietness, perfectionism, withdrawal from human interaction, sensitivity and deep thoughts are indicative of his introverted temperament, and also of his severe and chronic depression. Incidentally, introverts also tend to excel at tasks that require fine work, e.g. counter-point guitar!

A closing thought as to why Nick's music is so deeply moving to the rest of us. One of my text books* posits an idea for consideration: i.e. that depressed people probably see the world and themselves more realistically than 'normal' people. That is, non-depressed people overestimate their chances of success and underestimate their chances of failure. It is a human coping mechanism (or defence mechanism) that allows us to navigate through life. Nick's view of life, as reflected in his music, hits a nerve with us – a part of our thinking and feelings we have

---

* Atkinson, R.L., Atkinson, R.C., Smith, E.E., & Bem, D.J. (1993). *Introduction To Psychology* (11th ed.) New York: Harcourt Brace Jovanovich (pp 644–645).

suppressed to enable us to cope. Indeed, in Nick's own words (speaking to Brian Wells) he describes himself thus: 'I can't cope. All the defences are gone. All the nerves are exposed.' The genius of Nick Drake was that he captured that intense vulnerability so precisely in his music. It's so gentle and passive yet miraculously manages to pierce your heart and leave you spinning. A taste of what it was to be Nick Drake, maybe?

Following Donnah Anderson's fascinating essay, 'Depression, Manic Depression and Mr N. R. Drake', in issue 11, there was one particular question that stuck in my mind: Could Nick have been cured of his illness?

I asked Donnah and she kindly replied with the following (from *PM12*, June 20, 1997): "It's a pleasure to try and provide some answers to your questions regarding treatments for depression. Firstly, there are no real 'cures' for depression, mainly because psychiatrists and psychologists haven't worked out just what causes depression. There are several theories, most of them looking at different parts of the elephant and none of them seeing the whole animal. Most probably, depression is one of those complex disorders caused by the interaction of several factors – including genetic predispositions, personality factors, stress, learned ways of thinking and an alienating society, all of which combine to leave certain vulnerable individuals feeling hopeless, helpless, deflated and suicidal. I'll now outline some treatments for depression, some of which were available in Nick's day and some more recent. In general, psychology has progressed a great deal in the last 20 or 30 years."

Drugs

Antidepressant drugs are prescribed by a psychiatrist, who is a medical doctor specialising in medical illness. (Psychologists cannot prescribe drugs as yet because they are not medical doctors. Psychologists study and treat mental illness without using drugs.) Antidepressants are not stimulants, as amphetamines are, and do not produce feelings of euphoria and increased energy. Antidepressants help elevate mood by increasing the availability of two neurotransmitters (norepinephrine and serotonin) that are deficient in some cases of depression. Antidepressant drugs were discovered by accident and there is still confusion as to how and why they work, and why they don't work for all people suffering depression. They were first available in the Fifties, and today there are three main types:

TRICYCLICS

This is the type prescribed to Nick. Tricyclics prevent serotonin and norepinethrine from being absorbed, thus allowing a longer period of stimulation by these chemicals in the brain. Side-effects include dizziness, drowsiness (which Nick took advantage of to try and help him sleep), blurred vision, rapid heartbeat (as Nick discovered on that fateful November night), dry mouth, excessive sweating and decreased libido. For these reasons many people stop taking the drug.

MAOIs: (MONOAMINE OXIDASE INHIBITORS)

These drugs block an enzyme that destroys serotonin and norepinephrine, thereby allowing them to remain longer than usual without being deactivated. MAOIs are usually only prescribed after tricyclics have proved ineffective.

Tricyclics and MAOIs take three weeks or longer to start giving relief (which has doctors confused as to how they actually work).

SECOND GENERATION ANTIDEPRESSANTS

Not available in Nick's era, these target single, specific neurotransmitters. For example, Prozac blocks the reuptake of serotonin. Prozac is controversial because it occasionally provokes suicidal thoughts and changes personality, but has fewer side-effects and is more predictable than tricyclics and MAOIs.

Non-Drug Treatments

ELECTRO-CONVULSIVE TREATMENT (ECT)

This treatment was apparently suggested for Nick, as it is usually successful for people who don't respond to drugs. Basically, an electric shock is given across the head (by suitably qualified medical staff) inducing a seizure. Patients are anaesthetised and do not remember the procedure afterwards. ECT was overused and misused in the Fifties and gained a poor reputation. As antidepressant drugs became available, ECT use declined. In the Seventies it made a partial comeback, with many modifications. Side-effects involve amnesia for one to six months after the treatment is finished.

SLEEP THERAPY

Most depressed people have difficulty sleeping, suggesting a disturbance of their biological rhythms. Normal people only have small periods of REM sleep (the part of sleep when we dream) in the first half of the night. This trend is determined by changes in body temperature. During the first half of the night body temperature declines and there is little REM sleep. After about 3 a.m., body temperature rises and REM sleep increases. In depressed people body temperature rises early and REM sleep begins early and occupies a great deal of sleep time.

Several methods of adjusting sleep patterns can alleviate depression. One method involves having the person go to sleep earlier than usual, in accordance with their body temperature (e.g. go to sleep at 6 p.m. and wake at 2 a.m.). On succeeding nights the person goes to sleep half an hour later until bedtime reaches a suitable time (e.g. 11 p.m.). The result is a relief from depression that lasts for months.

Most of the research on sleep therapy seems to have been done in the Eighties, although in 1973 research showed that keeping a depressed person awake all night produced rapid relief from depression, although the relief only lasted a day or so. Nick may have inadvertently discovered this effect for himself by maintaining a routine of working at night. There is also the tape of Nick talking where he stayed up all night.

COGNITIVE THERAPY

This has the same rate of success as drugs but improvement is more longstanding, whereas with drugs, a person would probably have to continue taking them indefinitely. Cognitive therapy involves ana-lysing a person's thoughts, expectations and interpretation of events. The therapist teaches more effective ways of interpreting and thinking about experiences. For example, depressed people appraise themselves in negative and self-critical ways. They expect to fail, magnify their failures and minimise their successes. The therapist tries to help clients recognise the distortions in their thinking through carefully directed questioning.

A programme for treating depression might include cognitive ther-apy, as well as relaxation training, increasing social interaction, increas-ing pleasant events and teaching social skills. (These therapies are usually the role of psychologists.) Also, a combination of cognitive therapy and drug treatment is common.

Success rates for treatments of depression

Tricyclics: 64% of people respond well. MAOIs: less than 64% of peo-ple respond well. ECT: 80% of severely depressed people respond well. Cognitive Therapy: about the same as tricyclics.

As far as I can gather, the only drugs available in the Seventies were tricyclics and MAOIs. I do know that far less people are hospitalised today than in the Seventies, mainly due to the success of new drugs and cognitive therapies.

A question I've often pondered is, does anyone know how many pills Nick took the night he died? In one quote Nick's father says Nick '...took the whole lot,' yet in other places it's said he took a few. It's just that if someone takes a whole bottle of pills they generally intend themselves some harm (or to block out the pain forever), whereas if they only take a few over the prescribed amount they might be trying to relieve their symptoms quickly. This is an example of what psychologists call 'creative non-adherence' – where a person adjusts or supplements their prescribed treatment regimen in an attempt to regain control over their illness...

Schizophrenia and Mr N.R. Drake
Donnah Anderson, *Pink Moon 11*, July 1997

In a few instances Nick's name is linked with schizophrenia. For example, Gabrielle Drake (in *Melody Maker*, July 1987) mentions Nick's schizophrenia 'for want of a better word'. Also, Nick Kent (in *NME*, February 8, 1975) describes 'Know' as a 'paean to schizophrenia'. Pee Pee Charlbury (*Panache*, 1977) describes 'Know' as 'practically a definition of schizophrenia'. I do not think Nick was schizophrenic, although several of his depressive symptoms do appear in some forms of schizophrenia as well. For example, lack of movement (catatonia), lack of speech, and lack of affect (i.e. emotional numbness, feeling like a zombie). Patients with this form of schizophrenia usually have abnormal brain structures and a history of poor social and educational functioning prior to the onset of the illness, whereas Nick's education and social interactions were normal (or even better than normal!) during his childhood.

Another form of schizophrenia has symptoms of auditory and visual hallucinations. If some of Nick's songs are taken literally, such as 'Pink Moon', 'I saw it written and I saw it say', and 'Voice From The Mountain', it could be inferred he had visions of an apocalyptic pink moon and heard voices calling him from the mountains, seas and his neighbourhood! However, he did read a lot of poetry and was entirely aware of the use of metaphor, so I interpret these songs metaphorically rather than literally. After all, his psychiatrist prescribed antidepressants and not antipsychotics!

The song 'Know' does not necessarily indicate or define schizophrenia; however it is applicable to depression. I think many people view schizophrenia as the situation where people have more than one personality, and may have taken the lyrics, 'know that I love you, know I don't care', to refer to the idea of conflicting personalities. The Dr Jekyll/Mr Hyde syndrome is really another disorder: that of multiple personality disorder (which Nick didn't appear to have either).

I interpret 'Know' as an expression of emotional numbness. For example, one knows on an intellectual level that one loves another person (e.g. we all know we love our parents – 'Know that I love you'), but when one suffers from depression one cannot feel or express emotion ('Know I don't care'). Nick can see the people in his life and their concern for him ('Know that I see you'), but he is not the person he was before the depression developed and cannot interact with the people in his life ('Know I'm not there').

So, in my humble, totally fallible opinion, Nick was severely and chronically depressed, but not manic or schizophrenic.

Who Can Know the Thoughts of Nick Drake (Why He Flies or Goes Out in the Rain) Christina Giscombe, *Pink Moon 15*, 1998

I was fascinated enough by Donnah Anderson's article to write in and offer a few comments of my own. Although I only have a BSc(Hons) in Psychology, during my course I found psychopathology particularly interesting, and my studies also gave me a healthy scepticism of the psychiatric profession with all their dependence on drug therapy and labelling; psychiatrists coming from a medical rather than psychological background.

I agree with Donnah that Nick was not manic depressive, just depressive. She says that she does not think Nick was schizophrenic because of his seemingly normal childhood. However, although I doubt Nick was ever a full-blown schizophrenic, he could have been borderline. After all, his headmaster at prep school said of Nick at a very early age that they did not feel they knew him well, a strange comment to put on a child's school report unless they thought it worthy of comment. Anyway, the first onset of schizophrenia often starts in late teens/early twenties, so you can be afflicted in spite of a normal childhood.

Patrick Humphries in his biography *Nick Drake* (Bloomsbury, 1997) confirms that apart from Tryptizol, Nick was also being prescribed Stelazine and Disipal. According to my copy of the GPs' bible, *The British National Formulary*, which comes out annually as a guide to prescription drugs for medical practitioners, Stelazine (Trifluoperazine) is prescribed for 'schizophrenia and related psychoses, tranquillisation in behavioural disturbances, psychoneuroses', so obviously his psychiatrist at least thought he had psychotic tendencies. Disipal (Orphenadrine

Hydrochloride) is prescribed for 'Parkinsonism (the shakes) particularly with apathy and depression; drug induced extrapyramidal symptoms', in Nick's case probably to counter the effects of the antipsychotic drug, although one person at least is quoted in Patrick Humphries' book as saying they saw Nick shaking like a leaf as a result of his illness.

Tryptizol (Amitriptyline Hydrochloride) is described as an antidepressant of the tricyclic group, and is deemed innocuous enough to prescribe to children as young as six for 'nocturnal enuresis' (bedwetting). Interestingly, its side-effects are listed, among many, as 'cardiovascular: postural hypotension (low blood pressure), tachycardia (irregular heartbeat), and syncope, particularly in high doses. 'Syncope' according to my Oxford English Dictionary means 'failure of the heart leading to unconsciousness and even death'.

Donnah is right that schizophrenia has nothing to do with 'split/ multiple personality'. The main symptoms are auditory/visual hallucination and disassociation of the personality. Schizophrenics often use words bizarrely and sentences often consist of word associations that are homophonic or rhyme. Nick's line in 'Way To Blue', 'Have you seen the land living by the breeze?' could be a classic example of a schizophrenic line except, thankfully, songwriters and poets are allowed artistic licence. This line is the only line I could see in Nick's lyrics that could be remotely described as indicating schizophrenic thought. Compare and contrast this with the lyrics of Syd Barrett, with all his trips to Heave and Ho and Gigolo aunts and Bay lemonades and all sorts of fabulous creatures (bless him). There is nothing in Nick's lyrics to suggest schizophrenia.

Personally, I have little truck with the psychiatric profession and all their labels and pills. However, the fact is five weeks after the release of *Pink Moon* Nick suffered a major nervous breakdown severe enough to get him hospitalised for five weeks. We should not underestimate the severity of his illness, and I'm sure the psychiatric staff were only interested in helping him as much as they could.

Donnah Boyce makes a great point in *PM12*, 'if someone takes a whole bottle of pills they generally intend themselves some harm (or to block out the pain forever) whereas if they only take a few over the prescribed amount they might be trying to relieve their symptoms quickly.'

In *PM13* Mark Fogarty comments that his therapist informed him that the therapeutic dose of Tryptizol is in the tens of milligrams, the lethal dose in the hundreds of milligrams, 'so an accident would be unlikely'.

Patrick Humphries in the same issue of *PM* says that he believes it was an accidental overdose as for suicide there has to be an intent to take your own life, and because Nick was happier then than he had been for a long time. It is said that if he'd meant it he would not have done it at home and caused pain to his family. But for a painfully shy and retiring person this might have been the obvious place, surrounded by the people who loved and understood him.

However, it is well known that when someone makes a decision to commit suicide they very often do lighten up in mood and appear to others to be more carefree. A coroner at an English inquest is always very loath to give a verdict of suicide unless there is no other conclusion to come to. It is still a stigma, and was even illegal until the Sixties. A suicide verdict can cause problems with insurance for relatives, but it seems even the Drakes' high social class did not deter the coroner from pronouncing a suicide verdict.

Rodney Drake is quoted as saying in an interview that Nick 'took the lot'. Patrick Humphries in his book says it was anything between three and 30 tablets, and that Nick could not have been aware of their lethality. However, think about it, would a psychiatrist prescribe a drug on which it's easy to overdose (three tablets and you're gone) to a clinically depressed patient? I think the practice is only to prescribe a few tablets at a time to depressed patients to pre-empt overdoses. This suggests that perhaps Nick collected the tablets until he had a large quantity. Surely if he overdosed on, say, the 10 he was prescribed, then should that not be a 'misadventure' verdict because the psychiatrist over-prescribed? This is a real puzzle. To me the facts seem to point to Nick having taken such a large dose that there were no two ways in the coroner's mind that it must have been intentional. An existential philosophical treatise on suicide, *The Myth of Sisyphus*, by Camus, was found on his bedside table. As Stephen Greenhalgh says in *PM12* in his poem 'For Lilac Time', 'It was claimed there was no note ... Hell; what were the songs you wrote?'

If Nick chose suicide we have to respect his decision as a valid one.

Thoughts on Nick Drake
Donnah Anderson, *Pink Moon 17*, October 1998

As part of my university studies I've recently been reading about the relationship between stress and depression. It's often mentioned that there were no traumas in Nick's life to 'cause' his depression. There have been numerous studies about different types of stress, and apparently some individuals react to minor stress or chronic strain with depression, while hardier individuals require serious stress to become depressed. The types of people who buckle under minor stress are sensitive, perfectionist types with high expectations and low self-esteem. Minor stresses in Nick's life could be his move from Cambridge to London, giving up uni, going against his parents' idea of a suitable career, his records not selling, having to attempt to perform, lack of money, living alone etc... Apparently, these less hardy people think about things in rather negative ways too. I found the lyrics of a song that Nick never recorded (in the *Scrapbook* series from David Housden, book no. 5) called 'Leaving Me Behind'. The lyrics of one verse go like this: 'The chances they've come/But the chances they've been lost/ Success can be gained but at too great a cost/For some there's a future to find/ But I think they're leaving me behind.' Likewise, in 'At The Chime Of A City Clock', Nick sings about himself: 'A city star/Won't shine too far/On account of the way you are.' I think these lyrics and others like them say much about Nick's thoughts. Nick seems to have attributed his 'failure' to something within himself rather than some external factor (i.e., an internal attribution of negative events), probably his reserved nature.

An example of an external explanation could be putting a failure down to 'bad luck' or 'the economic climate' or 'someone else's actions'. Nick seems to have blamed himself and with this frame of mind success would cost him too much because he'd have to change his basic level of responding to the world. Also, if he did feel he couldn't perform because of his shyness (in the only interview Nick ever did he said he wasn't enjoying his performances), he would see this trait as something which he couldn't change and something that affected everything he did (what psychoanalysts term a stable, global attribution of negative events). Internal, stable and global attributions of negative events are correlated with depression. If this was the way Nick was thinking, then perhaps cognitive therapy would have benefitted him. Nick was intelligent, so he would seem a good candidate for some gentle cognitive challenging.

Another point that occurred to me when reading that Nick told his mother that his troubles seemed to start when he moved to London from Cambridge, was that this move would have changed Nick's self identity. He stopped being a student and started being a serious professional musician. He also stopped living in a residential college (where meals are provided, your room cleaned and mundane chores are almost nonexistent) and started living by himself in a large city to write his music (think of the lyrics to 'Place To Be': 'and now I'm older gotta get up clean the place'). In 'Hazey Jane II' the lyrics illustrate Nick's lack of coping ability in the city: '... when the world it gets so crowded that you can't look out the window in the morning'. I think the move to London involved a substantial change in lifestyle and identity. All changes in life are stressful, even 'positive' changes such as starting an exciting career with endless potentials such as fame and fortune, especially when he knew he was an innovative musician, but he was also aware of his natural reserve. Nick's high socioeconomic status and public school background were also at odds with his chosen path in life, someone in Patrick's biography says it was almost 'like slumming it really'. Downward socioeconomic mobility is cited as one of the risk factors for depression. So, in all, Nick could have been experiencing stress, albeit not traumatic shocking stuff, but insidious, chronic strain which may be harder to cope with than a sudden terrible event that you can identify, grieve over, work through and then get on with your life.

The role of stress as a causal factor in depression is not proven. However, it has been shown that stress is a mediating factor which may bring out a predisposed illness. That is, you have to be predisposed to depression (or anxiety, or schizophrenia or most other mental illnesses) to manifest the symptoms, but stress can speed up the process and maybe precipitate the first, or subsequent, episodes.

Film and Television

According to the BBC, an incredible half a million people watched Tim Clements' documentary, *A Stranger Among Us: Searching For Nick Drake*, which was screened in 1999. Speaking to the *Birmingham Post* about the film, which cost £70,000 to make, Tim Clements said: "He is better known now than he ever was when he was alive. His death was barely reported at the time. My aim is to get people to buy his records. It would be a dream to help get one of his albums in the charts. As a fan I wanted to share this wonderful musician with other people. Professionally, it was the challenge of making a film about someone who barely existed. There is no film footage, no girlfriends, almost nothing..."

A second Nick Drake documentary, *A Skin Too Few*, by Jeroen Berkvens, was released in late 2000. Writing in *Pink Moon 19*, Jeroen described the film: "I can tell you something about the film: it is finished, being approx 50 minutes, is shot on film, printed on 35mm for projection with very nice stereo sound and is called *A Skin Too Few*. People involved are Nick's sister Gabrielle Drake, producer Joe Boyd, college friend Brian Wells, musician Paul Weller, sound engineer John Wood, arranger Robert Kirby and photographer Keith Morris.

"*A Skin Too Few* tells Nick's life in a biographical way, starting in Burma. Because of the intimate nature of the subject it is a quiet film. The camera observes the landscapes which Nick lived in and described

191

in his lyrics in wide totals. Nick's music has its own special place in the film. For instance there is a scene with John Wood and Robert Kirby in which they show, by playing the original 8-track master tapes, how a Nick Drake song is built up.

"From an audio recording with his parents we hear in a very revealing way about the personal impact of their son's mental deterioration and about the terrible discovery of his lifeless body. These parts of the film include shots of Nick's room where he was raised and ultimately died. The deserted room changes during the course of the film because of the changing of the seasons and minor events.

"The title of the documentary is taken from an interview with Nick's sister, the actress Gabrielle Drake, who says: 'I believe that Nick was born with a skin too few.'"

In April, 1999, I interviewed Robert Kirby, for *Pink Moon 18*, and I asked him about his involvement in the film:

Jason Creed: I hear you were at Abbey Road studios recently, with John Wood, working on a new film about Nick, can you tell us what was going on there?

Robert Kirby: Jeroen Berkvens phoned me – it was last year actually – saying he was going to make a film. We were there on the 21st of January, I think control room 2. He phoned up and said they were doing a production – for their [Holland's] equivalent of the BBC – and he said John Wood was going to be there, would I go along? So, yes, I went along. I'd been working with Paul Weller, since the beginning of the year, on some tracks. I mean, he contacted me basically because of Nick. He came to Nick quite late apparently, getting on for 1990, or late Eighties, but is really into it. Anyway, when he heard that I was doing it, he asked if he could come along. So they spoke to Paul as well about his experience of Nick's music.

Jason: And they just sort of interviewed you there?

Robert: Yeah. Basically, we were up in the control room of studio 2, and John Wood brought along the original 4-tracks of *Bryter Layter* and *Five Leaves Left*. The gist of what we were doing was; John and I were at the desk, John engineering basically, but sort of talking generally about our reminiscences of Nick. It was a very non-hands-on method of film-ing. It was quite good: he (Jeroen) would ask you one question and then leave you to it, basically just wanted us to talk as if we were normal, you know, not like we had cameras pointed at us; and John just brought the faders up on various tracks and left them. And the main thing I can remember is them turning round and saying, 'Well, aren't you going to fiddle around with all these knobs that you've got there?' I mean, OK, it was a lot more basic back in Sound Techniques in the Sixties, but there were still quite a few knobs; but on Nick's tracks you could see it was just these four tracks sitting in the middle of a 48-track bench! And, of course, once John had brought the faders up, he sat back and we just chatted, and Jeroen said, 'Well, haven't you got things to do to it?' The stunning thing that came out of it, people forget, is what's on the record is what it sounded like in the studio. There's no sort of tarting about, you know, changing EQs, taking bits out, changing levels; I mean, the volume that something was playing at when it came in was the volume it was playing at when it finished, and you didn't touch it. So, that was the whole essence of the way John and Joe worked together, they got the sound correct to start with. I'd rather forgotten this over the years as well. But it was stunning, once we'd put the track on, and John had set them all to the level he wanted, you could just sit back for the whole track, and it sounded exactly like it does on the record. So, that was basically it. We went through various tracks.

A DVD of *A Skin Too Few* was included in the 2007 remastered edition of the *Fruit Tree* box set.

In 2000, Volkswagen used 'Pink Moon' as the soundtrack to its latest Cabriolet advert in America. David Browne wrote the following for *Entertainment Weekly*: "In recent years he has been the subject of a biog-raphy as well as tribute concerts in New York and London. His songs have been covered by Lucinda Williams and Kelly Willis and used in the film *Practical Magic*. But those nods pale next to that of Volkswagen, which last November debuted a commercial for its zippy Cabrio con-vertible. During the alluring minute-long spot, collegiate-looking kids take a night time drive through a wooded area on their way to a party, to the accompaniment of the wafting chords and whispery voice of 'Pink Moon'.

"The response was instantaneous, particularly from the twenty-somethings who may have never before heard Drake's timeless goth-folk. 'Pink Moon', which, according to SoundScan, had been selling between 85 and 108 copies in the weeks before, shot up to as many as 1,858 in a single week – not including the more than 5,000 copies sold on Amazon.com, which is linked to Volkswagen's website. Drake's 1994 anthology *Way To Blue* saw a similar leap. Capitalising on the interest, Drake's label, Hannibal, will soon be pitching 'Pink Moon' to radio, followed this summer by the release of remastered versions of Drake's three original albums. Later in the year, the label will bring out a previously unreleased demo tape recorded in 1967, which has Drake-ites drooling in anticipation."

The *San Francisco Examiner* reported that sales of 'Pink Moon' jumped from 6,000 in 1999 to 74,000 in 2000 as a direct result of the advert.

An often discussed topic in the pages of *Pink Moon* was the possibility of the existence of lost film footage of Nick Drake. In his article 'Caught on Camera?' from *PM19*, Julian Meek-Davies wrote: "I am curious, and in spite of myself I would like to see what the living, moving Nicholas Rodney Drake looked like. How did he walk, and how did he hold his guitar? I know from the *Complete Home Recordings* what he sounded like when he talked, but how does the voice relate to the whole – can some kind of picture be built up? If the alleged sighting of him at a James Taylor concert in 1970 were to prove to be authentic, it would be an interesting prize, one which I should be rather interested to see, along with anything else which might be lurking in the back of someone's cupboard.

"But would footage of Nick have to be stashed away like that? It could be that a piece of film showing him as a schoolboy is in fairly wide circulation. Interest has already been expressed by at least one *Pink Moon* reader in the film made by the late John Betjeman during the late Sixties of Marlborough College, at which the one-time Poet Laureate was a pupil, during the Twenties, and where Nick later studied before going on to Cambridge. The piece is typical of many such topographical films made by Betjeman for both the BBC and independent channels, and was part of a series on West Country towns commissioned but never shown by TWW. In it Betjeman provides a verse commentary on shots of Marlborough College, observing the boys as they go through their daily routine, speculating on their thoughts, hopes and dreams, and revealing his own past. As a period piece it is black and white film at its best, and as thought fodder, for those wishing to concentrate on things Nick must have seen and experienced, it is excellent value – the Polly Restaurant is featured at reasonable length, along with life in Upper School and in a senior study.

"Whether or not Nick actually puts in a fleeting appearance is not clear to me, but if one looks at the dining hall scene in the film, one boy, sitting at the head of one of the tables, bears such an uncanny resemblance to him that I immediately dashed to the nearest call box to contact Jason Creed! By way of 'directions' for anyone wishing to look for themselves, after entering the dining hall the camera pans down a line of boys, then down the tables. 'Nick' is the boy at the head of the third.

"Of course there are certain difficulties in making a final identification. The date of the film is unclear – between 1962 and 1964 – and it may be that it was shot before Nick's time at the school. The image is also subject to the criterion applied by Patrick Humphries to the James Taylor clip – 'there were a lot of boys in London who looked like Nick Drake' – and presumably at Marlborough too. Only someone who was there could authenticate it..."

On the 'place to be' chat room, February 19, 1999, Rob Bridgett wrote: "I have a video copy of the James Taylor concert in 1970 in which Nick is rumoured to be in the audience. He is only on screen for a couple of seconds laughing at a snuff commercial JT has just played. I don't know if anyone else has seen this but it does look uncannily like Nick right down to the boots. It is incredibly hard to verify anything like this but I would love to find out if it is him."

Speaking to Jason Creed on the phone on June 20, 1999, Robert Kirby said that he had recently received, from Gabrielle Drake a complete copy of the letter from which she read in Tim Clements' BBC2 film

A Stranger Among Us. In the letter, Nick mentions that he has recently been to a Francoise Hardy concert in London, which was filmed by the BBC, and writes about how he may well have been caught on camera. The concert was in London in 1967, but it's not known if the BBC still has the recording.

Still, no film footage of Nick as an adult or playing live has ever been found. The only known footage is a homemade Super-8 film from a Drake family holiday, shot when Nick was just a few years old. It was first shown to the public in 2000 as part of Jeroen Berkvens' documentary film *A Skin Too Few*.

Below is a transcription of an amateur tribute film made by Chris Brazier, entitled *Way To Blue*. It featured in *Pink Moon 19* after being discovered by a student at Cardiff University, in 1998. The film was made around 1985 and features an original interview with Nick's parents.

Way to Blue: A Tribute to Nick Drake
Chris Brazier, 1985

Chris Brazier.   It was on the tube, somewhere between Ladbroke Grove and Mile End, that I discovered Nick Drake, some five years after his death. I'd just come across the boxed set of his complete recorded works and bought it out of instinct. I didn't know then how much it would come to mean to me; and though I thought even then he looked a little like me, it was only later I found out we had the same birthday.

As the train journey went on my surroundings dwindled into insignificance and the story of Nick Drake's life, work and death opened up before me.

He was born in Burma on June 19, 1948. His father worked for a lumber company and met and married Nick's mother in Rangoon. The young family had a brief stay in another ex-imperial outpost, Bombay, before returning to this house which stands in a village near Stratford called Tanworth-in-Arden. With its rural charm and its 11 acres it suited the Drakes' upper-class Englishness perfectly, as did their choice of school for their son. Nick was sent to public school at Marlborough where he was in the same year as Mark Phillips, and where his own distinction was as an athlete.

Already he'd set himself apart though; the intolerant ebullience of public school life inevitably isolated him and he channelled his feelings into music. He bought a guitar which his parents thought appallingly expensive and taught himself to play it with another boy. He wrote sad songs about princesses and his romantic isolation. 'I was born to love no one,' he sang, 'no one to love me, only the wind in the long, green grass, the frost in a broken tree.'

All that year I listened to him, but only in the quietest, most solitary moments. It was as if I would be committing a sacrilege if I played Nick's first record, *Five Leaves Left*, to anyone else. It's an extraordinary debut. With its princess of the sky on her journey to the stars, and its river man with a plan for lilac time, the writing is certainly adolescent; but it's impossible to stand back from his strange, rich voice, its haunting, fragile beauty. In a way, its faults are its virtues; *Five Leaves Left* is the perfect encapsulation of poetic adolescence. It's the kind of record Keats might have made, had he been a rock singer.

Nick did enough at school to qualify for the last piece of the privileged educational jigsaw and went up to read English at Cambridge in the autumn of 1967. Nick loved Cambridge at first; its sense of the past fitted his introspection like a glove. He dressed in black, made midnight pilgrimages to the sea, and read the French symbolist poets. But the influences weren't all literary; the hippie underground was just hitting Britain and filtering through to the Cambridge that spawned the Pink Floyd. Nick smoked dope and listened to Van Morrison with the few friends that he'd made. He hated performing and usually just stared at his shoes while he sang, but he did pluck up enough courage to take part in an underground 'happening' at the Roundhouse in London, and there he was noticed by a member of Fairport Convention who introduced him to American producer Joe Boyd. Together they made *Five Leaves Left* and, on the strength of its good reviews, he left Cambridge to commit himself to a musical career.

In view of what happened later, do you think it was a mistake, Nick leaving university and committing himself so completely to music?
Rodney Drake: Well, looking at the thing in retrospect, I think it

wasn't a mistake. But, at the time, we certainly felt it was a mistake, and we tried as hard as we could to dissuade him from leaving Cambridge. It seemed to us a great pity that he shouldn't complete his degree.

Molly Drake: Yes, I think any parent would have felt the same. He only had nine months left to go, to take his degree, and it seemed a reasonable thing to do, but at the same time you had this feeling that maybe he was right, that this was his life and perhaps this was the obvious thing for him to do, not to waste any more time getting an English degree when he could be sort of forging ahead and getting into the life that he really wanted to. Don't you think so?

Rodney: Yes, I think that's so. And I think at that time, of course, we didn't know how good his music was; and I remember trying to persuade him not to leave by saying that if he could get a degree he would have a safety net, and his reply to that was that a safety net was the one thing he didn't want. And I think, yes, it was the right decision to leave Cambridge when he did. In fact, it might have been better if he'd left earlier.

Chris: Nick's first album didn't sell, despite the critical respect, but he made the second within a year. *Bryter Layter* is his best work; still sad, but more mature and less ostentatiously melancholy, and it contains his most perfect song, 'Northern Sky', the thought of which reduced me to tears one morning deep in the Himalayas and six months from home because suddenly it was as if Nick Drake came to symbolise everything that was of value in the culture I'd left behind.

Nick wrote *Bryter Layter* in the course of a bitter winter that he spent alone in a flat in Hampstead, huddling under blankets for warmth as he wrote; but when it too failed to sell, he lapsed into chronic depression and retreated home to his parents.

What was Nick's depression actually like?

Rodney: Well, you're talking about the last three years of his life, which he spent here at home with us; and it was a very difficult time for all of us, most of all I suppose for him. He used to spend a great deal of time sitting, not doing very much, and there weren't very many times when he was prepared to talk to us a great deal. He listened to quite a lot of music, and used to play quite a lot of his own music, but he rarely, rarely opened up to us; less to me than he did to his mother. In fact, I think she could tell you more about it than I can.

Molly: It was terribly distressing because you always felt, all the time, that there was something you could be doing, helping him, and you didn't know what it was; and whatever you seemed to do seemed to be the wrong thing. And you felt, terribly, that you needed someone to help you and guide you. I used to say to Rodney, there ought to be a training college where we could go, so that we could find out what was the best thing to do for Nick. Sometimes he wouldn't talk for weeks on end.

Rodney: He often used to get up at night and go downstairs to the kitchen, and we always knew that he was bad then. And Molly usually used to hear him and, often, in the middle of the night, she'd get up and go down and talk to him downstairs at about 2 or 3 o'clock in the morning. And he'd talk quite a bit more then, wouldn't he?

Molly: Yes, he would.

Rodney: But, there you are. And of course he used to, erm, rush off... He had his own car...

Molly: I think driving was a sort of therapy to him; it gave him tremendous comfort. He used to drive for miles and miles and miles because – I don't think he drove particularly anywhere, but he just drove, and I think it was something for him to do. And of course, many times, he tried to go off to London, or other places, and he couldn't make it, and he used to come back...

Rodney: He'd sometimes drive out somewhere, and he'd run out of petrol, because he couldn't bring himself to go to a petrol pump and order petrol, for some reason or other. And then he used to ring us up and say, 'I'm afraid I've run out of petrol.' 'Where are you Nick?' 'Oh, I'm at the beginning of the M4,' or something like that, and off we'd go and pick him up and bring him back.

Molly: Yes, it became sort of part of the normal pattern of life, you know, and you didn't do anything else really at all in your life. And you didn't want to, because you just felt that if you were there and you could somehow do something that was going to make him – not exactly happier, because he wasn't ever happy – but make life a little easier for him, you know, it was your greatest joy. And if he ever did have a good day, the happiness that would come over you in feeling that he was better...

Chris: The depression lasted three bleak years, most of which Nick spent closeted in this room which opens off the Drakes' lounge. It contains a piano and a tape, but Nick spent most of the time just staring into space or looking at his shoes. He'd occasionally visit friends, but sit for hours without saying anything, then leave. 'I wish I could meet someone who's gone through what I have,' he said. 'I can't cope; all the defences are gone, all the nerves exposed.' What do you think caused the depression?

Rodney: Well, that's really awfully difficult to say. If you're trying to look for a cause, it may be that he felt that he wasn't getting his message across, that his music wasn't being listened to as much as he hoped it was going to be listened to. He did actually say once that he felt he'd failed in everything he tried to do.

Molly: Yes he did. He had this profound feeling that he wanted to help people, with his music. And I think to begin with he was absolutely sure he was going to be able to help people with his music; and then he felt that he hadn't, and he said to me, 'I've failed in every single thing I've tried to do,' which was despairing. Of course, I said, 'Nick, you haven't,' and tried to point out to him how very much he hadn't failed. But he had this feeling, didn't he?

Rodney: Yes, and he felt that he couldn't make it with people and he couldn't communicate. And of course he couldn't communicate with people – that was one of his problems. And really he was loved by all his friends, but they didn't really seem to know him, and I think he felt that very much. We thought, when he was here, that we couldn't communicate with him just because we were his parents, you know…

Molly: Generation gap.

Rodney: Generation gap and all that sort of thing. But it was only really at his funeral, when so many people came up from London and all sorts of other places, and they all said the same: they said, 'It's not just you; none of us could get through to him.'

Molly: Paul Wheeler said that he just went away gradually further and further into a world of his own where none of us could reach him. This was his actual contemporary, one of the people who'd been at Cambridge with him, and Robert Kirby said much the same thing. It was sad for them as well, I think, because he did inspire a great deal of love; which is extraordinary really, because he didn't ever put himself out particularly for his friends, and yet they continued to love him and revere him too in a way.

Rodney: But to go back to your original question, whether his depression was due to all the things we've just said, or whether it was something in him, some sort of mental trouble, I wouldn't like to say. It's really more for the experts.

Molly: Yes, except the experts didn't know either. They were quite baffled by Nick. They were totally baffled. They gave him all sorts of different drugs and that sort of thing; and he hated taking the drugs, he simply hated taking them. And one time he threw them all down the loo, but – and, you know, we had to go and get another lot, sort of thing – but we knew they did help him, and he came to realise that they did help him, but it was a struggle to get him to take them. In fact, at one time he said, 'I'm going to get through this thing on my own. No more drugs from now on.' But he didn't get better, did he? He got distinctly worse. And so then he did go back onto those various things – Tryptizol and things like that – which of course was finally what killed him.

Chris: Nick made just one more album. Gone were the baroque arrangements, the gentle beauty; on *Pink Moon* Nick sings alone and unadorned, and his songs are bleak, uncompromisingly depressed. After *Pink Moon*, Nick sank even deeper into depression. He checked into a mental hospital for five weeks and then checked himself out again. He wrote a terrifying song about a black-eyed dog coming to get him, but for the most part he could barely speak, let alone work. 'I'm numb,' he said, 'dead inside.' Then suddenly Nick seemed to come out of his nosedive. He went to Paris to stay on a barge; he even started to write again. He seemed to be enjoying life, but on November 25, 1974, he was found dead in his bedroom. The coroner decided it was suicide. He overdosed on an antidepressant drug prescribed by his doctor, yet the bottle wasn't empty, and he had recently been happier. Do you think Nick took his life deliberately?

Rodney: No, I don't. During the sad three years he stayed with us there were times when we were afraid he was going to do something of that sort; and if this had happened six months before it did, I think we should have felt it was a deliberate act. But, the time when he did it, things were beginning to go much better for him, and we were very happy for it. He'd been over to Paris, he'd been getting going with his music again; he'd been improving his French with a linguaphone course, which was all spread out in his room. He did have bad nights and he did do things on the impulse, and I think he took a lot of these Tryptizol pills, which – we didn't know they were dangerous, and possibly he didn't either. The coroner said that he committed suicide, but personally I don't believe it myself.

Molly: He was a great chap of impulse. I think he was having a terribly bad night. He did have some terribly bad nights. In fact I knew that he'd taken Tryptizol from time to time as a sleeping pill; but I think he was having a bad night and he said, 'Oh, what the hell…' and took some extra ones. He'd been downstairs and had some cornflakes in the kitchen; this he did quite often, because he didn't sleep very well. And quite often I would hear him going down, and I would go down and we would have a chat and a cup of tea. But, of course, as cruel fate would have it, I was very tired that night: I was sleeping very heavily, and I didn't hear one single thing at all. And I think he went downstairs; and he'd been downstairs and he'd been playing a Bach Brandenburg Concerto; we found this on the turntable downstairs in the music room. It was a terribly cold night. He came back up to his room and the next morning he didn't appear – but that often happened because, you know, if he'd had a bad night he did sleep in quite often – but about 12 o'clock he still hadn't come down, so I went up to his room and found him lying across his bed. As I said, it was a terribly cold night: he had on nothing but his little, you know, little pants that he wore at night. His dressing gown was lying on the floor… And there it was…

Chris: No one will ever know if Nick Drake committed suicide, but his death turns one of his earliest pieces, 'Fruit Tree', into the saddest song I know. Had he lived, this film would never have been made.

Do You Recognise This Man?
Jason Creed, *Pink Moon 17*, February 1999

My first meeting with Tim Clements (film-maker/director) was when he came to my house with his sound man Billy, production assistant

Cerise, and David Housden of the 'Scrapbook' series, on June 13, 1998, to film David and I for his forthcoming TV documentary, *A Stranger Among Us: Searching for Nick Drake* (screened on BBC2, February 1, 1999). I was nervous for about a week before they arrived, but was soon put at ease by their friendliness, and we spent a good two or three hours filming, as David and I answered questions about our fanzines and their subject, Nick Drake.

My second meeting with Tim and his crew was on June 24, after Cerise had phoned and invited me along to the Glastonbury Festival to do some more filming.

We met up first thing in the morning at Tim's place in London and, after loading the car with all our gear and half the contents of a local Tesco, set off and soon made it – after three or four hours, as many wrong turnings, and in brief showers of drizzling rain – to Glastonbury.

Tim had decided, for reasons that will become clear, that we would be camping in a field which was at the opposite end of the site from our designated parking area; and, when he told me that, what with all the mud we had to trudge through, it would take us almost an hour to walk there, I thought he was joking. He wasn't; Glastonbury festival is huge.

Something I noticed about the festival in the short time I was there (and this is a very basic way of looking at it, because two days isn't nearly enough time to explore half of it) is that the majority of the people there seemed to fall into two separate groups. On the one hand you have the area where most of the stages are, and this is mostly populated by those who have come to watch the bands, roll around in the mud and generally get out of their heads; and the shops selling silly hats, and the hot dog vans and the like, make it seem a bit like a giant fun fair. And on the other hand, you have the area which we were heading for, which is mostly populated by more traditional 'traveller' types who set up all kinds of wonderful little cafes and stalls and exhibitions, and generally sit around playing the bongos and getting out of their heads.

We eventually arrived at a field called the Dragon Field (so called because it had a big stone dragon in it; a feature which so excited some people they couldn't help but urinate up it!) and planted ourselves down. The filming began straight away with, of all things, me putting my tent up; something which Tim thought would be highly amusing to use in the film. (It will be apparent to anyone who's seen it that very little of the film we shot made it into the final programme. In fact, out of the three days filming I took part in, only about 30 seconds actually made it onto the screen!) Then, after I had had a miniature microphone attached to my chest with the aid of some toupee tape (a hairy-chested Joe Boyd also had to endure this when he was interviewed for the film and apparently found having it removed very painful!) we went in search of our first victims.

Tim's main idea behind going to Glastonbury was simply to walk around the site, select people at random and ask them if they'd ever heard of Nick Drake; and with Tim doing the camera work, Billy the sound, and Cerise busiest of all getting everyone we filmed to fill out consent forms, it was down to me to find the people to approach and, if they'd heard of Nick Drake, ask them a few questions. But instead of simply asking people straight out, I took a large picture of Nick with me, and asked everyone I approached, 'Do you recognise this man?'

And, quite surprisingly, lots of people did. In fact, the very first person we spoke to had heard of Nick. We then went on to spend the whole afternoon selecting people at random and the response we got (for me, who thought we would be lucky to find one or two people) was quite startling – despite the fact that three people thought the picture was of Brad Pitt! But, from people who remembered the odd track, to casual fans who had an album or two, to die-hard guitar-wielding devotees, we met the lot. As we walked around the site, we went into cafes, up to food vans and stalls and innocent bystanders, and, it wasn't a majority, but a large number of the people we spoke to that recognised the picture of Nick were more than happy to talk about him. We also invited everyone who had heard of Nick to join us in a field called the King's Meadow the following evening for a special 'get together' that Tim was planning. And that was the reason we had trekked all the way to the Dragon Field to camp, it being next to the King's Meadow, which is a 'sacred space', and features a circle of standing stones.

So, after our first, very successful day of filming, we retired early (which isn't really the done thing at Glastonbury) at about midnight, because Tim wanted to get up at four the next morning to film me talking about Nick by the sacred stones as the sun came up.

Now, it's a curious thing, but my predominant memory of Glastonbury is one of bongos. Seemingly everywhere you go, people are banging them or (if they can't find any, as one man in a tent nearby to ours proved) plastic buckets. So, having crawled into bed, a party which had been slowly getting underway in the King's Meadow, featuring a man who had possibly the biggest pair of bongos in the whole of Glastonbury, if not the world, really kicked off. And he banged them, and people sang, danced and shouted, and he banged them some more, until I was still awake at four in the morning when we were supposed to be getting up and going to work. By that time, however, thankfully, it was wet and overcast, and impossible for us to do any filming; and we all had the chance to get a couple of hours sleep in.

We didn't achieve too much on the second day. Tim went off in the morning to meet up with a friend, the legendary singer-songwriter Sophie Smith (at least that's who Cerise told the press people Tim's friend Sophie was, in order to get her a free entrance and backstage pass), it rained for most of the early afternoon, and all we could do was lay back in our tents and listen to the sound of beating buckets. We did manage to venture out again though later in the afternoon, and this time Tim set the camera up in a busy place (next to some toilets to be exact, which didn't smell too nice when the sun came out) where some huge artificial flowers had been planted, and we gathered as many willing people as we could and asked them if they would answer a quick question before the camera. They came up one by one, and I asked, 'Have you ever heard of Nick Drake?' and it was great fun capturing their reactions.

We were also very fortunate to have been given backstage passes, and afterwards went in search of some rock stars and celebrities to interview. This was still only Thursday though, a day before the official start of the festival (we were there early because of Tim's busy filming schedule) and, although we wandered around the backstage enclosure hoping to bump into Bob Dylan in a nice cosy tent full of champagne and sandwiches, we weren't too surprised to find only a small army of music journalists and Keith Allen of 'Vindaloo' fame, who quite frankly looked far too menacing to approach. We then decided to go and do a little bit more of what we'd been doing the day before, with the picture of Nick, but this time on the large field in front of the main stage, where various groups of people were gathered; but none of the Robbie Williams fans we spoke to there had ever heard of Nick Drake.

Back then to the sacred space for the grand finale. As I mentioned earlier, we had been asking all the Drake fans to meet us at 8 p.m., as we were hoping to get a large gathering of people together and play them a song by Molly Drake; a song which Tim played to everyone he interviewed for the film, recording their reactions. But unfortunately, despite promises from many of the people we met and a mention on the local radio station, only a handful of people turned up; and then we couldn't actually film amongst the stones because the bongo players were out in full force. But we did eventually get everyone sitting down in a circle, and played them the wonderful song by Molly. Gabrielle Drake said in an interview recently that their mother was a great musical influence on Nick, and this song certainly proves it. With just Molly singing and playing piano, it sounds eerily similar to Nick himself. Anyway, we played the song, and I talked to everyone to get their reactions and, despite there not being the crowd we had hoped for, a good time was had by all.

And that was about it really. We packed the filming gear up after that and spent the last evening enjoying (a little too much in my case) the various opportunities for relaxation that such a place as Glastonbury has on offer; and late next morning we got up in the rain with aching heads, did the whole tent thing backwards, and trundled off homewards through the mud.

Despite the weather, and the lack of people at the final gathering, Tim was more than happy with the results; the first day's filming especially exceeding everyone's expectations. And if it hadn't been for the rain, I would have stayed for the whole weekend; but seeing the muddy pictures in the music mags the following week, I'm glad I didn't. I can still hear those bongos though!

Tanworth-in-Arden

Tanworth-in-Arden is a small, typical Warwickshire village, situated south-east of Birmingham, with a population of around 3,000. It has one pub, the Bell Inn, and the 14th-century St Mary Magdalene church, with a Sesquialtera Stop organ donated 'In memory of Nicholas Drake and his music by his family in 1977'.

A vast area surrounding the village was once covered by the Forest of Arden, which was cleared during the industrial revolution. The word Arden is derived from the Celtic word ardu, meaning 'high land'.

Over the years, Nick's grave has become an increasingly popular destination for fans, and now there is even a yearly 'gathering' in the village to celebrate his life and music. On the occasions that I visited the Tanworth-in-Arden churchyard, I always found a small number of notes or flowers left on or around the grave. Occasionally, however, fans paid their respects in more unusual ways. Andre Huckvale, from a letter dated June 22, 1998, wrote: "I made a slight detour and stopped off in Tanworth-in-Arden, not sure what I was expecting to see that I haven't seen a couple of times before but it was a beautiful fresh picture postcard sort of start to the day. Someone had left a bunch of dried flowers, spray painted pink, on the grave. A local guy walking his dog stopped and chatted and told me about how, a couple of months ago, a female Japanese admirer had erected this huge wooden crib type construction around Nick's grave, painted with pink moons and all these astrological and spiritual symbolisms. Well all of a sudden I didn't feel so strange standing alone in a graveyard, at 7 a.m. on my birthday, I can tell you.

"Since that incident a large engraved wooden sign has been attached to the tree next to the grave, not surprisingly requesting minimal signs of respect only to be left."

The sign reads: "The Drakes' family grave is private property. Please do not place any adornments apart from small floral tributes and messages on or near the grave space. Thank you."

I was often asked for information about the yearly recital of Nick's songs, on the anniversary of his death, at St Mary Magdalene church, Tanworth-in-Arden, as mentioned in T.J. McGrath's article 'Darkness Can Give You The Brightest Light'. In a letter to a *Pink Moon* reader, the vicar of Tanworth wrote: "The previous organist, who knew the Drakes, used to play one of Nick's songs as a voluntary before and after the Sunday Service which was nearest to the anniversary of his death; no other commemoration has been made so far as I am aware, and I have been here myself for 16 years."

In 2000, Andrew Hicks sent me a copy of a wonderful article he had written, called 'A Memoir of My Childhood Friend'. The friend was of course Nick Drake, and the article was all about Andrew's experience of growing up in Tanworth-in-Arden with Nick, travelling to school with him, going to parties at his house, and much more. It's a lovely, detailed piece which gives the reader a very good idea of the place and times that Nick grew up in.

It was intended that the article would first appear in the *Pink Moon* fanzine, but issue 19 had just come out and there never was a 20. It was first published on my website, nickdrakeworld.com, which I created at the end of the Nineties, featuring all of the *Pink Moon* fanzine and other, newer, material. The site lasted for a couple of years but was killed off by the rapidly escalating costs of hosting it. Since then the article has appeared on the Estate's website and, an edited version, in the *Family Tree* CD booklet. You can read the full article at the end of this section.

A visit to Tanworth-in-Arden
T.J. McGrath, *Pink Moon 5*, 1995

I was doing freelance work for various music magazines. My editor gave me approval to write an article for *The Trouser Press* magazine. I contacted Drake's parents over in England, and they agreed to an interview.

So, in the summer of 1982 I found myself flying over the Atlantic Ocean and wondering what I would say to Mr and Mrs Drake about their son's music.

Renting a car, I drove up to Tanworth-in-Arden. I called the Drakes and they gave me excellent directions to Far Leys, the family home. The house looked large and comfortable, and the grounds perfectly suited for garden walks.

Molly and Rodney Drake were charming and friendly. They spent the entire day with me, showing me photos of Nick and answering my many questions about his music. When the time came to interview them, I felt totally at ease. I could tell they were very proud of Nick's talents. When they showed me his room I was astonished ... everything was just the way he had it back in 1974. It was as if he had never left; his books, his clothing, postcards from John and Beverley Martyn, his notebooks ... everything. I was more than a little overwhelmed by the experience.

When it was time for lunch the Drakes insisted on taking me to the local pub. Rodney and Molly seemed to know everybody there. We took a short drive to the cemetery to visit the gravesite. I remember that the day was lovely, the views were wonderful, and that someone had planted a single flower on Nick's grave. It was so beautiful and so chilling.

When we got back we were amazed to find a young couple from Texas there to see the Drakes. They, too, were Drake fans. Rodney and Molly told them to come in. They came in and sat down, and they brought out a guitar and began to sing 'Northern Sky' and John Martyn's 'Spencer The Rover'. I thought to myself, how many people show up at the door to Far Leys? I am sure the Drakes never turned anyone away.

I finished interviewing the Drakes, said goodbye and thanked them for their generosity, and drove away. Back in America I worked on the piece for the longest time. It seemed a difficult article to write. Too personal and too private.

The article was finally completed and sent in. I received many letters from other Drake fans after it was published. Rodney and Molly Drake and I kept in touch throughout the years.

Darkness Can Give You The Brightest Light
T.J. McGrath, *Dirty Linen 42*, 1992

(The following is an edited version of the original article.)

His room is quiet now. The bed is neatly made. A picture of a rough-and-tumble sea storm is framed over the bed. His old desk, complete with coffee stain and pen, is pressed against a far wall. Volumes of Chaucer, Blake, Flaubert and Shakespeare peer down from a corner bookshelf. An old-fashioned radio sits ready and lonesome. His shirts are carefully folded in the dresser; his black sports-coat hangs loosely in his closet. Nick Drake isn't coming home tonight...

Far Leys is a comfortable brick house at the end of a tree-lined cul de sac. It is a warm and charming retreat. The rooms are painted in subdued swirls of yellow and blue, and the practical furnishings put the guest at ease. The grounds are lovely, with carefully tended flower gardens and walkways that overlook a sweeping view of the distant hills. Far Leys is the house where Nick Drake grew up, and where he spent his final hours.

Nick's parents, Rodney and Molly Drake, still live at Far Leys. They accept the occasional late-night phone call from one of Nick's fans as part of his legacy. They welcome tourists with open arms. Young and old Nick Drake purists arrive sometimes without warning...

It was there, in the large, snug house called Far Leys, that Nick first displayed his talent.

'As a baby he loved to conduct,' recalls Molly. 'Whenever the music started he would be up out of the chair waving his hands. I think at one time that he had an ambition to become a famous conductor. He dearly loved classical music and listened to it all the time.'

'He picked up on the piano quite early and was rather good,' Rodney chimes in. 'He was fascinated with some of the legends and myths incorporated into classical pieces. He loved a good story, even if some of them scared him half to death.'

Nick made many tapes; his favourite spot for practising and recording was an orange armchair, and he used to lounge around for hours slumped in that chair working on chord progressions and tunings. Nick worked best at night. Often while working on a new song he never slept at all. 'I used to hear him bumping around at all hours,' Molly Drake says. 'He was an insomniac. I think he wrote his nicest melodies in the early morning hours.'

Rodney Drake owns these tapes and plays them for visitors. 'Nick recorded them right here in the sitting room on a primitive tape recorder. He was quite a perfectionist and was always erasing songs he deemed inferior. I managed to grab a handful of tapes one day before he found out.'

After *Pink Moon*, Nick retreated to Far Leys. He refused to see his friends or talk to anybody. He just sat on that old orange armchair and looked off into space. His parents tried to seek professional help and doctors prescribed antidepressant pills.

On November 24, 1974, he was up and about as usual at night, planning and writing songs. Nick still had trouble falling asleep and his parents were quite used to him pacing the floor. He was apparently in a good mood as he had a Brandenburg Concerto on the turntable. His mother recalls him going into the kitchen for a midnight snack of cornflakes. 'I usually would wake up and join him at the table. For some silly reason, that night, I rolled over and went back to sleep.'

Nick lies buried in the Tanworth-in-Arden churchyard, his crumbling gravestone overlooking a wide expanse of closely cropped hills and carefully tended meadows.

Journey to Tanworth-in-Arden
Jonathan Wolff, *Pink Moon 15*, 1998

If I had kept annual playlists of the music I listened to most frequently, then Nick Drake's albums would have held their position firmly at the top of the list for each of the last 23 years – this despite my ownership of an increasingly large, and very varied, collection of records, CDs and tapes. My initial introduction to Nick's work had come at the beginning of his career, like many long term fans it was through the songs included on the Island samplers, *Nice Enough To Eat* and *Bumpers* ('Time Has Told Me' and 'Hazey Jane I' respectively). Whilst those two tracks were favourites, at that time any money I had spare for buying records tended to be invested in the latest releases by Led Zeppelin, Free, Jethro Tull, King Crimson etc ... However, five years or so after first hearing 'Time Has Told Me', Nick Kent's *NME* article inspired a guitarist friend to hold forth in the university bar about the brilliance and tragic loss of Nick Drake. I borrowed *Five Leaves Left* and *Pink Moon* and became hooked. From then on, with missionary zeal, I introduced Nick's music to anyone who would listen. *Pink Moon*, in particular, became a regular backdrop to our late night conversations in smoke draped student rooms.

During the interval between my introduction to Nick's music and the point at which I became a fan, there is one related memory that stands out. On September 18, 1971, I was at the Oval Cricket Ground for a one-day rock festival headlined by The Who and The Faces. During one of the interminable equipment changes between bands, the DJ (Jeff Dexter) played a track by Nick. The song was not one of the two I was familiar with at the time, so I can't identify it, but I recognised its style as being definitely Nick Drake, a fact confirmed by the DJ when the track finished. Looking back, the weird thing is that I attended dozens of rock festivals, so must have heard many hours of music played between acts, and yet, despite not really being a Nick Drake fan at the time, this was the one and only occasion on which a record played over the PA system even entered my consciousness. I can still vividly remember the ethereal quality of the music as it floated across the stadium and the feeling that, although very good, it seemed curiously out of place in that big arena. Even if it wasn't a live performance, I suppose at around 15,000 that may stand as the largest group of people, in Nick's lifetime, to have all listened to his music in the same place at the same time.

I resided for most of the Eighties in Coventry, only a few miles from Tanworth-in-Arden. I now regret that, despite my proximity to Molly and Rodney's home, I never paid them a visit. Inspired by Arthur Lubow's *Fruit Tree* notes, I thought many times about calling in on them and on one occasion actually got in the car to head off for Tanworth. Having turned the ignition, I sat in the car with the engine running for a minute or so, then switched it off again and went back into the house. As I remember it, I had a sudden impulse that, despite Arthur Lubow's words, the visit was all wrong – that my arrival would be an unwanted intrusion for Mr and Mrs Drake. I know now that I was probably mistaken but I'm sure Nick would have understood.

It was only on November 22, 1997, three days before the twenty third anniversary of Nick's death, that I finally made my pilgrimage to Tanworth-in-Arden. I have Patrick Humphries to thank for that trip. On a rare weekend away from the kids, staying in Stratford-on-Avon, I had purchased a copy of Patrick's long awaited biography and was thumbing through it over a lingering cup of coffee. Suddenly inspired, I persuaded my wife that we should make the short journey to Tanworth that afternoon. The whole visit evoked the pastoral mood of *Five Leaves Left*. As we approached the village, luminous autumn sunshine lit the surrounding countryside and a pheasant bumbled absentmindedly into the road in front of us. The only living soul we spotted, in the time we were there, was a gardener tending a bonfire in a corner of the graveyard. I was surprised by the worn state of Nick's headstone and slightly taken aback by the testiness of the shabby notice discouraging fans from adorning the grave. My discomfort was more than compensated for, however, by the splendid view across Warwickshire fields, the sense of stillness and the aura of timelessness summoned by the scene. On our way back we stopped off in Henley-in-Arden for tea and crumpets before returning to Stratford and an excellent production of *Romeo And Juliet*. It was all very autumnal, very English, very Nick Drake. I ended the day by sitting up until 4.00 a.m. reading Patrick's biography, the wonderful account of Nick's family life and schooldays complementing the fresh experiences of the afternoon. I felt that the journey to understanding Nick Drake had been completed, as far as I needed it to be. I can now put Nick's recordings more firmly into context. Ultimately, what really matters to me is that wonderful music.

Visiting Nick Drake
Ryan Foley, *Stylus* magazine, 2007

The visits made Gabrielle Drake apprehensive. Strangers in off-putting attire from places like America or Australia, arriving unannounced at her parents' brick, Queen Anne home. They climbed out of vans in groups, or sauntered up individually on foot, never put off by Far Leys' rather uninviting characteristics: the dark Georgian windows, the large, wooden gates at the foot of the driveway, its location at the end of a hushed, leafy Bates Lane.

After raps on the portico-covered front door, Gabrielle's parents always ushered the strangers inside, where they clinked teacups and toured the grounds. And that's usually when the concerned daughter's fears were assuaged. Though brimming with an unusual ardour, the visitors were always as quiet, introspective, and elegiac as the very artist they arrived in Tanworth to memorialise: Gabrielle's younger brother, Nick Drake.

'I am so often struck by how respectful and kind Nick's fans are,' says Martin 'Cally' Callomon, manager of the music side of Drake's estate, which released this summer's acclaimed compilation *Family Tree*. 'One never quite knows what is below the surface, but I sense a relief in them, a sense that Nick articulates a good deal of emotion they share together. So each fan seems to build a unique personal relationship with Nick's songs.'

Drake's career commenced at the tail end of the Sixties (*Five Leaves Left* was released in 1969), a period when pop music was at its most communal: bedroom LP delight with allies, a music-charged subculture, and television serving as the unifier of the pop masses (i.e., The Beatles on *The Ed Sullivan Show*). Akin with the work of England's Romantic poets, Drake's music demanded a more singular experience: a listener detaching oneself from the outside world in order to become fully immersed in the idyllic, undulating melodies and fragile candour. And, naturally, such independent experiences forge a granite-strong bond with the artist, listeners reflecting on their emotive responses and drawing their own conclusions without the sting of others.

One of the great ironies of the entire Nick Drake story is the very machine that helped orchestrate his rebirth (the Internet) is an integral part of the world fans seek to fade out from when indulging in his catalogue. In a brilliant piece for a 2000 issue of *Mojo*, Ian McDonald wrote, 'Day by day, reality thins further into physical matter as that obsolete spirit-stuff evaporates. Nowadays "spirit" is being squeezed out of our materialist society.' For many, Drake's music duly returns that sapped spirit – an artist deemed inept at caring for himself, now taking care of others with his music.

'Nick's records give you the rare opportunity to step sideways away from the world for 30 minutes, and come back to it renewed and refreshed and somehow uplifted,' says Matt Hutchinson, who heads up NickDrake.com. 'His music still speaks with a voice that connects directly. Put on *Pink Moon* with headphones late at night and you're almost in the room with Nick when he sings.'

'In this world that keeps changing faster and faster,' says Denise Offringa, 'where everything is going faster and faster, those who journey more on the inside than on the outside seek something that says it understands. And in Nick's music many find just that.'

Over the last four years, Offringa has done considerable work in moving the Drake experience beyond its soloist culture. She helps organise the annual Nick Drake Gathering, a summer event held in Drake's hometown of Tanworth-in-Arden that draws hundreds of fans from across the world. Offringa became involved with the event because of a 'sense of injustice' regarding Drake's frequently overlooked oeuvre.

This year's gathering took place August 3 and 4, and featured free concerts at Tanworth's village hall and church, as well as workshops where Drake's songcraft and life were discussed. 'We exist by the sole grace of donations on the days themselves,' explains Offringa. 'That makes it an event for the fans by the fans – or Drakeaholics, as some prefer to be called.'

Aside from the annual gathering, the Drakeaholics still flock to Tanworth. The visits to Far Leys (pronounced *Lees*) have long since ceased, Molly and Rodney Drake's generosity dying with them many years ago. (The Drakes would allow fans to snap photos of their son's still kempt room – his black sportcoat still hanging in the closet; his writing desk still carrying a coffee stain – or hand out copies of his Beocordtaped, home compositions.) Other village spots have become popular: the Church of St Mary Magdalene, featuring a pipe organ that carries a brass plaque dedicated to Drake and a guest book Drake's mother urged visitors to sign; and the adjoining cemetery, where Drake's ashes are interred underneath an oak tree very much like the one pictured in the artwork to *Bryter Layter*.

'I used to think it strange when people visited Gracelands,' says Jayne Westwood, a devoted fan who's been to Drake's grave, 'but I understand a bit more why people make the journey and go there. I can't really put into words how I felt. It was just so quiet and peaceful, and felt good paying my respects and giving thanks for the music and lyrics he left us with.'

Fans are stuffed with an infinity of Drake minutia, but that's just for debunking myths – like the much-told yarn where Drake dropped off the quarter-inch stereo mix of *Pink Moon* at Island without saying a word to anyone (this is false; he chatted with Chris Blackwell). Drakeaholics are known for being keenly self-aware of any behaviour that drifts towards idolisation, perhaps in part because their hallowed artist was never seen in such a light during his lifetime.

'In the past, some fans scraped little bits of the grave to take home, which is of course a disrespectful thing to do,' says Offringa. 'There are always some who go a bit over the top and do idolise, but most don't. Most just sit there and touch it, and have a quiet moment to thank Nick. It remains first and foremost someone's family grave. The lettering has faded quite a bit through the years, as people touch it and move their hand over it. It's the closest thing they can think of to "meeting" Nick and saying thank you.'

Despite the elbow grease of individuals like Offringa, the release of the aforementioned *Family Tree*, and occasional jaunts into the mainstream consciousness (see VW's shilling of its Cabrio with the jeremiad 'Pink Moon'), Drake is still tagged with the label 'obscure genius'. Which means his phylum of fans, despite the ardent passion and purpose, remains relatively small and grassroots.

Offringa talks of folks like Philip and Annabel Littleford, Tanworth locals who have opened their home to Drake fans much like Molly and Rodney once did decades earlier. Or the efforts to not only maintain

Drake's grave (removing dead flowers, planting bulbs, sending the more elaborate memorial items to Gabrielle), but that of the Drake family nanny, Rosie, whose ashes are interred at the graveyard.

It's a legacy maintained through simple, informal gestures. Drake would certainly be humbled by such doting and fussing.

'He once said to his mother that if only his music would have really touched one person, it would have been worth it,' says Offringa. 'I think this shows it was worth it. Because he has touched so many and in such a deep way, as well.'

A Memoir of My Childhood Friend
Andrew Hicks, 2000

It is strange that although Nick Drake was one of my closest childhood friends, I only came to know his music relatively recently. I was born a little more than a year before Nick and I spent all of my childhood at our family home just outside the Warwickshire village of Tanworth-in-Arden where Nick was brought up. It is all an awfully long time ago. I saw a lot of Nick when we were small. It was not his fault that he broke my leg as he was totally without malice. After so long, one is left with a strong but general impression of an old friend's personality, though the details have mostly faded.

It has been a strange experience for me in the last few years becoming addicted to his music. At any time I can put on a CD and Nick will sing for me. I can recognise his voice. Memories of him have stirred and I have come to know something of him as an adult. Now free of commitments to a growing family, I have more time to renew contacts with old friends from the distant past. I feel the loss keenly that Nick cannot be one of them. Instead I visited his grave on his fiftieth birthday.

All I want to do now is to share a few memories of the childhood of a gentle and happy person. So much has been written of the later stages of Nick's life, often creating a shadowy mystique of a strange and haunted individual. This bears no resemblance to the person I knew, to the real Nick. I do not want to dwell upon his tragedy as so many have done; I hope to celebrate what he really was and to shed a little light on the impression he left on one of the young companions of his early childhood.

I remember Far Leys, the Drakes' Tanworth home, from before the Drakes moved in. It was the home of Jim Smith, a stockbroker with Albert E. Sharpe in Birmingham. His daughters Judy and Rosemary were the same age as my elder sister and I. They appear as attractive children gazing out of a number of sepia photographs taken in our garden. At one of my parties Rosemary bit my arm leaving livid teeth marks. I forget what I did to warrant this. My sister and I used to go to the Smiths at Far Leys for a little pre-school or playgroup run by a Miss Tonks. When the Smiths moved to a house in Edgbaston, I thought Drake, the name of the newcomers a bit strange; a sort of family of ducks.

As I remember, Rodney Drake worked for Wolseley Hughes, an engineering company, and not Wolseley, the car company as stated by Patrick Humphries in Nick's biography. (Wolseley is now a major listed company with varied interests including a builders merchants.) The Hughes family lived in the large house in its own grounds with crunchy gravel drive next to Tanworth church. That connection could be what brought the Drakes to find a house in Tanworth.

The most accessible private schools were in Henley-in-Arden. Patrick Humphries says that Nick 'attended local primary schools'. To be more accurate he and Gabrielle were sent to Hurst House, a pre-prep school in Henley. I have the Holiday Circular for the end of the summer term (I think of 1953), the term when Nicholas Drake along with six others joined the school. At the end of the same term Gay Drake (sic) and my sister left, both to go to Edgbaston Church of England College for Girls. I was one year ahead of Nick. My parents and a number of other families shared a car pool with the Drakes from the time they arrived in Tanworth for the trip to Henley and later taking the girls to Edgbaston until the end of their schooling. So for over ten years we were closely connected with the Drake family and were in and out of each others' cars and houses on a regular basis.

I remember my first day at Hurst House, proud of my independence in not being taken by my mother, but by one of the other mothers, possibly Molly Drake. As you leave Henley on the road to Stratford, there is a steep private drive to the right signed to Ardenhurst School. This is the amalgamation of Hurst House, the pre-prep school and Arden House the prep school to which I later went aged eight. Hurst House is the square 1830s house on the right, now in private occupation, as you go up the drive. My impression of the school is still etched in my memory; of each class room, the swings at the side, the entrance hall, the stairs that I had to be carried up after breaking my leg at the Drakes' house.

Nick would have started in Miss Jones' class in the room on the right at the bottom of the stairs. After lunch we sat or lay on blankets and had 'rest' and were read a story. Then in our second year we progressed upstairs to Miss Franey's form, and then Mrs Ince and finally downstairs to Miss Smith, a fire breathing Catholic. When I fell heavily on the hard slate floor, she interpreted this to me as a punishment from God for infringing the school rule of not running along the corridor.

The school was run by Dennis and Jill Bennett (and I believe owned by Jill's family, the Nelsons). Their older son Jeremy is now a distinguished writer and producer of historical and other television documentaries. The younger post-war children, Mary and Oliver, were my contemporaries and were at the school. They were close friends for many years after I left and until, as invariably happens, we lost touch. Then there was Marcus, the dachshund who appears front centre in all the school group photographs. I have several of these photos showing about 60 attractive, optimistic, smiling children of ambitious middle-class fee-paying parents, arrayed in front of the school's solid Victorian facade. Gabrielle is in the photographs I have, but they must pre-date Nick's arrival.

It was an easy going, happy school where we learned the basics of reading, writing and arithmetic. Like me, Nick had his sister to see him into school, at least for the first term, and I am sure he settled in well. I do remember that both the Drake children were appropriately good at swimming, a skill learned in the Far East. The Holiday Circular I still have shows Gay Drake as winning the One Length Swimming Race, and coming second in the obstacle race. It also requests children not to bring sweets to school in future. Morning school begins with prayers at 9.20 a.m. and ends at 12.30 p.m., while afternoon school finishes at

3.40 p.m.. All children should arrive and be called for punctually. Those under seven should bring a pair of dungarees for games wear. Rubber boots should be marked with marking ink. And what's more 'a successful flower show was held on Monday June 22.' But it was expensive. My bill for Christmas term 1953 came to £22 and 18 shillings, including £1.11s 6 pence for dancing classes and 1s 6 pence for a marionette show. Such was life's pattern, safe and so secure and middle class, a world away from the classless milieu of the media and popular music.

We travelled to and fro in our Standard Eight, Molly Drake's succession of Morris Minors and the cars of a number of other parents. Rodney Drake's Humber Hawk or big solid Rover always did the run to Birmingham to the girls' school and the office. We knew every inch of the five mile journey to Henley, the old windmill at Danzey, now in the Avoncroft Museum, and of course the mushroom tree. For Molly and Rodney, dull or sullen silence in the car was anathema. Partly to subdue fighting in the back, but also because performance should be a universal pleasure, stories were told and songs were sung as we travelled. After leaving Danzey we always sang, 'Shall we see the mushroom tree' to the tune of an old nursery rhyme. For the Drake family, successful performance, both music and drama, were a way of life and an essential value.

The Drakes' house was sometimes the collection point for the children. I have a strong recollection of Far Leys from the many times of waiting there to be picked up by my mother and of children's parties there. In summer we played in the extensive garden behind the house. The lawns sloped down to the fields and to a marshy stream flowing out of a pond on the other side of the road where Nick and I would happily get covered in mud.

On one occasion we were playing inside in the upstairs corridor between Nick's bedroom and the playroom (later presumably the music room). The game was to rush down the corridor together and throw ourselves onto a mat and slide along on the polished wood floor. On this occasion I fell badly, Nick on top of me. The pain in my left leg below the knee was excruciating. One of the two Burmese amahs, known as nanny, came and carried me to the couch in the playroom. I was howling. She massaged my leg. My mother was called urgently and

I was taken to Solihull hospital where X-rays diagnosed a fractured tibia. I was plastered right up to the groin and was on crutches for six weeks.

The accident was nobody's fault but the Drakes were most concerned that it had happened while in their care. Molly and Nick visited me, still prostrate in my bedroom. They brought me some presents; activity games and a Noddy book, and signed my plaster. I distinctly remember Nick saying that I had been very brave; strange how a trauma preserves these little details.

Tanworth was a beautiful setting for a childhood, but it was not all dreamy, soft-focus summer days. There was still some rationing in the early Fifties and much austerity remaining after the war. Rooms were cold, we relied on coal fires, and many of the luxuries of today were absent. But we were among the better off. In the Drakes' playroom was a wind-up gramophone and downstairs in the drawing room a spool-to-spool tape recorder. This was the first time I had ever heard a voice being recorded. I now realise that the purpose of this expensive tape machine was to record their own music.

Tanworth attracted many of the business owners and managers from Birmingham and its industrial hinterland. While it was in unspoiled countryside, it was close to the factories and had good communications. From the age of eight, at risk from rough boys, I donned my red school cap and took the North Warwickshire line to Arden House in Henley. The trains had three maroon carriages with separate compartments, a leather strap to drop the window, to lean out and open the door, and were drawn by a tank engine that still went puff puff through the countryside.

In Tanworth the Post Office was manned by a loquacious gossip, Miss Chattaway and her mother. The tiny store was run by the Tibbles family, the butchers by Mr Simmons. Jack Hood, the ex-champion boxer, was publican of The Bell, and Canon Dudley W. Lee then Mr Willmott the vicars. There were still characters around from an earlier agricultural age, from before the industrialisation of farming. For example there was Mr Hussell, always clad in old tweed jacket and trousers, heavy boots and a cloth cap that he would doff to my parents. Was he farm labourer, gardener, carpenter? His grave is marked by a simple wooden cross that will soon decay and is just a few yards from Nick's headstone.

Far Leys stands in a lane just off the village centre. Opposite, a track leads to the village cricket pitch. Next to the track lived the Pattersons, Muriel and Pip who built there in the early Fifties. I was often at their house as my mother was a close friend, having lived in the cottage next to their house while my father was away at the war. Pip worked for Dunlop, had a well-polished Triumph 2000 and plus fours. He smoked a pipe with herbal tobacco which he collected from the hedgerows and dried in his garage. Then in the next house there were the Richards whose daughter rode with my sister and in whose pool we occasionally risked hypothermia. He was a senior executive with Scaffolding of Great Britain and his Jaguar was numbered SGB 1; a little flash perhaps, not as sedate as a Humber Hawk. Then next to the Drakes was a large late Victorian house down a long drive where village fetes were sometimes hosted; Mr Onions, a retired industrialist, and his wife, the sister of Mrs Williams, our much loved next door neighbour at Old Forge Cottage. And opposite in one of the houses built in the late Fifties or early Sixties, my friend from a later school, Nick Hallam, now a doctor. The place was small enough that we knew most of the families.

Such was the context, all positive, except perhaps a little too sleepy, a little isolated, perhaps unstimulating in comparison to the city, and suffering a shortage of companions. On thinking about it, Nick was one of the very few accessible contemporaries of about my own age that my parents would have seen as an appropriate social fit. I became used to my own companionship, went for long bike rides alone or walks through the fields with the dog. Perhaps Nick was the same.

We all went to the same parties. Nick would be immaculately turned out in neat shorts and cotton shirts, Clarks sandals and, horror of horrors, white ankle socks. I would rather have died horribly in a pool of piranhas. He was always a delightful companion, never aggressive or pushy, always dependable. He would not knock down your castle when you left the room, eat your sweets or hide your favourite toy. Nor punch you in the face when you were down. Childhood is red in tooth and claw and you gain permanent insights into those around you. Nick was not the most boisterous but he was sociable, joined in all the fun and got messy like the rest of us. With adults his behaviour was impeccable; his goodbyes and thank yous perfectly rehearsed, always addressing an adult, Mr or Mrs X or Y by name. Even unbroken, his voice had a hint of the low huskiness we hear in his singing. He was the good looking, delightful, ideal child that every parent would want their own offspring to emulate.

Likewise his family represented all that was charming and attractive; everyone would aspire to be like them. With great warmth they were able to express an interest in everyone of all states and conditions without any condescension. They excelled as hosts and I remember their adult parties to which we were invited. At Christmas the church choir came and sang carols in the large hallway. I stood awkwardly on one leg speaking monosyllabically while adults chatted volubly, passed round drinks and fiddled with small eats. I remember Molly and Rodney so strongly in this context, Molly beaming, Rodney and my father standing together ramrod straight gripping their glasses, discussing what they had in common; wartime experiences, Suez, fuel consumption, engineering, Wolseleys; both their fathers bought early examples of this car.

Gabrielle was generally there, strikingly lovely with that special capacity of putting people at ease, no doubt passing round drinks, asking the right questions and dazzling everyone. She was the rising star of theatre and screen. We watched her career with pride and delight. We went to see her on stage whenever we could. My father was a particular fan. He would always buy us tickets; I remember Malvern, Nottingham and going backstage to see her afterwards. She was a hard act for a younger sibling to follow. We did not even know of Nick's musical aspirations.

Were the Chatwins at those parties? After Hurst House, Nick did not go on to Arden House but to board at another prep school. I remember a sense of disappointment and mild betrayal as I would then not see him daily as before. Patrick Humphries documents his time at Marlborough where he boarded from the age of thirteen. Humphries mentions a number of famous old boys of the school, one of them the travel writer and novelist Bruce Chatwin. What he did not mention was that the Chatwins were a Tanworth family and were almost certainly part of the Drakes' social circle.

The parallels are strange; both sons of upper-middle-class families, Bruce Chatwin and Nick Drake were strikingly good looking men who would never go unnoticed. Both were of artistic temperament, both brought up in Tanworth, going on to Marlborough, both dying young and being lionised in death with biographies and growing critical acclaim and attention. Chatwin of course achieved much success in his lifetime, being well-known as a social animal and a bisexual. They both leave much behind and are remembered not only for their respective tragedies.

Early deaths are not uncommon. In the school car pool to Henley was another family with two sons. Again a managing director, good looking and charming people, the older son brilliantly clever at school, the younger perhaps struggling socially and academically. Unable to compete with his older brother he took up artistic interests, studied art, suffered mental breakdowns and finally killed himself in his twenties. It happens, it is not uncommon, mental ill health is normal. Apart perhaps from the pressures on the children of successful families, Tanworth does not show a special cluster of such tragedies. Any village would see such cases. Most are an absolute waste. In contrast Bruce and Nick's short lives were remarkably full and productive and are now widely remembered and valued.

Nick and I were now at different boarding schools and so I rarely saw him; just the occasional parties in the holidays. My sister travelled to school with Gabrielle every day in term time. The last time I saw Nick was at a party to which we invited him at our house. We had an old barn attached to the house which was perfect for noisy parties. Ring round friends with a date, get in some kegs of beer, set up some music and wait for them all to arrive. I am not sure which party it was; possibly the one on the evening of my sister's wedding which took place of course at Tanworth church. The Drakes came to the wedding and the reception; their familiar presence is in the wedding album. Gay and Nick were asked to the party afterwards in the barn. This would have been May 1968 when I was at University reading Law.

Whichever party it was, I retain a very clear image of Nick entering the barn and coming up to me and chatting. All was very familiar but also much changed, with our diverging experiences and interests, me feeling a bit conventional and boring, Nick, all studied cool and glamour. He had by then his standard image of long hair and dark jacket, possibly a polo neck, and dark trousers that didn't taper. He was very tall, slightly stooped, with a pleasant warmth but evidently shy, at a distance, not quite engaged, just as everyone has described. I am so sorry I did not have time with him on his own. Like me, perhaps he functioned better on a one to one basis and not in a crowd of people pushing and yelling over the loud music.

During the evening one of the girls there came up to me and said, 'Who is that gorgeous man?' I had to introduce her to him, but she was way out of his league, whatever league that might have been. As people do, he slipped away some time during the evening and I never saw him again.

My best Warwickshire friend at the time was Jane. She had been in Nick's year at Hurst House so knew him well. She was a competent guitarist and she and I loved nothing better than to sit around singing to the guitar, popular but pedestrian stuff. I am haunted by the possible memory that she said to me after the party that Nick had arrived with his guitar hoping to sing, looking for an audience. It was far too big and raucous a party, not the moment. But had it happened, had he played, we would have been transfixed by his talent; we must surely have met up again. Even then I knew nothing of his growing musical career.

After graduating in Law from Southampton, I spent two years with a law firm in Birmingham, then became a solicitor in London. Inevitably I drifted away from the safety and security of the friends that I once knew in my childhood. Then I accepted a lectureship in law at a university in Nigeria to enable me to join my girlfriend who was working there. This was towards the end of 1973. My mother recently told me shortly before her death that Molly Drake had said at that time that Nick was at home in Tanworth and would I come over to see him. I have no memory of this, but then it is a long time ago. At that time Nick did not have much more than a year to live. I am not sure how a meeting between us would have gone. I was on the crest of a wave, having given up my career in private practice to follow my heart on an immensely exciting trip to Africa. He would have found my high profoundly depressing. And I could not possibly have understood his predicament. At that time we so little understood or acknowledged mental illness, and at that age I had no insight or experience into it.

I remember where I was when the news of Kennedy being shot

reached me. But I do not remember being told of Nick's death. It may even have been some years after the event. Letters to Nigeria took many weeks, if they got there at all and phones were only for decoration. We were now confirmed expatriates with new lives, substantially out of touch with our old ones. We spent fifteen years abroad in West Africa and the Far East, the major cost being separated from our roots and old friends. I distinctly remember before a visit to Burma thinking of the possibility of writing to the Drakes to ask after their amahs who had retired there. But with only a week's visa allowed, meeting up with Nanny and Ngor was probably impossible; though it would have been a wonderful experience.

Returning to UK in 1988 with two small children and two careers to establish here, life was hectic. I rediscovered Nick to my great surprise being listed in the *Telegraph* colour supplement table of the 100 best post-war albums, or whatever it was. I was aghast. I had no idea of his critical acclaim. I had been on another planet and had missed it all. I went out and bought the *Way To Blue* CD but didn't have a CD player. I took it round to the flat of some Malaysian Chinese friends in their mid-twenties and listened to Nick's husky voice for the first time with great interest and pleasure. As the print of the sleeve notes was so small and I could not read it, Tieng read it out. It gave the account of Nick's life and achievements and of his death, a poignant description of Molly and Rodney's terrible loss. Tieng and Say were then amazed to see me, a middle-aged greying law lecturer almost twice their age silently listening to this moving account to a background of Nick's songs, in floods of tears.

Since then I have played Nick more than any other music that I have ever listened to. And I still do not always manage to do so without tears. Six years ago after a severe virus, I began to suffer from an unexplained chronic illness which left me in much physical distress and with too much time on my hands. Nick became a daily feature of my life, a special pleasure never rationed, who released many tensions and emotions for me, and helped me through a barren and difficult time. His music is haunting and sombre, but its beauty never fails to lift me. I do not always feel robust enough to face its emotional challenge, but when I do it is always to good effect. It is an immense pleasure, a tonic, even if moving and sometimes disturbing. Life and work can be emotionally deadening and Nick is the antidote. It is so strange that I knew so little of his music for so long but now am addicted.

It was during this time that my mother became ill and was dying of cancer. I came up to Cheltenham to see her. We talked together in the hospital about the Drake family and about Nick. I can date the time because it was May 1998, 50 years after Nick's birth. On the fifth, which would have been his fiftieth birthday, I went back to Tanworth for the first time for many years. As I walked among the graves looking for Nick's, I saw so many names that I had known in life. At last I found the headstone, so simple. 'And now we rise and we are everywhere.'

In the church I leafed through the visitors' book. There were numerous entries from people who had come to Nick's graveside on that particular day, his birthday, to say thank you for the music. I added my own entry with Don Maclean's line about Van Gogh; 'This world was never meant for one as beautiful as you.' I do not have to say that it was for many reasons a very emotional time.

Psychologists are fine until they pretend that they are beginning to understand the human psyche. Amateur psychologists who pontificate or jump to conclusions are even worse. But I have to observe that the personal pressures on Nick could have broken a much stronger man. In a family such as his, achievement is assumed and appears easy. How impossible to go from the strong support and discipline of such a home, through the institutionalisation of private schooling and Cambridge and then to drop out into nothingness. No routine, no structure to one's life, no community, just time stretching out ahead, during which one must produce creative and magical work. It must not only be good; it must be good of the type that bewitches a broad public and sells records. The alternative is commercial failure, rejection; hard for any artist who wants to be heard.

Then there is the difficult transition to be made from Old Marlburian and Cambridge undergrad; to transform from being rather pukka and patrician into a cool, classless artist with universal appeal. Did he curse where he came from? Did he swear in the night? And when unable to communicate with those around him, perhaps suffering an attack of diffidence, would he retreat into a slightly patrician distance? 'I'm a poor boy; I drive a Rover.' These were real contradictions that would have challenged anyone. The Sixties and Seventies were fast moving; it was no time to feel like a remnant of something that's past. When the ban on feeling free was lifted, when the prohibition on sweets in school and on many more powerful pleasures no longer applied, the total freedom from formality, commitment and routine must have been immensely difficult.

If I now want to conclude anything from these rather parochial and personal ramblings, it is this. Do not forget Nick. Enjoy and treasure his work. But do not, in anything that is said or written about him, play up the mystery of the shadowy tragic artist figure who nobody ever knew. This is all rubbish. I knew Nick; he was lovely, normal, sociable in a quiet way, a pleasure to know, real and substantial. And I also want to add that clinical depression, or whatever you may call it, is normal and is all around us. It hits the best people, including the cheerful ones, and it is often not apparent. Be sensitive to it; support them, whether they be young artists or people of whatever age or condition. Your involvement could be crucial to their recovery.

I sense that if Nick had been born twenty or thirty years later things might have turned out differently for him. The turn of the Sixties was a particularly difficult period, more of a revolution than it would seem in retrospect, requiring much of those wishing to reinvent themselves and to be their own person. It is still not easy to escape the expectations and conditioning of your upbringing, but now society is much more mobile. There is also perhaps a greater realism; we know that the world does not owe us a living and it is a hard world out there. We know we have to plan cautiously before making the big gamble. The Sixties was a melting pot in which people took great and romantic risks. There are many risks in life to be eagerly embraced. But for Nick, if only things had turned out differently; if he could have had a whole long lifetime, if he could have stayed for more.

Acknowledgements

It has been a great pleasure putting *The Pink Moon Files* together. I hope it proves to be worthy of its subject and pleasing to its contributors. I would like to say a very big thank you to all of the writers and interviewees whose words appear in these pages, and to the following people for their generosity and support: Joe Muggs, Ryan Foley, Will Stone, Andrew Hicks, Jeroen Berkvens, Robin Frederick, Kevin Ring, Vivian Fowler, Michael Organ, Robert Jones, Michael Burdett, Donnah Anderson, David Browne, Julian Meek-Davies, Iain Cameron, Richard Skinner, Patrick Humphries, Andre Huckvale, Janet Davis, Lyn Dobson, John Stokes, Anne Leighton, Christina Giscombe, Steve Greenhalgh, Luca Ferrari, T.J. McGrath, Brian Cullman, Charles O'Meara, Colin Betts.

I would also like to say a special thank you to Chris Charlesworth at Omnibus Press, who made it all happen; and Robert Kirby, David Sandison and Scott Appel, supporters of the original *Pink Moon* fanzine, who have left this world behind.

It has not been possible to contact everyone whose work appears in this book. I would very much like to hear from those I have been unable to trace.

The following articles appear courtesy of their respective copyright holders: 'Get Together' by Colin Betts from *Frozenlight*, published by Floating World, © Colin Betts 2010; 'Of Brilliance and Darkness, The Bittersweet Saga of Nick Drake,' by Charles O'Meara, © Charles

O'Meara 1988; 'Nick Drake' by Brian Cullman, © Brian Cullman 2010; 'A Visit to Tanworth in Arden' by T.J. McGrath, © T.J. McGrath 1995; 'Darkness Can Give You the Brightest Light' (extracts from) by T.J. McGrath, © T.J.McGrath 1992; 'Singing for Nick' by Robin Frederick, © Robin Frederick 2010; 'Who Can Know the Thoughts of Nick Drake (Why He Flies or Goes Out in the Rain)' by Christina Giscombe, © Christina Giscombe 1998; 'Scott Appel Interview' by Anne Leighton, © Anne Leighton 1987; 'The Direction Home (If you know the Way to Blue)' by John Stokes, © John Stokes 1999; 'Bryter Layter in Brooklyn, New York' by Janet Davis, © Janet Davis 1997; 'Nick Drake Tape Find' by *Record Collector,* © *Record Collector* 1998; 'John Martyn interview' by Richard Skinner, © Richard Skinner 1986; 'Meeting & Listening to Nick' by Iain Cameron, © Iain Cameron 1998; 'Depression, Manic Depression and Mr N.R. Drake', 'Schizophrenia and Mr N.R. Drake' and 'Thoughts on Nick Drake' by Donnah Anderson, © Donnah Anderson 1997/1998; 'Strange Face' by Michael Burdett, © Michael Burdett 2010; 'The Biography book launch and review' and 'Patrick Humphries interview' by Jason Creed and Patrick Humphries, © Jason Creed/Patrick Humphries 1998; 'The Sad Ballad of Nick Drake' by Mick Brown from the *Telegraph Magazine,* © Mick Brown/*The Daily Telegraph* 1997; 'Poor Boy, so sorry for himself' by Suzi Feay, from *The Independent,* © Suzi Feay/*The Independent* 2006; 'Joe Boyd and the Crazy Magic of Nick Drake' by Kevin Ring, © Kevin Ring 1992; *Five Leaves Left* LP review by G.C. from *New Musical Express,* 04/10/69; *Bryter Layter* LP review by Andrew Means from *Melody Maker* 13/03/71; *Pink Moon* LP review by Mark Plummer from *Melody Maker* 01/05/72; 'The Leave Taking (an interview with Gabrielle Drake) by Kris Kirk from *Melody Maker* 04/07/87; and a short extract from 'Requiem for a Solitary Man' by Nick Kent from *Melody Maker* 08/02/75, © IPC Media LTD 2010; 'A Memoir of my Childhood Friend' by Andrew Hicks, © Andrew Hicks 2000; 'Nick's Secret Garden', 'Elegy To Nick Drake' and 'Far Leys' by Will Stone, © Will Stone 2010; 'Way to Blue, the Songs of Nick Drake' by Joe Muggs, © Joe Muggs 2010; 'Visiting Nick Drake' by Ryan Foley, © Ryan Foley 2007.

Lyrics written by Nick Drake © Nick Drake/BMG Music.

Jason Creed, August 2010.

Lightning Source UK Ltd.
Milton Keynes UK
UKHW051841280222
399331UK00016B/359